STILL HOPE FOR SUZI

By

JOHN DUCKERS

Grosvenor House
Publishing Limited

This book is published by
Grosvenor House Publishing Ltd
Link House
140 The Broadway, Tolworth, Surrey, KT6 7HT.
www.grosvenorhousepublishing.co.uk

This book is a work of fiction. Any resemblance to
people or events, past or present, is purely coincidental.

A CIP record for this book
is available from the British Library

ISBN 978-1-78623-400-1

Preface

Every journalist is supposed to have a novel in them and as a journalist for nearly 35 years it has always been at the back of my mind.

But you know how it is – long hours in the office, a family to feed, commitments ... and somehow it never happened.

However, the years went by, I became semi-retired, the children were grown-up, my wife had sadly passed away, boredom and loneliness were wolves at the door – this was the moment, for once time was on my side.

Yet how to begin to construct a very different story than I was used to – 80,000 words minimum as against the short, sharp, bash it out and onto the next, disciplines of journalism? In short, would I simply dry up or, even more likely, lose interest? And did I have anything new and compelling to say? Could I excite the reader?

Plenty of people have written about plane crashes and plenty of people have written about love across the generations.

Then it struck me – why not combine the two? It was the new twist I needed. Not quite the proverbial eureka moment in the bath, but similar.

And I found that the words flowed – even the sex (extensive but not gratuitously so and definitely not autobiographical!) and the violence (restrained and in context).

There are some things you just have to do in life and for me this was one of them.

So I hope you enjoy it because I had a lot of fun writing it.

Prologue

"The position seemed hopeless. Here he was, virtually a non-swimmer, in what seemed a vast ocean, he knew not where, not a sight of land, hope of rescue at least in the immediate term non-existent.

Where do you start? What can you do?

Easier to let go. Slip away. Nice to have known you. Mum, Dad, sister Vicky, would be distraught, but they would rebuild their lives in time.

Now that outlet was denied.

Why had that bloody baby appeared? He had no choice ... he would have to fight, he would have to suffer, he would have to push his body and soul to the limits.

He could give up on himself, but how could he give up on a baby?"

Struggling in the ocean, Kevin and Suzi, the only survivors of a terrible plane crash, would cheat death. But there was no-one to show them how to survive life as their days, weeks and then years became one long crash.

This is a story which examines emotions in the raw.

How do you cope when the whole world is looking at you and the gaze never goes away?

Or perhaps you don't.

Still Hope for Suzi

They say that drowning is one of the worst ways to exit this world … now Kevin was about to find out whether they were right.

Worse still, he had already given up, resigned to his fate, thrown in the towel – it seemed a suitable moment for clichés.

He'd never been much of a swimmer. Oh, sure, he'd had lessons as a youngster. But never taken to it. For some reason, he didn't know why, it seemed an alien environment, you might even say that he was frightened of water. He could manage about half the length of a swimming pool but that was it and he had no inclination to get any better.

As he had grown into adulthood nothing much changed on that score.

He would flap about in the sea for ten minutes, never daring to get out of his depth. It was kind of pleasant as the sun shone down. But he was quickly bored so he would make his excuses, sidle up the beach, grab a towel and say how much he had enjoyed the dip.

It was a lie, but only a small one.

Living in Sydney, Australia, it was all somewhat dysfunctional given how much the lifestyle was based around sand and water.

Lots of his friends were terrific swimmers, quite a few were also expert at snorkelling.

Bronzed gods, both male and female.

Kevin, red-haired and with a delicate complexion which burned easily, sometimes felt like an outsider.

His chums teased him about his ability to access every piece of shade on offer.

At 15, with the sensitivities of a teenager, it bothered him a lot though he did not let on. You know how it is when you want so much to be accepted as part of the gang. But at 22 he had learned to live with it. After all, if you loved life, you had to work with the body the Lord had given you. And Kevin loved life.

He loved partying, he loved banter with the lads, and he loved flirting with the girls.

He loved the whole buzz and spontaneity about Sydney. The most beautiful of playgrounds – iconic structures such as Sydney Harbour Bridge and the Opera House, the bustling ferries, the mix of peoples, the diversity of the food … it just went on and on.

Oh to have just one more pint of cider down at The Fortune of War, a great little bar in The Rocks, one of the oldest parts of Sydney. It claimed to be the city's most ancient watering hole, dating back to 1828. Would he ever see it again?

He loved sport too, particularly rugby union.

It was hard to put his finger on why it so consumed him – something about its primeval nature, going to 'war' with your brothers, putting your body on the line, the gladiatorial contest, yet all wrapped around respect for the opponent. Rugby was tribal – it harked back to an age where you fought for what you could get. And you had to do it together if you were going to be effective. It was about showing the girls that you were man enough to deserve their affections.

In fact, he was so keen on sport that, rather than go to university, he had somehow talked his way into joining a sports agency.

He had the patter, he had the looks, he had the drive and desire, he'd discovered early when on work experience and part-time summer jobs that he possessed sales and marketing ability, he was a young man in a hurry. He was good at networking. It was a world he felt at home in. OK, they had started him at the bottom, not quite making the tea, but equally not far removed. But he was quickly helping with the roster of lesser clients, looking to boost their careers, attract sponsorship and make the most of brand associations.

You needed loads of enthusiasm, you needed to be ambitious, always you needed to be positive.

But he was a million miles away from positivity as he struggled in the water.

That was until he saw the baby. It was bobbing about like a plastic duck at bath time. He knew it was alive because it was crying lustily.

And it changed everything.

The position seemed hopeless. Here he was, virtually a non-swimmer, in what seemed a vast ocean, he knew not where, not a sight of land, hope of rescue at least in the immediate term non-existent.

Where do you start? What can you do?

Easier to let go. Slip away. Nice to have known you. Mum, Dad, sister Vicky, would be distraught, but they would rebuild their lives in time.

Now that outlet was denied.

Why had that bloody baby appeared? He had no choice … he would have to fight, he would have to suffer, he would have to push his body and soul to the limits, he had to try and survive.

He could give up on himself, but how could he give up on a baby?

The baby had more or less all its life ahead of it.

It was one thing to rationalise death all alone, forsaken by the world. It was quite another to in effect murder the baby by doing nothing.

Kevin thought back to his Christian upbringing. The family had never been much into religion. Possibly they got to church once every couple of months. More recently he had barely attended at all. Yet there was a residue of belief still within him. The flame had not been extinguished. It continued to flicker.

He took a deep breath and said a quick prayer.

Dear God, I have been weak, I have ignored you, I have transgressed in so many ways, but please be with me in this my hour of greatest need.

It provided solace and an inner strength.

He thought too of Becky …

They weren't exactly boyfriend and girlfriend but they had grown up together, attended the same school, laughed together, cried together, had loads of fun, been intimate.

She was beautiful, she was bright, she was kind and caring.

He had never told her that he loved her. Damn, why hadn't he told her he loved her?

Perhaps because he was still too immature to embrace what seemed such a vast responsibility and commitment. Stupid, stupid, stupid.

He tore himself away from such melancholy – it was for another day if, that is, there was to be another day.

He reached out to the baby and sought to give it what he hoped was a reassuring cuddle.

Water lapped over them.

They were in it together and their predicament was dire.

How had he got into this? The explanation could not have been more mundane.

Someone had suggested a lads' jaunt to Bali. Perhaps surprisingly given it was not much more than a throwaway line, and despite the usual lax organisation, it had gradually come together.

They had been before and loved it, so the incentive was there.

Bali was dazzling, even temperature around 30C, spectacular scenery, idyllic beaches, just stunning. No wonder it was so popular with tourists. It rained a lot in the wet season but you simply avoided the wet season.

Five friends booked time off work, packed the suntan cream, raided the piggy bank, dug out the passport and bought nurses' outfits to wear the first night for a laugh.

Johnnie was the wise-cracker. He worked in insurance, had a penchant for karaoke, and dabbled in occasional stand-up comedy. He wanted to be a comedian – the rest of them said he already was!

Jack was a sex-obsessed car mechanic – dirty by day and, they joked, dirty by night.

Alex worked in financial services and was regarded as the brains of the party. He had been the one who had booked the flights and the hotel. A petrol-head, he loved fast cars and even faster women.

Phil, in the final year of a philosophy degree, was the quiet one. Never much of a drinker, he would indulge a day or two of boisterous behaviour around the bars and the nightclubs before taking himself off to learn about the temples, culture and history of the island.

Kevin would sometimes accompany Phil on his expeditions.

Bali was such a vivid location that it seemed obscene to do nothing but drink, lie on the sand and try and pull girls.

The others were well aware of Kevin's aversion to bumming around on beaches for any length of time. And, though there was a reward available for whoever did the most shagging, they all knew that Kevin always regretted 'cheating' on Becky. There had been girls but it never felt right. And besides, wasn't Kevin petrified about getting some sexually transmitted disease.

They wound him up unmercifully but Kevin wasn't bothered. He flung the occasional beer in the direction of his tormentors but he was only joshing.

Anyway, Alex always claimed the most notches on the bed post, going into great detail about their sexual performance. Nobody really believed him.

They had met up in high spirits at Sydney Airport.

There was the usual drudgery of booking in with their suitcases, passport control, ever more stringent security.

A round or two of drinks in the departure lounge, a cursory look round the shops, the first not-very-funny wind-ups ... and then onto the plane.

Some loud ribaldry as they worked their way past the posh seats at the front, just to piss off the executive dickheads who were already being served glasses of champagne.

And then they were battling it out in cattle class to get their hand luggage stowed in overhead lockers, settling into their cramped seats, and looking about to identify any 'fit' air hostesses.

A typical before take-off scene of people fussing over head rests, turning off mobile phones, fiddling with ear pieces, a babble of eclectic chatter, kids crying, lockers being shut. The rumbustious babble so familiar to the cabin crew.

There would be the urbane voice of the pilot welcoming all aboard, words enunciated in the tones of a high society cocktail party. Providing information on the time, the altitude, the goodness knows what – come on pal, get the thing into the air.

Then it was the safety blurb which all on board ignored apart from the nervous few who hated flying and were already twitching in their seats and feeling sick. Airlines were increasingly trying to liven up the mindless dirge by throwing wads of cash at celebrities who already earned far too much in the belief that it just might entice a minority to pay some sort of attention. But these were hardly Shakespearian performances and the cattle were far more interested in identifying what movie to view, how much free alcohol they could snaffle when the trolley came round, and watching with amusement the struggles of the obese bloke two rows up to get his seat belt to stretch far enough over his vast belly.

I mean to say, was there any point in knowing that your life jacket was under your seat when you were so squashed in like sardines that you would never be able to reach it.

And why would it matter either way given everyone was almost certain to be wiped out in a crash.

If your time was up then your time was up.

At last, after what seemed like endless taxiing across tarmac, the engines were in overdrive, or whatever the correct aeronautical term was, and you were speeding down the runway.

Take a tighter grip on the armrest, fidget a couple of times in your seat, sneak a glance at the taught faces around you ... and, thank God, it is off the ground.

Not being an engineer, it never failed to amaze Kevin that something which appeared so flimsy – wobbly wings, an interior overwhelmingly plastic, with engines that looked far too heavy for their supporting structure, all one feared held together with glue in the fashion of a boys own kit, could ever take to the air with so much freight and so many passengers.

One could only ever hunker down in one's ignorance and hope those paid to know what they were doing really did.

Relief.

But no escaping a long and tedious six hours-plus in prospect where however you tried to while away the time – film, magazine, book – nothing seemed to suffice.

It was a routine that never changed.

Except this flight was going to be different from all the others.

It took years for the official inquiry to report – understandable given the complexities – and then it couldn't quite decide between a bomb, human error, pilot suicide or mechanical failure.

The sea is always reluctant to give up its secrets.

It meant the newspapers, commentators and others could go to town on conspiracy theories.

Kevin recalled later that a sort of shudder went through the plane, it seemed like it was being shaken about, and it rapidly lost altitude.

It was mayhem in cattle class.

"There were terrible screams, people were fighting to put on oxygen masks, things were flying through

the air, those who had been in the toilet queue were on the floor dazed or unconscious. We were losing height all the time.

"It was total panic where I was sitting. There were people praying to their God, people crying, people frantically trying to send last text messages on their phones, grown men calling for their mothers.

"I think we all thought it was the end. I certainly did.

"You wonder what was happening with the pilots. Their training would have told them to get the aircraft below 10,000 ft. If they were still capable of functioning, I am sure they would have been fighting to try and stabilise the plane even though it proved a lost cause. I think we have to give them credit – that they managed to get off a mayday was in my view heroic enough on its own."

Back in economy the terror morphed into a weird form of calm.

"Many of us were frozen in the moment.

"It was when we broke through the cloud, with the ocean seemingly rushing up to meet us, that the dreadful screams began once more. They were such haunting, agonised cries, as if they came from the beginning of time. It was ghastly.

"I never saw us hit the water, I never even felt it, I suppose I was already numb. This then was death ... except oddly the more I thought about it the more I became convinced that I was maybe still alive. You have to remember that all this is going through your head in milliseconds.

"I became aware I was under water, I was still strapped to my seat, and I had this distinct feeling that someone was looking after me and I was going to make it. I could see distant light above me. I fought to rid myself of the seat. It was a form of suspended animation. Reaching the light became all-encompassing. It seemed to take an eternity.

"Then suddenly I broke the surface. I couldn't believe it. My lungs ached, a wave splashed over me, but I was alive. I was alive. It seemed impossible but it was true. This was not delirium. I really was alive."

And, if to prove it, seconds later the baby popped into view.

Clutching the child, Kevin tried hard to compose himself.

He looked at the little mite – it was hard to tell the sex, a girl, he thought. She was staring confidently at him as if she knew that survival was pre-destined.

He looked about him. There was some debris – a shattered suitcase here; what looked like a piece of plane wing there.

He grabbed at a passing seat – anything that might act as a buoyancy aid.

For the first time he realised that his left arm was hurting. All of a sudden he felt shattered and it was all he could do to hold onto that seat for grim death – maybe it would prove a grim death.

Now he noticed there were bodies in the water – fellow passengers who had hopes, desires, ambitions to fulfil. All snuffed out.

The baby was becoming agitated and grouchy. He'd never thought much about babies and their needs before.

Managing to remove the nappy, he wiped its bottom as best he could and hoped that would suffice. And he allowed the nappy to float off and join the rest of the flotsam and jetsam.

In the process he discovered that she was indeed a girl.

He had to trust that the Indonesian authorities had instituted an air/sea rescue alert.

They had.

Already planes and ships were being notified of the last known position of the aircraft. Others like Australia and Singapore offered their services. It quickly became an international operation. And it needed to be, given a vast expanse of water and the effect of ocean currents.

Kevin was weakening – the sun blazed down, salt tore at his skin, his grip on the seat and the baby was ever more precarious. What about sharks? Who cared about sharks? If they put him out of his misery then so be it. He had tried his best. This was not Hollywood – it went way past sharks.

He was having trouble focusing. He must not go to sleep – then the baby would die and almost certainly he would too. Rather like counting sheep, but with the reverse intention of staying awake, he kept on suggesting to himself all the female names he could think of that the baby might be called.

He decided on Hope.

It was surely not her real name but at least it boosted his spirits and he hoped Hope would bring them good luck.

Hard to work out how she was doing. She had gone quiet. Could be alive or dead. Nevertheless, every bone in his body told him she was alive. This baby had guts.

But their fate was sealed unless rescue came soon.

Momentarily she slipped from his grasp. Somehow he reached out and hauled her back in. Tough to hold onto the baby and the seat at the same time.

"That was probably the worst," he admitted later. "I thought for a second she was gone. I could never have forgiven myself."

As it happened, Capt. Hassan Suhendra was closer to the pair than he knew as he and his crew stared down at the seemingly barren seascape. Of course, he had no idea there were any survivors – only that 270 were on board. He recognised that it was a forlorn mission. All had surely perished. But you had to do your utmost whilst light and sufficient aviation fuel remained.

Kevin heard engine noise before he caught sight of the plane. Were his senses playing tricks on him? He tried to raise his injured left arm but couldn't. He dare not raise his right for fear of becoming detached from the cabin seat and the baby.

The aircraft was showing no sign that it had seen them.

Indeed no-one on board had spotted anything, certainly not survivors. Time was running out when one of the crewmen reported that he thought he had seen what could be wreckage.

They did a final sweep.

Was that wreckage? Was there evidence of an oil slick or was that just a darker patch of sea water?

Nothing to lose, thought Capt. Suhendra, in dropping a life raft. Just in case.

On hunches like that hang human lives.

Kevin saw it plunge from the plane and inflate in the water. He wanted to scream his thanks. He wanted to cheer his heart out. But he had the energy for neither and anyway knew full well how vital it was to try and conserve his remaining strength.

Was it a sign they had been spotted? He had no way of knowing.

And anyway it had hit the water perhaps 500 metres away, perhaps further.

What then use was it likely to be? He could not swim to it. The likelihood was it would simply float off, so near but so far.

As time passed he began to wish they had never dropped it.

Yet it appeared to be edging towards them. Was that really the case? Or were his eyes deceiving him in his exhausted state?

Many minutes went by. Now he was sure it was drifting nearer.

Hope really was bringing them luck. God must be taking pity.

Many more minutes went by. Now it was tantalisingly close.

In what seemed one of the most monumental decisions of his life his blurred brain told him to abandon his hold on the seat. He reached for the life raft, found the entrance and placed the baby aboard. He attempted to follow but couldn't. He tried again and failed again. He felt the last of his being ebbing away.

"No," he told himself. "Not now. You cannot let go now. You must get on board that life raft. You must."

He summoned up everything he had left and crying in his distress managed to lever himself half on/half off the raft.

Then, slowly and hurting, was able to squirm all his body all the way inside.

He collapsed, utterly spent, at the furthest reaches of his endeavour.

He lay there unconscious – for how long he had no idea. Perhaps about an hour and a half.

But at least it blanked out reality.

No further need to pour over the life or death quandary.

If the latter, maybe months later someone somewhere would find a tiny mummified body and a gnarled corpse inside a tattered life raft ravished by wind and tide.

Then at least the world would know they had fought as long as they could fight.

If the former, then both could bear witness to disaster and honour those who would never return to loved ones.

There would be times ahead when Kevin would question whether death might have been preferable to life.

By now the missing plane was leading the news bulletins.

Sombre announcers were telling how it had suddenly disappeared from radar screens on route to Ngurah Rai International Airport, Bali's main airport and Indonesia's second largest.

Close to the main tourist areas, it handles millions of passengers a year and can take all the big jets.

The airport is named after I Gusti Ngurah Rai, a Balinese hero who died fighting for independence from the Dutch.

Already a steady trickle of increasingly desperate relatives were gathering in the main terminal building anxiously waiting.

As is the norm in these sort of situations real news was at a premium, in part because the authorities themselves knew very little.

Officially the flight was still 'delayed', but with a search under way it was obvious that something had gone terribly wrong.

Relatives both in Bali and Sydney were now frantic for information, clutching at straws. Hoping against hope that there could yet be some innocent explanation. Refusing to accept the only possible implication – the aircraft had crashed into the sea. If that was the scenario there would likely be no survivors ... there never were.

Quickly the mood turned ugly. The weeping crowd vented their frustration at being told so little. They shouted at airport and airline officials.

Tall tales were already being bandied about; fantasists were laying down poison.

The plane had been hijacked to China so a democracy campaigner aboard could be silenced. It had hit bad weather, turned back and landed at Port Moresby on New Guinea, where for some unknown reason a news blackout had been imposed while the passengers were being checked over.

None of it was true.

Instead, the search was widening as freighters, warships and fishing boats made for the crash site.

One of the vessels was container ship, the Sola Spirit, outward bound from its home port of Mumbai.

She was on a tight deadline but the law of the sea is universal. Her captain had swung her onto a new course and now she was in the vicinity of where communications with the aircraft had been severed.

The crew knew that spotting a life raft amid the swells was a tall order; seeing wreckage remote.

Nevertheless, eyes were peeled. You had to believe it was possible. You could not just casually write off so many lives. And what if they had all perished? The families would want to know why. They would want to apportion blame. It was vital to pick up any clues to what had happened.

And, when straining not to miss the slightest lead, the ocean delights in fooling you – particularly if the light is poor. What seems like something tangible turns into just another lump of water. A body in the sea is revealed as an old oil barrel.

They had been at it for several hours when a cry went up from one of the sailors.

Could that be a life raft in the distance? And to everyone's astonishment as the ship eased closer it was clearly a life raft.

Excitement began to build. Container ships don't need a big crew – perhaps 20-30 personnel. But now they were all agog. This was a once in a lifetime moment.

Would there be anybody within?

They put down a ladder from the side of the ship.

A rope was tied around the waist of a young deckhand and he swam the few metres to the raft.

He looked inside, expecting to find nothing, and reeled back extending thumbs up to his comrades.

There was someone there, slumped on the floor – at that point he hadn't noticed the baby.

They pulled the raft close up to the ship and willing hands reached out.

Kevin gave a low moan and stirred ever so slightly. A further buzz of excitement surged through the Sola Spirit's crew – he was alive.

It was incredible. And they edged him up and onto the deck.

But, hang on, to be absolutely sure the deckhand had checked the life raft again and to his utter amazement there was a baby lying to one side.

Shouting his joy, his colleagues could barely credit it. In his arms he was holding a baby.

Unbelievable! A miracle.

Was it alive too?

They rushed the child on board ship.

At first they couldn't find any vital signs. The ship's first-aider took charge. Tilting the baby's head backwards, he blew a tiny amount of air into the lungs.

Then gently massaged the chest.

He did it again.

At the third time of asking the baby coughed.

A cheer rose from the onlookers.

The baby coughed again and now the chest was rising and falling as with normal breathing.

They peeled off her sodden top, dried the little one, and wrapped her in a blanket. Placing her in an old laundry basket, they transferred her into the galley for extra warmth.

She opened her eyes and another cheer went up.

For Kevin, events were largely ethereal. He felt there were people around him but he couldn't make out who. He knew stuff was happening to him but he did not know what.

He recalled: "Everything seemed vacant, like it was passing me by. It was the most foreign of sensations.

"It wasn't an out-of-body experience the way people close to death describe it, more like being completely divorced from reality. It was as if my mind and body could no longer connect. I was there but I wasn't."

The debilitating sun was no doubt a contributory factor. His eyes and lips were all dry and puckered from the salt.

Like the baby, they stripped him of his wet clothes.

He was weak, he was shattered but hopefully, they reckoned, he was young enough and sturdy enough to get over this.

They bathed his face and lips, rubbed soothing cream into his skin, dribbled water into his mouth as best they could – their medical knowledge did not extend to fitting a drip even had one been available – and put him to bed in a bunk. Sleep would surely be his best cure.

The captain set a new course, this time for Benoa Harbour, Bali's main port.

It was important to get the pair to proper medical facilities as quickly as possible.

He got on the radio to alert the port authority to his intentions while explaining that he had two air crash survivors on board who needed urgent help.

At some point Kevin was jolted awake, looked around wearily and indicated that his throat was parched. His rescuers brought a cup to his mouth and gave him more water. He smiled his thanks.

Then a frown spread across his forehead.

He tried to speak but his parched throat was just too sore. He tried again. They strained to pick up the words.

It seemed he was trying to mouth something beginning with the letter b, but they couldn't work out the rest.

Then the penny dropped. The word had to be 'baby' surely.

The baby was fine, they told him. He raised a shaky hand in salute. The trouble was his eyelids seemed so heavy, and were already coming down like metal shutters on a shop front. Within seconds he was fast asleep once more.

And the baby did appear to be fine.

Indeed at that very point it was crying that it was hungry.

They found an old lemonade bottle, did their best to sterilise it in hot water, boiled some milk, poured it in, left it to cool, tested the liquid on their skin to ensure it was more or less the right temperature, and fed it to the baby.

The baby gulped it down enthusiastically.

Word of the developments leaked, then spread around Bali like wildfire even before the Sola Spirit had docked.

Benoa is a busy commercial port at the best of times – fishing boats at one end of the spectrum and huge cruise liners at the other.

Now there were ambulances and police cars at the quayside. A crowd of onlookers had built up. Members of the media jostled to get the best spots to take pictures that would go worldwide.

This was the biggest thing to hit Benoa in decades.

And with Ngurah Rai International Airport situated at Denpasar just seven and a half miles from the port many of the plane crash families were dashing down there hoping against hope that there might be one of their loved ones aboard. With information so scant no-one was prepared to trust what little they were being told. Perhaps rumours of two survivors meant 22 survivors.

Soon the police were struggling to keep back a swaying, near hysterical throng.

It is the way of huge incidents such as this.

And all the time there were fresh rumours like another lifeboat had been found with other survivors in it.

Sadly it was not to be.

With several ships now on site, bodies had been picked up. So had a small amount of wreckage. But there was no sign of further life.

Not news that families listening to their radios and scanning through their mobile phones wanted to hear.

At last the Sola Spirit was tying up alongside. The gangway was down and police and a medical team headed aboard.

After an initial assessment on the ship the baby was rushed to a local hospital for a full health examination.

You can imagine the chaotic scenes. People craning their necks to look. Reporters almost fighting over scraps of information. Photographers battling for pictures. Crowds reluctant to part with police having to force a corridor open. Wailing sirens from the emergency vehicles.

And it was much the same for Kevin.

It took longer to remove him from the vessel. Awake but very woozy, he was this time aware of people all around him, people taking his pulse, checking his breathing, looking at his eyes, setting up a drip.

His hand was still hurting him and so were his ribs and he tried to indicate the problem areas.

But he was just so, so tired. His legs were like jelly. His body felt like a steamroller had run over it. Muttering his name took a huge effort.

He thought of his family and wondered whether they knew yet. He assumed not.

Naturally, the airline was checking the passenger roster and looking to establish identities.

But, wisely, no-one wanted to make any media statement until they were absolutely sure. It would be the same when the bodies started arriving. This had to be thorough, it had to be right, and if that took time then so be it. That was so hard on the families. But it was vitally important they were not put through new traumas because someone, however well-intentioned, had made a mistake.

It was the correct approach even if it exacerbated the hostility of the families, who were already fed up with the endless waiting.

Waiting, waiting, constantly waiting.

Of course that simply spouted further speculation layered on top of tittle-tattle – tough for investigators to disprove.

A temporary mortuary was set up in one of the port cargo sheds. There were no occupants. But the first batch of bodies was on its way.

Above everything there was this awful doom-laden sense of loss.

Kevin decided he must have drifted off again because when he next came round he was in a hospital bed.

A huge bandage was tied round his chest. His troublesome hand was in a plaster cast.

They told him later it was two broken ribs and a cracked bone in his wrist. He had got off extraordinarily lightly.

He wondered how long he had been lying there.

It subsequently transpired that the sedatives he had been given had knocked him out for 24 hours or so.

Trying to fix his eyes on what was around him he suddenly realised that Mum, Dad and Vicky were huddled by the bed.

It was reassuring – he wasn't on his own.

He tried to smile. Mum was holding his good arm and tears were flowing down her face.

He tried to speak but nothing emerged.

Dad held a finger to his lips – that could come later.

Mum was talking about how much they loved him. But it was all too much to take in and sleep enveloped him once more.

The next time he woke up Becky was there at his bedside too.

It sparked within him a complicated frisson of diffidence and desire. She must love him too to come all that way. She looked gorgeous.

She was wearing a blue skirt and a white top. He marvelled at her wonderful legs, her trim waist, and her flowing brown locks.

"Becky," he murmured, hoping he hadn't injected too much passion into his voice in the presence of parents and sister.

She smiled that so sexy smile which brought out the dimple in her cheek, then she leant over and kissed his forehead.

His heart rate leapt; his loins felt they were on fire.

"Becky."

His voice trailed away as his gratitude for her being there mixed together with how much she meant to him.

He wanted to explain so much to them about what had happened, convey the horror, how scared he had been,

But it was all too much.

Becky was telling him there was loads of time for explanations – for now he needed all the rest he could get.

"It will be fine," she confided. "We're going to get there."

And then the question he had to ask.

"The baby?"

The baby too was doing fine – the apple of the eye of all the nurses and midwives.

The gurgles of happiness, the cherubic smile, even the tiny belches of air … they all felt the urge to mother the little thing.

Devoting so much attention to their wonder baby while, like Kevin, trying to guess her name.

Angelique? She was such an angel. Storm? She had already survived so much at such a tender age. Sandy? Bali's beaches were such a draw to so many visitors.

Physically she was already good. Nobody wanted to think what harm might have been done to her mind.

Especially as she was now an orphan – the authorities had worked out who she was and to be ultra-safe had conducted a DNA match with relatives.

She came from Normal in Illinois in the United States.

It seemed appropriate because nothing could ever again be normal for Suzanne Elizabeth Duthie.

In McLean County, Normal lies adjacent to the perhaps better-known Bloomington. The twin centres have a population of roughly 130,000.

It is where father Robert, a lawyer, and mother Rose, a teacher, had chosen to raise a family. Suzi was their first born.

Rose had so much wanted a girl and it had come true.

Suzi was absolutely adored and no doubt destined to be utterly spoiled. At least until a brother or sister arrived which was the couple's fervent hope.

Why was she travelling at an age when she hadn't even taken her first steps?

They were headed for Dubai where Rose's sister Abby, a worker in the hospitality industry, was on secondment.

The sisters were very close, it was to be Abby's first sight of her nine-month-old niece in the flesh and she was very much looking forward to it.

It being such a distance Robert and Rose thought they might as well make a long vacation out of it, take extended leave from their jobs, and maximise what they could get out of the steep air fares.

So they went west rather than east, and made a first stop in San Francisco. You think you know your own country but there were vast tracts of the United States they had never visited. They took sight-seeing trips like any other tourist – Alcatraz, the Golden Gate Bridge, Fisherman's Wharf, a boat cruise on San Francisco Bay, and the proverbial cable car ride.

They had a wonderful time. What a city.

Back on the plane next stop was Sydney, and they hit the locations that Kevin would have been so familiar with – the Opera House, Sydney Harbour Bridge, and Bondi Beach.

They didn't have time to do it justice and determined that they must return one day and properly explore its delights.

And then what more beautiful a location than Bali to visit on route to Dubai.

They were really looking forward to seeing the island if only to work out why so many raved about it.

It wasn't to be and they had perished along with so many others with similar stories to tell.

Stories of human achievement and human frailty.

Robert and Rose were proud of living in Normal even though the name never failed to produce light-hearted comment.

Advertising types were for ever seeking to link it with Bland, Missouri, and Boring, Maryland.

With the town of Oblong also being in Illinois, a headline in the local Bloomington-Normal Pantagraph – itself one heck of a title – supposedly featured "Oblong man marries Normal woman".

Nobody seemed quite sure whether that was real or fanciful.

And how did Normal get its name?

The Chicago Tribune explained it thus: "Normal is not named Normal out of an excess of Midwestern humility. The town that has given the world Steak 'n Shake used to be North Bloomington but, in establishing its own identity in the mid-19th century, decided to borrow its new name from the local college."

What is now Illinois State University was then Illinois State Normal University, the normal deriving from a French innovation, higher education for teachers and women in what were called *ecoles normales*.

Incidentally, for anyone who does not know what Steak 'n Shake is, which is probably more than half the world, it features a combination of premium burgers and milk shakes, a concept founded in Normal in 1934.

But Normal and Bloomington have far better claims to fame.

Both lie on the iconic Route 66 and there are all sorts of connections to Abraham Lincoln, revered 16th President of the United States, who owned property in Bloomington, had many friends in the area and, as a travelling attorney in his early years, acted in local court cases.

Robert and Rose had met in senior high school.

It was in essence an attraction of opposites.

He was relatively reserved until a combination of Rose and law school brought him out of himself. He loved sport, American football and soccer to the fore.

The name Duthie is Scottish in origin. Indeed you will find Duthies all over the world. Perhaps unsurprising given the Duthie motto in Latin is data fata secutus which translates as follow my destiny.

Go to Aberdeen in Scotland today and you will find Duthie Park, situated by the banks of the River Dee, 44 acres given to the local council in 1881 by Lady Elizabeth Duthie of Ruthrieston, in memory of her uncle and of her brother. It is particularly noted for the winter gardens complex – tropical and arid houses, many exotic plants, a sanctuary which continues to draw in around a million visitors every year.

Rose di Matteo was, as the name sounds, of Italian descent.

Like many Italians, she possessed a flamboyance, an outgoing nature which sometimes got her into scrapes, an exuberance to make the most of life, a front foot approach and a willingness to try different things.

They became friends in the school choir. He fell in love with her looking at the back of that glorious neck and the shimmering dark hair. Her smell was enough to send him almost insane.

Music, arts, dance ... Rose loved it all.

Rosa was a name bestowed on di Matteo women from way back but had somehow become Americanised with that part of the family which had emigrated to the mid-West.

Robert was her rock.

In turn, he was captivated by how she took him in mind and body to places he could only dream about.

It was a grounded relationship – they attended their local church most Sundays and they tried to live their lives imbued with moral values and the difference between right and wrong.

It was a partnership which could perhaps be summed up in the words of a great hymn which includes the lines: "Let love be real, with no manipulation, no secret wish to harness or control; let us accept each other's incompleteness, and share the joy of learning to be whole."

They made a good team.

It seemed so cruel they should have been taken in so dreadful a manner.

Frantic phone calls were taking place between relatives of Robert and Rose.

A shaken Abby was already on route to Bali.

The first she had known of the tragedy was a knock on the door of her rented apartment located in a popular area for overseas workers.

It was two representatives of the US Consulate General's Office and instantly she realised something terrible had happened.

She had been so busy at work such that the disaster had passed her by.

They broke the news as gently as possible, but there is never a good way of imparting such a black message. That Suzi was alive, the child Abby had never seen, was at least something she could hold onto.

But in her mental turmoil at first all she could think about was Robert and Rose.

Would they have known what was happening in those horrific last moments as the aircraft hit the water? Had they suffered? Surely they must have been petrified.

She sat there in floods of tears, unable and unwilling to get her head around what was already a nightmare.

And, of course, David and Nancy from the Consulate had no answer to those questions.

Nancy put her arm around Abby. Crying was a release; best to let it all out.

She was trained in bereavement counselling and aware that it would be far worse were Abby to bottle it all up and sink into a private world of grief.

Neither did it take bereavement counselling for Nancy to know that people reacted differently when confronted with great loss.

She had started out as a local news reporter but after three years or so had chucked it in, realising she wasn't cut out for all that journalism could throw at you. She hadn't felt a failure. It wasn't quite for her and it was important to admit it. There was no shame – she had made many friends and she had experienced things which would stand her in good stead for the future. And, once she had settled on where she wanted to go from journalism, the change of career worked.

Journalists refer to it as the 'door knock' when they are ordered by their bosses to speak to the bereaved.

There was a knack to it and some hacks were much better at wheedling their way into homes than others.

Some parents, husbands, wives, in their heartache, needed to talk. They wanted to tell this complete stranger their loved-one's life story. They got out the family picture album and reminisced. They were anxious that the world should know even as they mourned. Quite remarkable.

But sometimes it went the other way.

Nancy had gone to the door of a family whose eight-year-old daughter had been killed after being thrown from her pony. Something had spooked it. And, though wearing the proper head gear, the girl had still received fatal injuries. In the seconds after the door had been opened by the father and Nancy had explained who she was and the purpose of her visit, the mother, totally out of it, flew at her, chasing her down the garden path, screaming abuse, before dashing back inside. The husband, desolation convulsing his face, spoke calmly, said he did not dispute why she was there, but quietly requested Nancy take her leave.

The whole business unnerved her.

Perhaps sublimely it was why she subsequently went in for bereavement counselling.

It felt like hours but in reality was probably only about twenty minutes before Abby began to think more rationally.

David and Nancy explained in general terms what had happened to the flight, how it seemed certain there were just two survivors, and one of them was Suzi.

Suzi. Poor Suzi. How lost and frightened she must be. Both her parents gone. In a strange country. Strange people …

Abby knew she had to get to Bali as soon as she could.

David and Nancy had been working on that basis. Leave it to the Consulate, they would get her booked on a flight, sort out arrangements, would have their counterparts in Bali meet her off the plane.

Abby started flapping. She would need to pack a case, perhaps two. Where was she going to get baby clothes? Where had she put her passport? She must phone her employers and explain the situation. She must phone her mother and father and Robert's mother and father. What was to be done for the best once she got to Bali?

She was in a complete stew.

Nancy and David told her they were there for her. Not to worry. It would all be OK. Just take it slowly.

Abby concentrated on putting together a plan.

All that mattered now was Suzi and her welfare.

The thought that Robert and Rose's bodies might never be claimed back from the ocean pained her enormously. Bodies or no bodies? Funeral or memorial service? She kept telling herself that Nancy and David were right – it would come together eventually.

She must be strong, cleanse her mind of the obtuse and inconsequential, and get to Suzi as soon as she possibly could.

Generally quite a practical individual, she began to organise herself.

Soon she was speaking to both sets of grandparents back home in McLean County. All four were stunned and hurting. They already knew and were trying to take in the immensity of it – the Sheriff's Office had been in touch and DNA swabs provided.

Abby breathed a sigh of relief – at least she wouldn't have to explain it all. She had the feeling that in the next few months she would be doing a lot of explaining to well-meaning folk who only wanted the best for all concerned. It would be demanding.

Both sides of the family were supportive of her decision to fly to Bali.

Did she need help? Did she need money?

Abby told something of a white lie, promising she had everything under control. All four were getting on in years and had only ever been outside the US on rare occasions. A trip of that magnitude would be arduous and stressful. She was determined not to put them through it.

Anyway, they were more than placated when she told them she intended to take Suzi back to Normal as soon as the authorities would let her. Even at the end of a phone she could feel the sense of family and the warmth it generated. It was the proper thing to do, they told her. They would see their precious grand-daughter soon enough.

She phoned her employers and briefed them on her dilemma.

They could not have been more understanding and offered all the support she required. Her boss said he appreciated that she would want to take Suzi back to Normal and get her settled. He promised leave of absence for as long as necessary. It wasn't appropriate to talk money but he pledged she would remain on full pay even if it took a year.

It was generous of him. Neither said anything but both spoke in tones hinting of an acceptance that Abby was probably unlikely to ever make it back to Dubai.

It was a great pity, it had been a quality job, but she was now embroiled in a bigger picture.

Back to packing.

You know what it's like when you are in a fluster – you're mind goes blank.

She found her large suitcase and searched about for a second, slightly smaller one, she knew she had somewhere – they would have to go as hold baggage but it would be worth any extra cost, not that cost was a consideration given the situation.

She packed a load of clothes aware it could take days before she had time to think about throwing things in a washing machine. She went round the flat retrieving treasured mementos, photographs and ornaments. Her laptop computer went in, her wash things, her make-up bag, first aid case, jewellery (such as it was), music tapes, lots more.

Goodness – what else would she need?

Come on, think, Abby, think.

Nancy did her best to lend a hand, making suggestions, checking that Abby had her phone, her phone charger, passport, all the real essentials.

Not to worry about baby clothes, nappies, wipes and all the rest. That could be left to the Bali end. People would rally round.

David and the team at the Consulate were working on the flight – they managed to book her on one for that night.

As she waited for the taxi Abby was understandably anxious.

She was 27, three years younger than Rose. There had been boys but nobody truly standout had walked into her life. The only babies she had encountered were those of friends, where you could sit them on your knee, bump them up and down, make suitably quirky noises, and hand them back. Now she would be thrust into spontaneous motherhood, at least for a while, in a manner she had never imagined.

No time to prepare, no antenatal classes, she would have to wing it.

Nancy went with her in the taxi – it was a one hour drive but, for Abby, passed like the blink of an eye as thoughts tumbled around her brain.

Nancy put her hand on Abby's – repeating it would be all right, she would be fine, no point in worrying.

Abby smiled weakly.

Presently the taxi arrived at Departures – the lights were bright, there was an incessant bustle of people, vehicles, planes taking off and landing, the heat tore at the throat ... like most big airports around the world it was non-stop.

An airport official met them – briefed to look after Abby and smooth the way for her.

Abby and Nancy hugged.

"Thank you so much for everything you have done," said an emotional Abby.

It had been less than a day but somehow she felt she had known Nancy all her life.

Nancy smiled.

They hugged again.

"All the very best for what lies ahead," said Nancy. "Give the baby a kiss from me."

And then Abby was heading off, steeled to jumping the usual airport hoops most of us know so well – checking in, luggage, passport control, security, waiting for the gate number to come up.

Finally, she was on the plane, embarking among the first as the airline had fixed a priority seat for her.

Nancy thanked her lucky stars that things had gone well and in particular the media hadn't cottoned on to there being a Dubai link to what was increasingly being billed as the Bali Baby disaster.

She had seen news scrums before with journalists thrusting tape recorders in faces, photographers battling to get the telling shot and TV crews pushing and shoving with the best of them – total hypocrites who were for ever claiming the moral high ground while being as intrusive as everyone else.

The media pack in full pursuit mode was not always an edifying sight.

Nancy feared for what Abby was likely to be walking into at the other end and fervently hoped whoever was her counterpart could provide the necessary protection.

It was a nine hour flight to Bali. The cabin crew were attentive. Abby got a little sleep, but, so typical of air travel, the turbulent type which never seems to refresh.

She felt apprehensive, weary and not a little scared, but as they neared touchdown it was, she told herself, vital to get her act together.

She must step up to the plate to meet the trials and tribulations that were bound to come her way.

The cabin crew were going through the usual routine of checking all the passengers had their seatbelts fastened, items of baggage were put away safely and there was no-one left in the toilets.

It was a smooth landing and soon they were disembarking.

Abby thanked the stewardess as she left the plane.

"Good luck."

They both knew she was going to need it.

The local Consulate was on the ball. Abby was met by a tall, lean, angular representative.

He announced himself as John Munro.

They smiled at each other – Abby felt an instant attraction. She tried to put it on the back-burner. This was not the time or place.

He told her that a car had been set aside for her – once they had got her luggage they would smuggle her out of a side door. It had all been approved.

"That's very thoughtful of you," she said softly.

Their eyes met and she almost fainted.

"Are you all right," he exclaimed, taking a grip on her arm.

"Yes, honestly, I'm fine," she just about managed.

Then, trembling, added: "It's been a long trip."

At baggage reclaim she pointed out her suitcases and he pulled them from the conveyor belt.

He guided her away from the milling crowd and through a side door indicated by an airport staffer. Soon they were in a restricted area and getting into the back seat of a Buick.

The driver pulled away and headed for a little used exit gate.

A handful of media had peeled off from the hospital stake-out. All but one were at the front. But a maverick photographer had gambled on subterfuge being put in place.

Kerpow! The flash went off and blinded them for an instant.

The snapper wasn't quite sure what he had got. He recognised it as a consular car and he recognised one of the consular officers in the back. But who was the pretty blonde?

He decided there had to be some connection and phoned ahead for a reporter colleague to be aware.

Nobody had got any shots of Kevin or the baby so far – deemed still not fit to be exposed to public view.

Forty-eight hours in and the press corps were getting twitchy.

"Damn it," muttered John, aware they had been rumbled.

He tried to explain to Abby the massive interest in the 'story' and cautioned that it could get messy.

Abby absorbed his advice, but nothing could have prepared her for their arrival at the hospital.

The place was mobbed and the car surrounded before they could spirit her inside.

The tumult was scary. People were bashing on the windows so hard Abby feared they might break. And she edged closer to John.

The car drew to a halt, local police were attempting to clear a path through to the main entrance, between John and the driver they got the door open and pushed their way out. She hung onto him as if her life depended on it, thrust close into his body as they battled their way through.

It would have been lovely had it not been so frightening.

But at last they had made it.

Ruffled and a touch breathless, she was glad of his arm around her.

He guided her to a seat, got her a glass of water, and offered reassurances that she was safe.

She thanked him and, unable to stop herself, plunged into the deep brown pools of his eyes.

Suddenly embarrassed, she inquired whether there was somewhere she could freshen up.

This time it was he who was embarrassed. Of course this attractive young woman who he already felt so at ease with would need the ladies after such a hardball encounter.

He pointed her in the direction of the restrooms and silently reproached himself for his insensitivity.

Abby took time over her ablutions, tweaked her make-up and studied her face in the mirror as if bizarrely this was the end of innocence.

She determined she would not turn into the stereotypical helpless and over-emotional female.

She would emerge from the toilets ready to face the music; when it came to departing Bali she would be a tougher, more worldly-wise individual. She just hoped she would not put in jeopardy the values she had been taught to uphold.

John was waiting for her. He was now accompanied by one of the hospital's administrators. He led them to an office, sat them down and arranged drinks to be brought – John chose white coffee while Abby opted for sparkling water.

The administrator kept the briefing succinct not wanting to tax her.

He ran through Suzi's condition on arrival, the extensive checks doctors had carried out to ensure there were no major issues, she was eating and drinking, and was generally "in rude health". It would be wise to keep her in for another couple of days for monitoring, just in case. But then she should be fit to go home, wherever home was.

He assumed Abby would be eager to see Suzi as soon as possible.

"Yes, that would make my day," responded Abby.

He promised to sort her out with a room in which to stay. They would bring her belongings up from reception where the driver had deposited them.

She should make herself comfortable and not be afraid to take advantage of the hospital facilities – she must be hungry, any of the canteens would be at her disposal.

He motioned for a colleague to come in, take a head and shoulders photo, and sort out a temporary security pass.

Did she have any questions?

She felt as if she ought to have a million questions but couldn't think of anything in that instant.

He explained that they would want a longer chat with her to discuss Suzi's future plus how best to meet all the media interest – but all that could wait for morning.

Abby smiled her thanks and the three of them set off for the ward.

It took a good few minutes – all hospitals seemed to have endless corridors and endless numbers of doors. But finally they were there.

It was the usual busy scene with nurses scurrying about, children crying, concerned visitors.

And there was Suzi …

It was her first sight of the girl who meant so much.

They handed her to Abby who cuddled her, kissed her forehead and tried to reassure the little one.

She thought Suzi looked nonplussed, reserved, wary even.

But Abby told herself the poor darling had been through such a battering that she was bound to be bewildered. And here was another grown-up she had never met before in her short life – who was this? What did she want?

John made his excuses – not wishing to intrude into such a private, family affair. He said he would wait for her outside and she should take as long as she needed.

She smiled happily, glanced at the baby in her arms, and looked back at him. As he stepped out of the door John thought she looked perfect. One day she would make a wonderful mother herself, he decided. Already, though it had only been a few hours, he could feel himself becoming smitten while at the same time cautioning it would be out of order for him to get involved with someone in his professional charge.

Abby spent half an hour playing with Suzi as they sought to get to know each other.

She told Suzi all about herself, how she was Suzi's aunty, how Suzi was very much loved and that Mummy and Daddy had gone to heaven.

Obviously Suzi would not understand any of this. Abby just hoped she was making a connection.

It was a start which both could work on.

Abby handed Suzi back, promised she would return soon, waved and said bye-bye.

Then she was gone.

John was there with the administrator. Her temporary pass including photo were complete – that was fast – and she put them around her neck.

The administrator asked how Abby's first meeting with Suzi had gone.

"Fantastic," she replied, beaming.

It said a thousand words. Nothing else was needed.

Another walk along corridors and then the three of them arrived at Abby's room for the night. Her suitcases were already there.

She looked around. It was pleasant, neat, light and airy.

Was this suitable?

"Yes, yes, absolutely fine," she stressed. "I very much appreciate all you are doing for me."

Now it was the administrator's turn to smile.

He told her that if there was anything she needed then she had only to ask. And he gave her a mobile number to phone.

Then he took his leave.

That left the two of them alone, of which John was all too conscious. This was inappropriate.

He suggested leaving her free for half an hour to get herself unpacked. Perhaps, afterwards, they might go and find that canteen meal?

She said she would very much like that, and they parted.

He went off, found a convenient bench and frittered away the time glancing through emails and replying to vaguely important ones.

When he got back she was sitting on the edge of the bed ready – he decided efficiency and punctuality must be two more of her talents.

They walked out into the main complex and followed the restaurant signs.

It was like so many canteens the world over – tired décor, difficult to marry up the food with the menu, piles of cutlery in various stages of cleanliness and bored yet impatient staff, all-powerful in their own domain, serving portions which wouldn't sustain a gnat.

She chose fish and rice; he opted for a mild curry.

From a vast room full of tables they picked one by a window and seated themselves down.

John looked around at the smattering of mostly sad souls dotted about – this was not the candlelit restaurant he would have chosen for a first 'date'.

Thankfully it turned out that the portions were not quite as minimal as they had first appeared.

They ate mostly in silence – hard to impress a girl when your mouth is full of food.

But at length, as they sipped water after finishing their meals, they got talking – all a touch constricted as is the case when you really know nothing about each other.

Abby told him a little about Normal and contrasted it with the lifestyle in Dubai. He did his best to outline the attractions of Bali.

She asked about his name, Munro.

He explained how like many Americans he was a complicated melting pot. Of Scottish extraction on his father's side, his mother was English.

They lived in London.

Dad hailed from Texas, in the oil business, and moved around a lot so it had seemed sensible to base themselves where Mum had relatives.

So, from the age of five, John, an only child, was largely brought up in the land of Shakespeare and Churchill, and, at the age of 13, he had been sent to public school – the fee-paying independent arm of the education system in the UK – Uppingham School, in the tiny, rural county of Rutland, roughly in the middle of the country.

It had meant a huge adjustment and he had to harden up fast. But virtually everything you could think of was on hand – from cricket to amateur dramatics, speech-making to carpentry, and much more beside. All under-written by top quality teaching.

He had enjoyed his time there. It was a period of experimentation and hard work – exams to pass, expectations to meet.

Bringing back the memories had dragged him away from the immediate.

He realised he had overdone the explanation because at that point she nearly fell asleep at the table and they agreed it was time to go.

He walked her back to her room.

"Will you be here tomorrow?" she queried. "I could certainly do with a bit of support with everything the hospital seems to have lined up."

John assured her that he would – his other work could just pile up, he told himself.

He shouldn't be spending so much time on this one 'project' but he wanted very much to do so.

"Until the morning," he said.

"You've been so very attentive," she told him and squeezed his arm.

They parted, hormones all over the place.

Kevin was getting stronger by the day and chatting away in his room to Becky and the family.

He was still in pain from the ribs but was proudly collecting signatures on the plaster cast.

Most of the conversation was deliberately casual in nature – the weather, life back in Sydney, and reading the thousands of get-well-soon cards.

An outpouring of love from so many around the world – people he would never meet.

Hopefully, he mused, he could thank them all via the good offices of the hospital.

But Kevin was already feeling that things were pressing in on him.

At some point he would have to go through with his loved ones the ordeal he had suffered. At some point he would no doubt have to give statements to police, air crash investigators and goodness knows who else. At some point he wanted to see the baby again and try and build a bridge to the baby's relatives. At some point he would need to do something to satisfy the media's agitation for interviews and pictures. At some point he would have to sort out where he and Becky were headed. At some point there would be the funerals of his friends – he ought to be there.

He did not feel up to it. Indeed, he dreaded it. Just thinking about it left him subdued and jittery.

His confidence was shot – he felt himself mentally curling up into a protective ball, wanting to hide away from the world.

He felt inadequate – not an attitude that had ever plagued him before.

Becky and the family were understanding. It was a natural defence mechanism after all he had gone through, they told him. They would nurse him back to health.

They told themselves he just needed time, let him recover at his own pace, recharge his batteries.

But his mood swings worried them.

Hounded to distraction, the hospital's two-strong PR team was swamped and, as soon as the police had named Kevin and Suzi, they were even more swamped.

Correspondents wanted far more than condition reports which was pretty much all that had been authorised to go out so far.

Being resourceful people, news organisations had uncovered a variety of pictures of Kevin on social media posts. Kevin larking about with mates, Kevin offering a toast complete with large glass of beer, Kevin kicking a ball around.

A trawl through Facebook had similarly turned up pictures of Suzi. They fastened on to one where she was in the bath – it tied in with being plucked from the water.

The heat was on to discover every available fact about the pair however obscure and however banal.

It almost seemed that anybody who had ever known them was having a microphone thrust in their face.

Feature writers and teams from women's magazines were interviewing baby experts, child psychologists, trauma advisers ... to build up a picture of how Kevin and Suzi might be reacting and what it might mean for the future.

All types of mischief was going on in a vicious battle to get the first interview with Kevin.

It was like a feeding frenzy.

Relatives back home were being approached, people were trying to bribe hospital staff to take notes in pleading their case, huge amounts of money were being bandied around for an 'exclusive'.

Something was going to have to give.

Hospital administrators decided it was time to get Kevin, the baby and Abby together and, if that worked reasonably well, then to develop a media strategy.

Next day John phoned her to see where things were at – just his voice was a thrill.

She said she didn't know what was going on – he said he would come in anyway.

There was a knock on her door – it was the official she had spoken with before. He presumed she would be keen to see Suzi again but would she like to meet Kevin too?

Definitely she would like to meet Kevin. This was the man to whom Suzi owed her life. Abby seemed to be forever thanking someone, but in Kevin's case thanks could never even come close to reflecting the family's gratitude.

"I'll go and set it up," the man told her.

He arrived at Kevin's room and went through much the same parallel procedure.

Kevin didn't immediately jump at the offer. He had worked out this had to happen sometime. Nevertheless, he dithered. What could he say? Would he and Abby get on?

Yet he wanted to meet her and he very much wanted to meet Suzi and see how she was adjusting.

So it was agreed.

An hour later and they were altogether in a staff room.

Kevin and Abby were first introduced to each other and, yes, it was a diffident opening.

Abby asked how Kevin's recovery was going.

He was basically fine, he told her … washed out, lacking energy, but glad to be in one piece.

He asked about her journey – she told him that Bali seemed very beautiful. It was just a pity she was there for all the wrong reasons.

"Spot on," said Kevin.

She thanked him profusely for what he had done to save Suzi.

"You must have been very frightened," she queried.

His smile back was more than a touch tangled.

"In many respects Suzi saved me," said Kevin. "I wouldn't have made it without her."

His voice dropped; his eyes looked distant.

This wasn't the time for a question and answer session. The man had suffered enough.

Abby went quiet, but was spared when thankfully the door opened and there was Suzi in the arms of a nurse.

Kevin's parents, Becky, Vicky and John had been trying to very much stay in the background, but with Suzi's arrival a host of voices were quickly welcoming her.

She looked around at everyone curiously, then got all shy and pretended to hide into the nurse's breast, dropping the white rabbit she was clutching in the process.

Screeching, she lunged towards where it had fallen as if to say 'somebody pick it up, will you'.

Abby reclaimed it for her and sensing the moment the nurse handed over Suzi.

"Hello, Suzi," cooed Abby. "Do you remember me from yesterday? I'm Abby, your Mummy's sister. You are lively today, aren't you?"

Suzi looked around all the smiling faces as if in wonderment.

"And, do you know who is here, Suzi?" went on Abby. "It's Kevin. He's the man you met when you were splashing about in the water. Do you remember splashing in the water, Suzi?"

There was an under-current of amusement from the others in the room – nothing like baby talk to break the ice.

Abby motioned to Kevin, suggesting he might like to take Suzi.

They both rose from their chairs and Abby passed Suzi to him.

At first Kevin stayed standing, feeling incredibly self-conscious, rocking the baby to and fro in his arms.

He looked into her eyes; she looked into his.

Was there a meeting of minds?

"We certainly remember each other well, don't we, Suzi?" he chatted to her.

"We were playing in the sea for a very long time. I'm so pleased that you are much, much better. I was worried about you. Were you worried about me?"

There was laughter in the room.

He was getting into this, he decided.

"Where did you get white rabbit from, Suzi?" he asked her. "Did the nurses give him to you?"

He wibble-wobbled Suzi's nose with white rabbit.

Big smile and chuckles from the little one provoked a flurry of sighs and 'ahs'.

Suzi was playing the room already – just a natural, he reckoned.

Far from being uptight, as she was entitled to be, she seemed to be revelling in the spotlight. The centre of attention.

As for Kevin he had lost himself in this girl who clearly meant so much to him.

Abby was beaming. The get-together had been a hit, certainly better than any of them could have predicted.

And the baby talk continued until, with Suzi beginning to get a little bit fractious, the nurse suggested she take her back to the ward – her next feed was due.

They all said their goodbyes to Suzi and as the door closed there was another spate of animated conversation.

"Isn't she terrific?"

"Gosh, she is looking well."

"You would never have guessed anything had happened to her."

There was a sudden hush.

A baby had brought this disparate bunch of individuals together and for a fragment in time they were almost as one.

The administrator broke the silence – plainly he was intent on getting down to business.

He thought Kevin and Suzi would probably be fit to leave for home in a few days. But there was no hurry, he promised. No-one was going to frog-march them out!

Kevin gave a wan smile. He was not at all sure he was ready.

But the administrator was already moving the meeting towards the issue of the media.

He had been in these situations before but nothing quite as big. The worldwide interest was staggering.

He made a phone call and invited the Head of PR to join them.

They ran through the options – a photo opportunity, a press conference, a statement released through the hospital.

Kevin said he didn't think a press conference was his bag.

Abby said she would be prepared to play ball on a photo opportunity, just as long as they didn't start firing loads of questions at her.

The Head of PR assured her he would lay down 'rules of engagement' to the media, would be there to guide her, and would certainly step in if things looked like getting out of hand.

He suggested to Kevin that they had a chat and then a statement would be produced taking in his quotes.

It wouldn't satisfy the Press but would help back them off for now.

Kevin recoiled.

The Head of PR stressed that nothing would go out with which Kevin wasn't happy. He suggested they give it a go and see where they got to.

It was made to sound so reasonable he felt he couldn't duck out.

It would all be in conjunction with a press release from the hospital updating on how both Keven and Suzi were getting on.

It was decided to coordinate it all for 11 am local time the next day.

The Head of PR would in the interim sit down with Kevin for 20 minutes and then go away and compose something.

They arranged a slot for the afternoon.

Aware that the meeting had dragged on far longer than envisaged, the hospital administrator quickly wrapped things up.

Everyone went their separate ways.

Kevin's party headed to an inner courtyard which offered some quiet and tranquillity amid gorgeously scented flowers.

Abby and John opted for lunch.

Fed up with the canteen, he offered to go out and come back with some street food, which he did – Lawar, a Bali dish created from a mixture of vegetables, coconut and minced meat mixed with herbs and spices ... plus a bit of salad for luck.

They ate it in her room and it was delicious.

She couldn't finish it all and said she would keep some back for her dinner.

They talked about the press conference and how best to handle it. Be confident, he told her, pose Suzi sufficient for the photographers to get good shots of her, lots of smiles into the lenses.

But it wasn't all serious – she teased him about the amount of time he was spending with her while he joshed about 'needy females'.

It was fun.

And John took things further suggesting that in the aftermath of the press conference when the media had plenty to keep them busy he might have a go at smuggling Abby out of the hospital and show her a bit of the island and its beaches.

She said she would love that, but perhaps best to see how the press conference went first.

She gave him a kiss on the cheek when he departed. He felt a million dollars.

Kevin had retreated into his shell again, thoughts racing around his mind about what he might tell this PR man. As little as he could get away with, he hoped.

Becky tried to nurture him, sorting cool pineapple and lemonade drinks all round, and doing her best to be relentlessly cheerful.

But it wasn't getting through.

Kevin smiled vacantly at her. How could he explain that he felt submerged by the whole process, everything was so OTT, all these strangers were wanting different pieces of him.

He made an excuse about wanting to rest and retreated back to his room which in the intervening period they had transformed. Vases of flowers designed to distract, looking out onto sedate gardens, the sea and sky in the far distance ... they hoped the aura given off might make it easier for him to come to terms with what had happened.

Kevin's Mum saw the worried expression on Becky's face as he headed inside, and moved over to sit beside her.

She took her hand and spoke softly about how hard it must be for him. It was bound to be tortuous, she noted. It could not be rushed. It was hard to know what mental anguish he might be going through. They needed to get him home and hope that in familiar surroundings, stimulated by family and friends, no pressure, no stress, it would all come right.

Mum told Becky she had a very important part to play. "I'm sure we'll get the old Kevin back – we need to keep at it."

Becky nodded, and promised to do all she could.

Neither woman was being entirely honest with each other.

Becky was already feeling a fish out of water and a bit in the way. She told herself she was being unduly alarmist. She must shake this off. His Mum was right – it was bound to take time.

Privately Kevin's mother felt much less assured than she had given away. Had all this never have happened she would have been completely phlegmatic about two young people and a burgeoning relationship. But with Kevin clearly not himself she wondered whether he could handle matters of the heart while at the same time getting himself together. Would it be too much for him?

If it was going to be a choice between mental breakdown and Becky then Becky would have to go. Ruthless but necessary. Maybe they could get back together at some later date.

But, she told herself, she must be fair to this young woman who clearly loved her son, and they were a very long way yet from taking such drastic measures.

For Kevin, time was ticking round towards when he had agreed to meet the Head of Public Relations.

With every minute which passed he felt more and more restless.

This is ridiculous – you've got to control your emotions, he told the walls in his room. The man was only doing his job. So what was this nervous sweat all about?

But it was no good. If anything, he decided, he felt more lost than when he really was lost out on that ocean with the baby.

There was a knock on the door.

Oh God, help. HELP.

The PR was standing there.

"Come in," said a voice from a million miles away which, Kevin presumed, must be his.

They sat down and for an instance there was a prescient silence as both men hesitated on making a start.

The Head of Public Relations got his notebook out and plunged in.

"My name's Gerry," he said.

Kevin knew that because the fellow wore a prominent badge which said Gerry Smythies, Head of Public Relations.

"Do you mind if I call you Kevin?"

"No, that's fine," said Kevin.

"Well, Kevin, probably best to work together along the lines we might want to develop in the Press statement."

He decided to broach things cautiously.

"I imagine you would want to thank all the doctors, nurses and other hospital staff for all they have done?"

"Yes, absolutely," agreed Kevin relieved. "They have been marvellous."

And I guess it would be good to thank the people of Bali and indeed people worldwide who have been offering their best wishes for a speedy recovery?

"Indeed," said Kevin. "It has been over-whelming."

Letters and cards had been piling up. Emails and Facebook messages continued to arrive.

Uplifting but also intimidating. It was something else on the 'to do' list, a list he didn't want to do. However his parents were gradually getting through them. His own mobile and laptop had gone down with the plane. A new phone had been delivered to the hospital but so far he hadn't the courage to use it, afraid he would disappear into a black hole of backed up trivia.

"Good stuff," said Gerry.

"You are looking well," he fibbed. "How are you feeling in yourself?"

Kevin fibbed too. "Good, thank you. I've been walking around the hospital grounds and spending time with my family. It's been nice."

"And reunited with your girlfriend?"

The question startled him for a second. Of course, Becky. He supposed she must be his girlfriend. After all, he loved her and he wanted her to love him, yet he was less sure about the level of commitment he could deliver. The 'to do' list was getting longer by the minute.

He thought for a second.

"She's been great," he noted. "It's reassuring to have her here."

His couldn't find anything else apposite to say.

The PR man had hoped for more. Better to have been told she was the love of Kevin's life, and he was going to propose to her. But Gerry was thankful for small mercies.

Should he push further and request Kevin and Becky do a quick photo shoot? But he didn't want to blow it.

Especially as he needed to ask about the crash. Did he remember much about it?

Kevin looked out of the window. He could talk about those terrible screams from fellow passengers as they prepared to hit the water. He could tell about how he thought he was gone too. He could tell about his lungs nearly bursting. He didn't mention any of these things. These were for the ears of the air crash investigators; he would instead play the "don't want to prejudice the inquiry" card.

"It all happened in a flash," he murmured. "It's painful. But I've been asked not to go into detail while the investigation is on-going."

That was a bit of a fib too – he hadn't yet spoken to the crash investigators though they had indicated they would like to speak to him as soon as he felt able.

Gerry said he fully understood.

Both knew that was a whopper.

"What was it like in the water?"

"At first it was hard to believe I was still alive," said Kevin. "I'm not a good swimmer so I was concentrating on staying afloat."

Time to bring the conversation round to the baby.

"What about the baby?"

"Yeah, she seemed to appear out of nowhere. I was caught napping so to speak. It is hard to think of such a tiny thing surviving such a gargantuan event. But she was clearly alive."

Gerry was scribbling furiously. "How did it feel to have saved her life?"

It was the wrong question, and it had been going so well.

Kevin scowled.

"I want it to be crystal clear that I am no hero in any of this. There are a lot of people hurting badly. I got lucky. And, anyway, it was the baby who saved me, not the other way around. She was my treasure."

It was almost a speech and suddenly it occurred to him he had got more animated than he probably should have.

And, he decided, the way Gerry was looking at him said much the same.

Gerry got the drift.

"We'll leave it at that for the present. I'll go away and write this up, then come back in an hour or two. We can go over it then, add and subtract as appropriate. Play about with the sense."

He fiddled in a bag and brought out a camera. Would Kevin mind having a photo taken which could be given out along with the statement? It would be useful for the media to obtain an 'in hospital' shot. What he actually meant was that it would promote the hospital in a good light.

Kevin shrugged. He just wanted this over now.

Gerry posed him sitting on the side of his bed. Click. A couple more just in case.

And finally it was over.

With profuse thanks Gerry beat a retreat. Across the piece he had pulled it off, he decided. But it still had to be tied up.

A talented ex-journalist who had switched to the 'dark side', coaxing out a story remained part of his very existence even though these days it had to be camouflaged in corporate image gunk, and, of course, every word approved.

He hit his computer enthusiastically and the words flowed. This was not a tin-pot little release on some charity gift to the hospital. This needed careful crafting … it brought out his professionalism. Not so tabloid in nature that Kevin might baulk at the whole thing and change his mind. Not so timid that it would come across as dull and uninteresting.

He checked it and re-checked it both so the facts were correct and the pitch was right.

At length he was satisfied and headed off to find Kevin.

After a bit of a search he discovered him seated in a waiting area staring into space.

A bit peculiar, thought Gerry. But didn't dwell on it.

He opened up a laptop and pulled up the proposed Press statement – he'd decided not to print it out because sometimes these things looked harsher on a black and white page, less threatening on computer.

An old dog's new trick.

Kevin glanced through it.

He could tell the guy to bin it. He could tell him he hated it all. He could go through it for an hour and a half, scoring bits out here and adding stuff in there, not that there was anything insanely inaccurate in it.

But his eyes had glazed over, life was too short (of all people he had come to know that) and it was simply too much effort. And he didn't want to be rude to this man who when all said and done was doing his best and trying to be supportive.

"Yeah," said Kevin. "Go with it as it is."

A relieved Gerry expressed his thanks and headed away to put it through his bosses.

That would probably test his negotiating skills. You normally had to drop the occasional line, just so the top man felt he had justified his position. Maybe add in some blatant PR guff about the hospital's expertise in accident and emergency, most of the media would likely dump the flowery stuff anyway. Massage the fellow's ego along the lines of how it all showed the hospital in such a positive manner, which actually it did.

And finally they got there. Job done.

After making the changes, he gave the final version to a secretary with instructions to print off 150 copies. He thought that should be sufficient.

Next he posted a statement about a statement, plus the photo opportunity, on the hospital's web site for all to access. And he phoned the local media, stringers and one or two particular pals alerting them.

The phones remained red hot for the rest of the day with media types fishing for an advance on what was going to be said.

Gerry talked it up, told them it would be Kevin's frank and fearless take on surviving against all odds, but wouldn't give away details.

This needed to be a success all round.

Gerry headed for home. An expat with a Balinese wife, he had had plenty of practice at keeping work and home life apart. He sank a beer. He would worry about the next day when it came.

That morning he was in early. There was an enormous amount to do.

He needed to check the room out where the briefing would take place, ensure the TV people with their lighting and their cameras were in place, microphones were working, there was a suitable medical backdrop, plenty of seats for photographers and journalists, copies of Kevin's statement were ready, all was well with Abby and Suzi, hospital officials knew the batting order.

Thankfully it all came together; no major snags.

The room was packed and noisy. The air conditioning made conditions just about bearable.

Gerry produced Kevin's statement – it and a photo were now available on the hospital's web site – and began to distribute them. It generated the usual eager rush, a bit of pushing and shoving but nothing too bad. Statements had fallen to the floor in the melee, some journos had taken more than they needed, others were clamouring for one. Gerry gathered up those that had hit the deck. Gradually, it all cooled as the media got down to reading it and preparing their questions.

Gerry took to the main microphone briefly and explained the order of events.

Then one of the doctors took over on a second mike, detailing the latest condition reports on Kevin Jackson and Suzi Duthie. In summary, they were making good progress and would likely be discharged quite soon.

He sat down again.

Gerry then went to a side door and ushered in Abby with Suzi in her arms. Flash lights lit up the room; cameras cheeped like birds.

Abby and Suzi took a seat at the front, then Gerry confirmed to the gathering who they were.

Abby smiled broadly into the line-up in front of her. Cue more flash lights and camera clicking.

Then she cuddled Suzi on her knee and made the sort of baby noises which she knew would enchant viewers when they saw the video.

"Isn't she the one," she announced to all and sundry. "And such a brave little girl."

The media pack started shouting out questions – they had been asked not to do so but only in a half-hearted easy-osy fashion. Gerry had expected it and was confident Abby would measure up.

"How is Suzi handling it all?"

"Brilliantly. She's been ever so good. Fingers crossed that it continues."

"Is she showing any signs of being affected by all that has happened?"

"Naturally she was dehydrated at the beginning but she has bounced back well. We're very pleased."

"How is she taking to hospital?"

"Fine. The nurses have been spoiling her and there is so much to absorb. Hopefully I can take her home to the United States fairly soon, but we don't want to rush things. Constantly adjusting to new situations is bound to be challenging for anyone never mind a nine-month-old."

"Has Suzi met Kevin since the rescue?"

"She has indeed – very moving for all of us. We owe so much to Kevin – what he did to keep her alive was above and beyond what any reasonable person might suppose. It must have been so terrifying and who could blame him if all he had done was try and save himself. I know he won't like me saying this but for us he is a hero."

"Is Suzi missing her parents?"

"I'm sure she must be but of course being so very young it is hard to tell. The extended family has come together and she will get lots of love. So we are hoping for the best. But clearly being orphaned in this way is a terrible tragedy."

"Do you fear that in time she could prove mentally scarred?"

Gerry stepped in to say he felt that was an unfair question, but Abby indicated she would take it.

"That is for the future," she said. "Hopefully not. We will have to try and address it if and when it arises. I am sure there will be medical help available if she needs it."

The sweet smile was there again. Flashes popped and cameras clicked.

Gerry intervened once more.

"Just two more questions – we don't want to tire the baby out."

A flurry of shouts from the mass and Abby just managed to pick up on one who was asking who would look after the child once in the States.

"We are still talking about that," said Abby. "In the first instance I am going to be there to provide continuity, but as to the longer term we shall have to see. However, she has caring grandparents, uncles and aunts, so I am sure we will work it out."

What a natural, thought Gerry, admiring how this composed young woman was taking all this in her stride, thoughts echoed by John who was standing at the back.

"Last question."

He pointed to one of the local Bali journalists knowing they would have a slightly different angle.

"Have you been impressed by Bali and the response of the Bali people."

Abby shone, provoking yet another flurry of flash lights and camera clicks.

"Everyone has been so kind. It is my first visit to Bali but I would love to come back. It is a beautiful island. The care provided by the hospital has been first class. I must thank the Consulate for their magnificent support. People of Bali – we owe you so much. The goodwill and love towards Suzi has been humbling."

She tried to catch John's eye. She hoped he was proud of her.

Abby and Suzi left by the same side door amidst a final few camera shots and generous shouts of 'good luck', 'all the best for the future' and the like.

John realised that the media weren't really the hard-hearted beasts they were made out to be. They were only human too, with human feelings. Who could not be touched by a survival story on such an epic scale?

Gerry was at the microphone again, having promised for the benefit of the visual media to read out Kevin's statement in full.

At the end there were a couple of inquiries about whether Kevin would agree to be put up for interview – the media is endlessly greedy for more. Gerry explained that Kevin was still fragile and did not feel he was quite ready for that yet. He promised to keep the media informed should he subsequently be willing to speak.

The room began to break up, cameras turned off, journalists and photographers gathering up their gear and rushing for the exits, looking to file for a myriad of global outlets.

Gerry was pleased. It had gone well.

John was pleased too. Maybe he could spirit Abby off to a secluded beach while they were all distracted. He hoped so.

He went in search of her.

No response when he knocked on the door to her room. He found her in the ward, playing with Suzi. Bound up in what she was doing, she never initially noticed his presence.

Meanwhile he kept quiet and just watched, enchanted.

He had only known this girl for a few days yet already he was captivated.

At length she spotted him standing there.

"Oh, hi John."

That same dazzling smile which tore at his heart-strings.

She turned back to Suzi. "Look Suzi, here's John, are you going to wave to him."

She took Suzi's hand and pretended to wave. Suzi blew a bubble at him.

Then Abby was snuffling her nose into the baby's neck to squeals of excitement from Suzi.

"This big, bad man is going to take me away from you for the afternoon," she teased.

She looked back at John. "Are you going to sweep me off in a gilded carriage led by a procession of Hindu gods?" she joked, the island being more than 80 per cent Hindu.

"Something like that," he responded, deliberately po-faced.

She laughed.

She placed Suzi back into her cot, handed her a rattle, told her she would see her soon, and meantime the nurses would look after her.

And then they departed, headed first for Abby's room.

"What's the chances of a swim?" she asked enticingly.

"Pretty good, I should think."

She found the bikini she had thrown into her luggage at the last minute just in case. Grabbed some flip-flops, a towel, sun cream, her handbag, sunhat, sunglasses …

John marvelled not for the first time how women never travelled light whereas men – this was drifting into sexist areas, he decided, mustn't go there.

"Got everything," he inquired.

"Think so."

She put a finger to her cheek and pondered – God, she was beautiful.

"Let's go," she announced, and placed a hand on his shoulder.

John's vehicle was in a visitor's spot in an overflow car park. He inquired whether it was a good idea to hide her under a blanket on the back seat in case any of the media were hanging around.

She tossed her hair and appeared all shy.

Then shrugged. "Let's just go as we are," she insisted. "It's a day to die for, I intend to have not a care in the world for this afternoon at least, and, anyway, the media are my friends now."

They walked to the car happily.

Soon they were on the road, driving through lush agriculture, past exotic temples, rice terraces, birds flitting about in the trees.

It appeared as idyllic as Abby had been told until John got his own back and teased her, telling her to look out for large water monitors and snakes including the king cobra and reticulated python.

Deliciously, she pretended to be shocked.

Beware too of the island's mountainous backdrop, with a number of active volcanoes.

"Now you are frightening me," she joked.

At length they arrived at a small but pretty beach well out of the way of the main tourist areas, and got out of the car.

There was hardly a soul about.

"Oh, John," she exclaimed. "It's scintillating."

And she squeezed his hand again, driving him almost wild with lust.

This time there was no way he was going to give that hand back. They walked onto the shimmering white sand hand-in-hand as the tropical trees swayed their approval.

They stood there for several minutes, arm-in-arm, so picture-postcard.

"I can't resist," she said, and for a split second he got the wrong idea. "I'm heading back to the car to get my swimming things."

"Good thinking," he stuttered.

She stopped and turned to him. "I take it that it is safe to bathe."

"Yes," he assured her. "I checked with the locals when I first came here. We should be fine."

She found her towel and bikini, then pointing very deliberately, stated that she was going behind a clump of trees fringing the beach to change.

"And no peeking."

He put on his trunks in the back seat of the car, and only peeked a bit.

She emerged in a sultry yellow bikini.

His eyes wallowed in her firm breasts, the willowy blonde hair, the slim waist, the long legs ... oh, those legs.

How he wanted to hold her in his arms.

She came over to him, and gave him a playful shove in the chest.

"Last one into the sea is a cissy," she exclaimed, and was off.

They raced down to the water and plunged in.

Well, actually, he plunged in. She was rather daintier, frolicking in delight, before pretending to splash him.

He pretended to splash her back.

She jumped on him and pretended to duck him under. He picked her up over his shoulder and spun her around, ignoring her protests.

They stood in the water laughing loudly.

Then she changed the mood and feigned being upset.

"Big bully," she jested. "Don't like you anymore."

And broke into a gentle breast stroke in the opposite direction.

He declined to follow, engrossed by the spectre of this feisty woman he had fallen for – so different to all the others.

They swam for quite a few minutes. The water was warm, the sun was shining, the setting was hard to beat.

The time came to emerge and both were soon drying themselves down with their towels.

She gave him yet another dazzling smile and his heart almost missed a beat.

She put her hand through her hair.

"I forgot my swimming hat," she groaned plaintively. "I must look terribly bedraggled."

He assured her that she looked as glamorous as a film star.

And he couldn't stop himself as his hands moved onto her waist as if by automatic pilot.

He held her to him and they kissed for the first time.

They kissed slowly and tenderly.

Then they kissed passionately and provocatively.

She felt elated. You were always supposed to know when it was the real thing. She knew already.

He felt he had entered into a serene new world.

A local walking his dog along the beach came into view, and the spell was broken.

She put a light top on and rubbed sun block cream into her legs and feet. She offered it to him and he did the same.

She placed their towels together on the sand and lay down, a strong arm around her and her face nestling into his chest.

Until she felt the urge to get back to Suzi.

After sorting themselves out, they returned to the car and drove home largely in silence, both pondering how much they had to give something which energised them both.

Suddenly, he had an idea.

"I'll spin you past my apartment block so you can see where I live," he declared.

"Why, Mr Munro," she declared, as though he had taken things too far. "Are you propositioning me?"

She looked coyly at him and they were laughing together again.

After the detour, he dropped her off at the hospital and promised to pick her up the following afternoon.

"Shall we do it all again," he almost implored.

"Yes, let's," she replied.

They kissed, she got out of the car and waved as he drove off.

She took a deep breath. Events were moving fast.

But the next day … oh, the next day.

It was towards the end of the dry season but there was little threat of a tropical downpour.

They stopped for lunch at a roadside restaurant, went for a walk up to a beauty spot vantage point and then found a different beach.

This time, because he didn't know it, they confined themselves to walking, cuddling, kissing and admiring the view.

She told him loads more about life in Normal and the work she did in helping to run a major leisure complex in Dubai. He told her about his route from public school in England, through university in the States, to joining the Bureau of Consular Affairs – he spoke three languages – and how the Bali posting had come out of the blue.

Once more it was time to head home.

They got in the car.

"Right," he said. "Back to the hospital."

"Actually," she said. "Why don't you show me this bachelor flat of yours? The spin past it yesterday intrigued me. I'd be interested in seeing more of how you live here in Bali."

"It's a bit of a tip," he apologised. "I would have cleaned it up had I known."

"Don't you want to show me?" she flirted.

"No, I'd love to," he responded quickly.

"Make it happen then," said Abby.

She had already decided that she wanted this madly attractive, suave, consummate gentleman, but he would need to want her.

He parked up – it was a clean-looking apartment block which seemed well cared for.

He put the key in the door and ushered her in.

It was a compact sort of place – kitchen divided off from a lounge/dining area, two bedrooms, one of which he used as a study, toilet and bathroom.

The lounge certainly needed a tidy up – DVD's lying all over the place, magazines dotted about, used coffee mugs.

He showed her the master bedroom.

"Is this where I am supposed to proposition you?" he asked cheekily.

"I don't know," she said. "Perhaps you had better try your luck."

They embraced and as they kissed breathlessly they knew that each of them very much wanted the other.

She unbuttoned his shirt and rummaged through the hairs on his chest.

He removed her top and then her bra – her mammaries were exquisite.

Quickly she dropped her skirt, slipped off her panties, and disappeared under the sheets.

Almost frantic with desire he tore off his trousers and pants and joined her.

They swept each other's body with their hands, their lips gorged on each other, he caressed her breasts longingly, he stroked her most precious gift, she held his erect penis.

Taking this slow was not on the agenda – that's how desperate they were for each other.

She opened her legs wide and he entered her.

She swooned her approval and held him ever tighter.

He groaned with pleasure as his pre-eminence throbbed with anticipation.

They came virtually together in a coupling which took them to Venus and back.

They continued to hold each other close as his tower subsided. Finally they split apart and lay panting on the bed. Then hugged – neither wanted to let go.

"Oh, John, that was magnificent," she whispered in his ear.

He snuggled up to her even more, kissing her neck and stroking her thighs.

They stayed glued together for many minutes before separating at last. Both felt utterly fulfilled.

She asked to use his shower and he pulled open a cupboard drawer and found her a towel.

He followed after her and by the time he had emerged she was dried and dressed and had taken a seat in the lounge.

He swiftly covered his own nakedness and then got them a cup of coffee.

It had been so good neither knew quite what to say. She held his hand on the sofa and simply told him how nice it was.

He told her she was special, and meant it.

The next afternoon when he found her in her room in the hospital her mood had gone from glorious to glum.

He knew why.

The Consulate had already told him that the hospital was releasing Suzi and he was to make arrangements for Abby and the baby to fly to the US.

He tried to cheer her up by telling her that it would be a fresh start for a child who in all probability should have been dead.

And someone who relied on her.

She gave him a half smile, and said she supposed so.

A tear trickled down her cheek as she looked at him with big, sad eyes.

He held her as they sat on the side of the bed and her despair tumbled out – what if they were never to see each other again?

She told him she could not expect him to throw in a great job in a great place for someone he barely knew. But she would always hold dear the memories.

He let her say her piece, all the time caressing her hair and face.

Her tears had left a sodden area on the front of his shirt.

"Oh, look what I've done."

She reached for some tissues and made a fuss over trying to mop it dry.

He took a firm grip on her arms and made her look into his face.

"Now," he said determinedly. "Listen carefully.

"I pledge to you that this is not the last we will see of each other – the absolute opposite is the case. Right person, wonderful place, rotten timing. But we are going to work this out. Already you mean everything to me. I will not give you up, come what may. We are going to write long letters to each other. We are going to speak on Skype as regularly as we can. All my leave is going to be spent with you, Abby."

It was the words she so wanted to hear.

"Oh, John," she sobbed, with tears of happiness this time.

She threw her arms over his shoulders and revelled in the warmth of his body.

"Oh, John, do you really mean that? Do you think we could?"

He told her they must strive for each other, must fight to carve out a future together, must keep telling each other that distance made the heart grow fonder. It would not be easy, it might fail, but they would never forgive themselves if they didn't try.

They examined each other with great seriousness.

"I want to make it work," she told him.

"I do too," he said.

They kissed in a manner which confirmed the understanding, how they had promised themselves to each other.

It could have been a prelude to ... to ... she pulled away.

"We mustn't, or I am going to want you more than I can resist ... and there is so much to do."

He smiled.

"Let's go to it," he said.

Abby had that morning been called into the administration office and given the great news about Suzi.

They discussed all the things she would need on route – nappies, baby clothes, carry cot and much else besides.

John had been phoning airlines and working out the flight combinations. He decided the best on offer were Denpasar to Chicago with just the one transit stop on the way.

It would take a whole day and more but that could not be helped. A long and tiring flight at the best of times especially for a baby.

John and Abby talked it all through, discussed what bags could go in the hold and what could be carried on board. He promised he would liaise with the hospital team and ensure there was no duplication. They would go out and buy stuff if required.

He got out his mobile and booked the tickets.

They exchanged pictures to put on their phones, they exchanged all their contact details.

He helped her pack for what would be an early start the following morning.

Already she was fretting about how she was going to manage. He told her there were mothers with infants doing it all the time. She would be fine.

This man's support meant so much. No longer was she alone against the world.

As she had said earlier, there was so much to do that the hours just slipped by. They grabbed a spot of supper but there was no time to dally.

She promised him she would get an early night. He promised her he would pick her up and take her and Suzi to the airport in plenty of time for the flight.

They kissed and parted.

A penny for their thoughts? Both were too tired.

He picked her up on schedule in the morning, placed her bags in the boot, everyone made a big fuss over Suzi, Abby said her thanks over and over.

"You must get off before you are late," they told her.

A quick pose for half a dozen dedicated photographers still on the beat and determined to get the bye-bye-baby farewell shot.

And it was off to the airport.

She checked in, luggage sorted, it was VIP treatment similar to her arrival, John soothed last minute fears.

They embraced and kissed deeply – neither cared whether any crafty members of the media were watching or not.

Then she was gone.

Kevin had decided it would be better not to see Abby off – she was bound to be mad busy.

But, it was right and proper that she found time to supply all the necessary contact details for him to keep in touch, and she made sure these reached him.

They arrived with a hand-written note expressing her admiration for him and what he had done – he would always be welcome to visit and the family would do their best to keep him in the loop about Suzi's progress.

It was good of her and he felt re-assured. He was absolutely determined to stay connected. Suzi would be a part of him for the rest of his life.

Meanwhile, like Suzi, it was time for him to head home.

His parents, Becky and Vicky tried to play it down.

But it was as if the here and now was destroying him. He seemed constantly on edge, nervous, frightened of what was round the corner.

He continued to be dogged by the guilt which tends to afflict survivors of many descriptions – why had he been spared when so many others were dead? How was he supposed to bear such a burden?

Whenever anyone looked at him he was instantly wondering what they were thinking? Were these the spirits of the departed returned to haunt him?

Becky had tried to give him space and when that didn't work she tried to flood him with love.

One night she engineered it that they were on their own.

They kissed but his heart was not in it. And she was greatly dismayed when having spent time on making herself as sexy as she could, plus putting on the flimsiest of flimsy outfits, he shrunk away from her embrace, saying he did not yet feel able to have intercourse with her once more – he had never used that expression before and its formality killed everything.

She had badly wanted sex with him – it had been a while.

Before, it had always been good – they had revelled in each other.

Her frustrations began to grow.

Vicky and his parents were doing their utmost to pull him out of this dark closet where he was sheltering.

They talked endlessly about happy family times, things Kevin had got up to when he was young, engaging him as much as they could in his love of sport. Yet even with sport he was largely disinterested.

Sport, he had decided, was just so frivolous and trivial compared to the wider world, death and destruction.

No longer did it matter.

Once more they told themselves that when they got back to Sydney he would snap out of it. There was no Plan B.

So when the hospital authorities announced he was fit to be released, they were keen to catch the first available flight.

However there was still the immediate issue of continuing media interest.

While the statement issued on Kevin's behalf by the hospital authorities had been well received, the hounds were desperate for his full, unexpurgated story.

The family and the hospital had asked more than once that his privacy be respected while he recovered, but that could only ever be a holding operation.

Could he say a few words? Might it not be cathartic? His family could be there to support him.

He flatly refused.

The whole world seemed to be ganging up on him. Eating him alive. Determined to feast on blood. He felt under attack on all sides.

Gerry had some sympathy with the media pursuit just as he had sympathy for Kevin. Kevin had thrown them one bone, if only he would be prepared to throw them another.

Alternatively, Gerry toyed with setting up some stunt to smuggle Kevin clear but feared the media would tear the hospital's reputation to shreds if he did.

At least might he smile and wave as he exited the main entrance, inquired Gerry and pressed the family to talk him round.

They urged him towards cooperation if only in honour of the hospital staff who had done so much to treat his injuries – the ribs were much improved as was the arm.

Becky offered to try and deflect attention by speaking to the media herself.

He caved in, and it was agreed.

It was decided to have him emerge through a group of nurses who had played a particular part in looking after him.

The plan worked after a fashion.

His parents, Becky and Vicky bolstered him as he came out into an unruly crowd of photographers, reporters, TV crews, flashing lights, hubble and bubble.

It shook him to the core and he would have turned back had that been possible.

Somehow, he pressed on, mumbled a few words to the nurses, managed a desultory wave, attempted to smile and was gradually eased to a waiting taxi and refuge inside.

He cowered down, physically shaking, as the taxi moved off, headed for the airport.

Becky held back and they converged on her.

She performed like a trooper as question after question was fired at her.

What was wrong with Kevin – even the media had been stunned at his distant look and sunken eyes?

She admitted he was still coming to terms with the whole thing. He would need support, kindness, love and as little stress as possible in the next few weeks, preferably staying out of the public eye.

Was he pleased to leave hospital? Yes, he was and the staff had all been truly magnificent.

What was the relationship between her and Kevin? She had already determined there was no way she was going to lie. She might not tell the whole truth but she wasn't going to lie. She said they were close friends, had known each other from childhood and he meant a lot to her.

Were they engaged? No, they weren't engaged.

What were their hopes for the future? Simply to get Kevin better – they weren't thinking past that.

What about the baby? They certainly hoped to remain in touch.

She cut it short, explaining that she had to catch the same flight back to Sydney. And they let her go without any hassle, acknowledging that she had been straight with them.

She got into a second taxi and they were soon making a steady pace down the road.

Becky closed her eyes. It had not been easy and she felt a little drained herself. It had allowed her the merest glimpse of what Kevin must be going through. It was dawning on her that there was going to be no easy fix. Was she in for the long haul? She wasn't sure.

She parked the thought at the back of her consciousness and tried to immerse herself in a last chance to soak in the beauty of Bali.

Kevin was seated beside his parents on the plane – a pity, thought Becky. She would have liked to have held his hand tight, tell him she was beginning to understand, put her head on his shoulder.

She dropped into a snooze insistent she would hold a candle for him whether they stayed together or broke up.

Arrival at Sydney Airport, she supposed, would mean yet more fuss – first photo shots back on home soil and all that trash.

It proved exactly so.

Sometimes these things were emblazoned over the television news, people falling over, cameras flying but who might ever imagine they would find themselves at the centre of such chaos.

Airport security did their best but were simply outnumbered.

Kevin looked riven with self-doubt.

As the cacophony of sound reached a new height, he managed just a few grudging platitudes in response to the barrage of shouted questions.

Yes, it was fantastic to be back on home soil.

Sure, the first thing he would do was open a cold beer.

No, he didn't feel a hero. He did what he could. He wished he could have done more.

His father finally got fed up of the buffeting.

"Come on, guys, give it a rest," he pleaded. "The boy is badly in need of convalescence – this is not good.

This isn't fair. You've had your pound of flesh. Now let us be. Please."

Nobody payed the slightest notice.

He held his temper.

Extricating themselves, they piled out into taxis, one carrying all the luggage.

It had been frenetic and it had taken its toll.

Tears rolled down Kevin's face and he began to sob uncontrollably.

All three women, his mother, Becky and Vicky, immediately moved to hug him. Mother got their first and tried her best to soothe and succour.

"Why me? Why me? Why me?"

"It's OK dear, mother's going to look after you."

He let out a piercing scream, loud enough to penetrate the heavens.

The taxi driver pulled to the side of the road and stopped.

"Is he all right?" he inquired. "Do you want to take him to a hospital?

They asked him to continue – they were headed to the family home in Manly, one of Sydney's main suburbs and one of its most upmarket.

Kevin lay sprawled, moaning intermittently, head in his mother's lap as though he were somehow reverting to being a child once more.

Vicky was shocked, her father was looking tense, Becky was upset.

Could Kevin be having some sort of breakdown?

Not a possibility the Jacksons would ever admit to. Jacksons didn't have breakdowns. The "b" word was verboten. Australians were supposed to be hard as nails, weren't they?

They arrived at last. The half hour drive had seemed like five hours.

They guided him into the house, Mum and Dad with arms around him in case he collapsed.

A crowd which had assembled – the odd newshound, a few voyeurs who had come to gawp and a vast number of well-meaning neighbours with banners such as 'Welcome Home, Kevin' and 'A Hero Returns' – weren't quite sure what to make of it all. A mixture of surprise, disappointment and concern.

As the gathering started to break up and people drifted away Vicky went back out and said a few words. She thanked them for their best wishes, explained that there was no intention on Kevin's part to snub them, just that everything which had happened post the plane crash coupled with his sorrow for the death of his friends had left him run-down.

He needed to take things slowly one step at a time.

Once he got better she was sure he would want to engage with the local community.

It produced a murmuring of empathy, the banners were lowered and little groups wandered away, whispering to each other in the way people do when somewhat confounded by a turn of events they had hoped would pan out very differently.

It was a shame for two reasons in particular.

Kevin's parents were well-respected in the area. Brett Jackson, semi-retired, had been a prominent shipbroker. June Jackson had been a midwife prior to her own children coming along. She had taken several years off when they were young – having brought so many babies into the world she wanted to ensure hers got the best possible start in life. She had never regretted that decision, was thrilled at the way both Kevin and Vicky had developed into fine young people, and opted for voluntary work rather than resuming her career.

Secondly, Manly was such an attractive suburb, admired by many.

Shimmering beaches, vibrant business community, laid-back attitude, renowned by many to be "as Australian as it gets".

Breath-taking walking trails, almost every manner of leisure activity, the playground of those who sought to flaunt wealth, influence, ambition and body beautiful.

With a population of around 80,000, it describes itself as "a must visit destination offering waterfront restaurants, attractions, adventure and entertainment for young and old – relax on the wharf, enjoy sensational views and simply take in the ambience of this cosmopolitan resort-style location".

In short, Manly prided itself in being a trendy place to live and having a window on the world.

For the first week the world backed off and Kevin was allowed the space he craved in order to grieve for Alex, Phil, Jack and Johnnie.

He paced around the house and garden caught up in his own self-doubts, not exactly relaxed, but a little less intense. Not exactly chilling – how could you in such hot weather … boom, boom – but no longer as weighed down.

Still largely uncommunicative, spending hours on an old garden swing, no appetite when he would normally tuck in, guzzling endless amounts of milk.

His mother couldn't make it out though encouraged that his manic behaviour had subsided.

Becky had gone back to her work as a beautician but dropped by whenever she could.

She found Kevin unresponsive but at the same time quite needy. He would ask her to hold him as though reverting to the foetus position inside the womb. She would oblige but felt distinctly queasy. Her heart ached for the return of the active, decisive, fun-loving, always-on-the-go boy she had fallen for at school.

He went for a 15 minute jog around the local area, something mother felt was a good sign.

He went for long walks, but always on his own, which had mother worrying for his safety in case he somehow wandered off. It was almost dementia-like.

And of course the world was bound to intrude into his world before long.

His boss at the sports agency came round to see how he was – he had advance warning of Kevin's troubles and took things softly-softly, staying clear of 'controversial' areas, passing on positive messages from his colleagues, asking how the firm could help.

He never said anything but it greatly concerned him that Kevin was so hard to reach.

Air accident investigators wanted to interview him – he hadn't felt up to it when still on Bali. Dad had spoken to them and asked that Kevin be given some leeway. They said that was acceptable, it must be very hard for him, but they needed to crack on with the probe, the public expected that of them.

Brett did his best to safeguard his son, while explaining how vital it was that Kevin should find it within him to speak to them. There could be things that seemed innocuous to Kevin which could be crucial to the investigation.

Kevin became resigned to cooperating but it put up his stress levels and the demands upon him in his fragile state were almost too much to bear.

He wasn't being bolshie. Why couldn't others 'get' that all Kevin really wanted, at least for a while, was to shut and bolt the door. What was wrong with them?

When it could not be dodged any longer he found the interviewing process took an enormous amount out of him. It felt like he was being hung, drawn and quartered. OK, they had a job to do ... but it was excruciating.

For both parties it was like pulling teeth.

Several times Kevin broke down as he told of the screams, the tortured faces, which all too often kept him awake at night. Each time they had to break for at least 15 minutes, drink a cup of tea, wait until he had composed himself, and then press on.

This was not uncaring officialdom but simply that it seemed prudent to drive the interview relentlessly forward, partly so all could then move on and partly for fear Kevin would be unable to persist if they tried to break it into several sessions

Kevin emerged suicidal. He went straight to bed, talking vaguely of topping himself.

Mrs Jackson called the family doctor.

The doctor seemed rushed off his feet, examined Kevin minimally, concluding there was nothing physically wrong with him.

He prescribed pills and beat a retreat. Kevin wouldn't take them.

Becky's next appearance found Kevin in bits.

She dragged him out for a walk, insistent that shutting himself away was the worst he could do.

She talked to him about anything and everything, her work at the beauticians, friends asking for him, the weather, politics, sport. She forced him to interact, partly through flattery, by continually asking his opinion, his wise advice, and mining his knowledge base. An acquaintance walked by – Kevin would have blanked him but Becky made a point of saying hello, prompting a conversation and sparking Kevin into playing his part.

After two hours they were back at the house. He thanked her, he said he felt better for the exercise, and for the first time since the accident he kissed her as a woman should be kissed.

It built her hopes but the next time she was round the improvement had receded – he was morose, aloof and switched off.

Feeling down herself as a result, she gave it ten minutes, made an excuse and left. And felt very guilty for doing so.

She would persist but she knew she couldn't do it for him; he had to help himself.

It was around this time that the letter writing started, and that was seriously weird.

For they all went to the same address – Suzanne Duthie in Normal, Illinois. But then confusingly they all began, Dear Hope.

Obviously, Suzi would be unable to read them and there was no attempt to use baby-speak. This was as though to an adult.

They were long letters too; almost confessionals.

Kevin told how he thought about her often, openly admitting he was struggling to come to terms with the accident.

Nothing seemed to matter any longer. Every day was just full of total tripe. He could not be bothered with it.

What meaning was there in the accident? Why had the two of them been spared? Were they destined for some sort of higher purpose? He felt himself conversing with the dead in his sleep – were they trying to point the way ahead? His impression was that he had entered a separate world where Becky, Vicky and his parents were peripheral figures. Perhaps, he said to Suzi, she would understand when she was older.

The letters kept dropping through the family letter box roughly every two months, and they found them disturbing.

Was this man mentally ill? Were they expected to respond? Should they phone Kevin's family and voice their concerns for him? Should they bin the letters or keep them?

Presumably Hope was a kind of pet name for Suzi?

There was quite a discussion about what to do and, because different opinions were expressed, it was decided to kick the can down the road. The letters built up into a bundle which was secreted away at the back of a drawer. Except that as time went on there was another bundle, then a further bundle, and gradually the drawer was being taken over. Meanwhile Suzi was growing – toddler, playgroup, schoolgirl.

But first, flashback time.

When Abby had arrived sleep-deprived and wilting with Suzi in her arms family members were there to meet her at Chicago O'Hare International Airport.

There was Robert's mother and father, Anne and Ed, Rose's mother and father, Sara and Jeb, plus Suzi's two uncles, Harris and Luke.

It was quite a reunion or at least it would have been in happier times.

All the more as TV crews, reporters, photographers, the usual media spectrum, had gathered to mark Suzi's homecoming.

Abby, who was getting quite a professional at all this, sparked herself into life, turning on the glittering smile, and showing Suzi off to the cameras.

Abby reckoned she now knew how it must feel to walk the red carpet at the Oscars.

Everyone wanted a shot of them and Abby tried to oblige.

"So happy to be back on American soil," she declared.

Suzi had been an "angel" all flight – another fib for she had instead been largely uptight and distressed before falling into a turbulent slumber.

A great fuss was made of Suzi by both the family and the media. The little one simply clung to Abby for dear life amidst this sea of faces.

The media were pacified and the family set off in convoy for Normal.

They pulled up at Sara and Jeb's home, it being rightly deemed far too morbid for Abby and Suzi to stay at Robert and Rose's house.

Sara carried Suzi out of the car – Abby had kept nodding off and for safety the babe had been transferred over.

Like at Kevin's it seemed the whole street had turned out to welcome them.

'We Love You, Suzi' banners, cheering, car horns hooting, apple pie, even fireworks – the latter being somewhat over the top to say the least.

It was a touching scene, the family thanked their neighbours profusely, and members of the media were on hand to record it all.

When they finally got indoors and closed the front door Abby slumped into a chair, took two sips of a cup of coffee and promptly crashed out.

Suzi, she knew, was in good hands. Anyway, Abby couldn't keep her eyes open one iota longer.

Sara and Jeb had been busy while Abby had been collecting Suzi.

Rose's old cot, which Sara had never been able to bear throwing out, was discovered under a dust sheet in the garage and been cleared of cobwebs and years of dirt. It was now spotless and re-assembled it was fit for purpose if a bit old-fashioned.

Baby food had been purchased from local stores while they had been inundated with kids' clothes from well-wishers.

They put her into a high chair which Harris had supplied and tried her with a chicken concoction and a peach affair.

She seemed to approve albeit plenty was splattered in all directions for good measure.

Sara and Jeb smiled knowingly at each other – it had been a long time since they had been wiping baby mess from the carpet, not something they ever supposed would be coming their way again.

Of course it brought back the memories with more tears shed for Robert and Rose.

Their bodies were not among those recovered though Sara and Jeb had not given up. Perhaps the sea might yet relent.

It was very important to give the devoted couple a proper funeral, a grave to which the family could return, be still and 'talk' to them. The thought of a memorial service for their lost ones seemed a poor substitute but one they knew they might have to embrace.

Time would no doubt make the decision for them.

They put Suzi down in the cot and she too went out like a light.

Her grandparents watched over her in the Land of Nod, then found a blanket to put round Abby who was still out cold in the chair.

Then they retired to bed themselves.

It had sapped their energy too.

Everyone slept in next morning even Sara and Jeb who were always up early.

It was time to take it easy for a few days while Abby recovered from jet lag, she and Suzi became accustomed to the house and the constant stream of callers were treated with politeness and civility.

Over Sunday lunch there was another family gathering, with Suzi once again centre of attention.

Interested parties wanting a cuddle should form an orderly queue, joked Abby.

Later in the afternoon all were partaking of the sunshine in the back garden when something prompted a tenuous discussion about what would be best for Suzi.

Sara and Jeb said they would happily look after her.

But, being in their late 50s, the question was posed whether it might prove all too much for them.

Luke and his wife Amanda had two young children, Jimmy, aged four, and Jane, aged two. They suggested that Suzi might be a good fit with their two.

Abby felt it vital that she be there for Suzi at least in the short term. She said it was unlikely she would return to Dubai and she would probably look for a job locally.

She then dropped her big news and how she had met John. She did not want to go overboard at this early stage, they had known each other for less than a week, but would like to explore where it might take them.

He hoped to come to Normal to visit in the next couple of months.

They were very happy for her realising from the tone of her voice that John clearly meant a lot. It sounded like the real deal.

So nothing got decided. But then did that matter? See how things developed. Let all the close family play a part in her upbringing.

Social Services would no doubt want a say, rightly determined to ensure her welfare.

But they could cross that bridge when they came to it.

Sara and Jeb became Granny and Grandad while for Anne and Ed it was Grandma and Grampa.

The next time Becky went round to see Kevin she found him composing one of his letters to Suzi … except she did not know anything about this growing obsession.

Her first reaction was to be pleased that at least in this way he was back communicating again, and her heart warmed to him.

"Who are you writing to?" she asked.

At first he didn't appear to hear her, completely caught up in what he was doing.

"Sorry," he said. "Did you say something?"

She smiled, trying but failing to make eye contact.

"I was just wondering who you were writing to – whatever it is you seem very focussed."

"I'm writing to Suzi – I write to her regularly."

"Oh," said Becky, somewhat startled.

At a loss to understand why he should be writing to a child not even past its first birthday, she could only reply: "How interesting."

A more fitting response might have been "how strange" but so many of us don't actually say what we mean.

Undone, she decided to park this revelation to when she could give it proper attention.

She changed the subject.

"Have you spoken with any of your friends recently?" she inquired.

"No," he insisted in a tone so hostile it effectively called a halt to any further discussion of the subject.

"Oh," said Becky, again stung by the response.

She attempted another approach.

"What about a decent holiday – it might do you the world of good?"

"No. I don't need a holiday and I certainly don't want a holiday."

He glowered at her and turned back to his letter.

Becky felt like blubbing.

"I think I'll go and make a cup of coffee."

She deliberately didn't ask if he wanted one – she didn't think she could take another rejection, however mundane.

He never even looked up as she made for the kitchen.

Mrs Jackson was there.

Becky, she decided, looked shattered.

"Oh, Becky," she commiserated and passed over the tissues.

Becky dabbed at her eyes and sighed.

This wasn't how it was supposed to be but Becky no longer cared about reticence or indeed getting into a state in front of what she had hoped might one day be her mother-in-law.

"Whatever I do I can't seem to reach him," she ventured between sniffs.

And Kevin's mum embraced the sensitivity of this nice girl who was so fond of her son.

This was certainly not the time to tell her that the family felt she and Kevin should have a break in their relationship, at least until he could regain his health.

"I don't know what to do for the best," moaned Becky.

Kevin's mother put an arm around her, steered her to the kitchen table, sat her down and promised that everything would seem better over a nice cup of tea.

By the time the tea was made Becky was more together. They sipped the hot brew.

"He has been through something beyond our understanding," opened Kevin's mother. "This may take very much longer than we first thought."

Becky nodded her head but once started her worries poured forth.

Kevin appeared a different person and she wanted the old Kevin back. The writing of letters to a baby seemed … seemed … well, plain odd. She hated to suggest it, but … could Kevin be really having the breakdown they had all feared?

Mum put on her most charismatic voice. The girl cared, she cared, they all cared.

The trouble was none of them, and not just Becky, knew how to rectify the situation.

Mum had thought about whether it was time to get mental health services involved, perhaps even pay privately to see a psychiatrist.

But that almost seemed like giving in. Time could sometimes be a great healer.

So she gave Becky the honest truth. That she had no magic wand either. She had no idea if or when they would get the old Kevin back. Becky, she urged, must decide for herself how much she had to give without putting her life on hold. You only got one life and you needed to live it. She must do what her head told her rather than go with her heart.

And it was all said with such fondness that deliberately addressed Becky as family.

For another six months Becky kept committing but gradually her energy faded.

Kevin's mum could see the tiredness in her eyes and the love gradually dissolving.

So sad was this to watch that she determined she would have words with Kevin – one final attempt to save the relationship.

She spoke softly to him, said Becky was a lovely girl who clearly loved him, he could do far worse, he was treating her abysmally, and he should make up his mind if only to set Becky free.

But Kevin was a million miles distant and said something quite bizarre.

He told her: "There's only one woman in my life now … and that's Suzi."

His mother told him that was ludicrous, he needed to get a grip, he had to re-connect with his old life, and by the way the world didn't owe him a living.

Indeed she got positively cross.

He simply went and moped. Back hiding away with his demons.

Becky came round less and less, and it all petered out as she decided she was effectively single once again and it was time to party.

The last time there was even a flicker was when the families of the missing four who had travelled with Kevin to what should have been a golden holiday decided they could wait for bodies no more.

The joint memorial service for Alex, Jack, Johnnie and Phil was a traumatic occasion in a packed church, 500 crammed inside and perhaps the same again gathered outside.

The hymns were beautiful and there was a reading from Psalm 23 including the immortal words: "Even though I walk through the valley of the shadow of death, I fear no evil, for You are with me; Your rod and Your staff, they comfort me."

It was a gathering of the grey, mothers broke down and had to be supported, people sobbed openly.

The wake was reserved – given the awful events of the air crash, laughter and bonhomie was out of the question. Friends and relatives remembered the best of times, spoke of four lives cut down in their prime and pondered the unfairness of it all. Why them? What had they ever done to deserve such a fate?

People payed their respects and slowly wandered away.

The media caught the mood and were equally respectful in their coverage.

Kevin was there with his family ... just. At first he had objected, saying he could not face it, that his presence – the sole adult survivor – would be an affront to the bereaved. He tried to explain that it was a past life to which he could not return.

His father lost his temper, grabbed the lapels of his son's jacket, banged him up against a wall, and told him he was attending the service be it kicking and screaming, come hell or high water.

It produced pandemonium in the household as the two were separated, Kevin's father red in the face, Kevin as white as a sheet.

Reluctantly he agreed to go, a sullen presence amidst an outpouring of grief.

Becky, wearing a black suit and looking drawn, said hello to him, took him by the arm. He acknowledged her. But there was no hint of all they had previously shared.

They parted and neither said another word to each other.

Kevin did not attend the wake. He could not face the intrusion. He could not look people in the eye. He would be in pieces again. Instead, he walked down to the sea and spent an hour and more just staring out to the horizon, watching the waves, marvelling as the seagulls soared, and doing everything he could not to think of the crash.

Of course he could not escape it – but he feared he never would.

Many in the congregation felt for him in his isolation; many others felt his attitude malign and disrespectful.

Either way, Kevin wasn't interested.

Babies grow up fast and Suzi was no different.

In the blink of an eye she was walking unsteadily, saying her first words, knocking over ornaments and shedding tears when she fell.

All the family adored her.

Sara and Jeb had gravitated into looking after her, relieved from time to time by Anne and Ed and Abby.

Abby did her best to carve out ring-fenced time for Suzi despite having landed a terrific job as deputy chief executive of a luxury sports and leisure complex.

It was a dream position, but, she told herself, Suzi was a dream girl.

They did not pick up the signs of what was to come, though in retrospect they were there. If only they had been spotted.

Her manners were non-existent, still hurling her food about, declaring it to be 'pig poo', referring to Granny as 'stinker' and branding Abby 'ugly'.

She and the family's collie Lady hated each other. As she grew up, Suzi took every opportunity to pull Lady's tail and kick her. The normally mild-mannered dog growled savagely, bared its teeth, and barked angrily. Suzi responded by throwing her toys at the poor thing. Lady developed such an aversion to Suzi that she went out of her way to avoid the child.

And it didn't stop there.

When she was four she tried to drown a pet rabbit in next door's pond. When she was five she hit a boy at a children's party so hard he had to be taken to hospital.

Whenever she was thwarted she screamed the house down at volumes which scythed through your brain.

Naturally, there were times she could be angelic.

Just a charmer when the media came round to see her blow the candles out on her birthday cake.

Before throwing a switch to turn back into Miss Nasty.

All this was put down to tantrums, a highly strung nature, and the fact that she was an orphan.

Jeb and Sara found it hard-going, struggled with discipline, but were determined.

Abby was worried for them. She could see them visibly ageing. She could take whatever Suzi could throw at her – often literally.

And she was torn.

Because by then, she and John, the remarkable love story, were headed to the altar.

He had made it over to Normal after about three months, their longing already fired up by Skype sessions and lots of letter writing.

Encouraged by the family, Abby had moved into Robert and Rose's house.

Lying empty, it needed some tender, loving, care. But Abby hadn't been sure, concerned she would be trespassing on the 'grave' of her sister and brother-in-law. Fearing too of walking with ghosts and the bad luck it might bring.

But she was persuaded that it was exactly what Robert and Rose would have wanted for her

She pledged to herself that she would make a new home there, be that temporary or permanent, and honour what they had begun.

So when John arrived over it was all spic and span.

She had explained to him that she could not take days off from her job having only just started it. He said he was coming anyway.

And when they fell into each other's arms the magnetism was alive and gushing.

Like in Bali, the sex was ecstatic and their loved-up aching for each other as torrid as before.

When she did get time off work they shut the door on the world for 24 hours and salivated in the thrill of exploring every inch of each other, mind and bodies entwined in desire and delight.

The visit lasted for just ten days but felt like ten weeks … no, it felt like ten years.

They had already known that what they had was unique to them, but they had taken it to new vistas.

When they weren't in bed she gave him a spin around Normal – her pride in the town shone through and he was happy for her.

Straight-away he decided it seemed a nice place with nice people.

She introduced him to the family and they were impressed.

Like any young suitor meeting her mum and dad for the first time, he was nervous. All a bit daunting. But they were very welcoming and put him at his ease.

Without being rude, there was some gentle probing into his background and prospects – was this man right for their daughter?

But he was polite, respectful, and it was clear to everyone that he and Abby were deeply in love.

When she saw him off at the airport they could barely tear themselves apart.

She cried – again!

"Oh, no," she told him. "Not for the first time I'm soaking your shirt with my tears."

And she was laughing, crying, unsure whether to be happy or sad.

He kissed her lovingly, picked up his bags and headed for Departures.

She returned home and slept for eleven hours straight, worn out but hugely satisfied.

She owed it to her new workplace to graft and that is what she did. She spent as much spare time with Suzi as she could, still startled at the little one's horror spats.

And in-between there was romance by Skype and US Mail.

Between work pressures and the mounting concerns over Suzi, she found her fond hopes of visiting him in Bali drifting. It wasn't her intention, she yearned for him ... and she told him so.

It was already four months and a part of her was frightened she might lose him.

And when he told her in one of their Skype love-ins that he couldn't wait any longer her heart missed several beats and her head was swimming.

But she should never have doubted him. He said he had requested some further leave and would arrive the following week.

She could hardly wait, but she would have to.

This time she did manage to get some time off too.

It was decided they would go away for a short two centre break, seeing the sights of Chicago and going on to Niagara Falls.

They took a stroll along the Riverwalk, which hugs the main branch of the Chicago River, restaurants, bars and attractions at every turn, complete with views of some of the city's most iconic architecture.

She showed him Soldier Field, home of the Chicago Bears football team.

And then they went on to beautiful Niagara, surely one of the wonders of the world.

Did you know that more than six million cubic feet of water goes over the crest of the falls every minute? Well, you know now.

They did what every tourist has to do and took a Maid of the Mist boat cruise, which has carried passengers into the rapids immediately below the falls since 1846.

Awesome, magnificent, spectacular ... adjectives don't do it justice.

They clung to each other as the vessel bobbed and weaved and emerged soaked to the skin, the flimsy protective rain jackets with which they were provided akin to cotton wool in a wind tunnel.

How they laughed, hugged and sucked in one of North America's great natural attractions – right up there with the Rockies, the Grand Canyon and Yellowstone.

Later that evening, watching the sun going down, sitting in the garden at the motel where they were staying, he proposed.

He did it properly, as all men should.

He got down on one knee, asked her to marry him and proffered a ring from a little purse in one of his pockets.

It was how she had dreamed it might be when a little girl.

"Yes, yes, yes ... yes," she shouted out loud, and flung herself into his arms.

This was the man she loved, this was the man she wanted babies with, this was the man with whom she would grow old. Women in love the world over say the exact same thing and it doesn't always pan out. Abby knew it would.

The ring didn't fit and she playfully told him he was hopeless, but of course that could easily be rectified.

She studied the ring and decided she absolutely adored it.

And, talking of love, their love-making that night hit new orgasmic highs.

They would always remember that quaint motel in Niagara.

Indeed, when they got back to Normal she knew full well that, like Suzi, her life would never be normal again either.

Abby went straight to her parents, and announced the news. They were thrilled.

She hugged her mum, she hugged her dad, she hugged John, John hugged her mum and was given a resounding handshake by her father.

Amid gasps, John formally asked her father's permission, which he graciously gave.

Champagne, lots of it, was broken open and there were toasts to the engaged couple.

Uncles and aunts appeared seemingly out of nowhere, the neighbours were invited round, and it turned into quite a party, many an admiring examination of the ring and lots of advice on where to get it sized properly.

Eventually, tipsy but elated, the happy pair poured themselves back home, clutching a full Champagne bottle ... because there had to be one last toast – to Robert and Rose.

That night there was no love-making – both Abby and John were far too smashed.

Somehow, Suzi slept through the party. But next day Abby and John called by to tell her of the engagement and show her the ring.

There were no smiles, she was generally sullen and unresponsive, more interested in pulling tufts of fur out of a small teddy and chucking them all over the room.

Abby was disappointed but accepting. Marriage was a difficult concept for a little girl to get her head round.

They telephoned John's parents in England. They too were very excited for him and expressed their natural desire to meet Abby as soon as could possibly be arranged.

Abby spoke over the phone and said John had told her lots about them.

She promised she would do her utmost to live up to being their daughter-in-law. They told her she would be welcomed into their family.

But the conversation brought them down to earth.

They sat down to discuss how to be together permanently rather than thousands of miles apart.

She offered to chuck in her job, leave Normal, and join him in Bali.

Knowing how hard she would find it to be away from those so dear to her, and her sense of responsibility for Suzi, he ruled that out. Instead he suggested he speak to his superiors and try and get a posting closer to the United States. Once that got sorted out then they could set a date for the marriage.

Aware that might prove difficult to achieve, she asked him whether he was sure it was the best route to take.

He joked with her how indispensable he was.

More seriously, he said he would check out the possibilities and explain the circumstances. Hopefully, they would be sympathetic.

So that was decided.

It was bound to take many months and in the interim they would just have to hope for the best, get back on Skype, and hit the letter writing trail once more.

And, she said, if it dragged on then as soon as she was due more holiday she would be straight on a flight to Bali.

When he left the next day there were fewer tears because both knew their destiny was to be together.

Somewhere along the line, amidst so many thrills, there had to be a reckoning – it was agreed with the church, like with Kevin and his four dead friends, that it was time to have a memorial service for Robert and Rose.

Their bodies hadn't been found and it was hard still to hold out hope that they might be.

The family were dignified – they wanted a simple service lauding two ordinary lives.

Naturally their wishes were respected.

On the day the place was heaving. Absolutely packed.

People spilled out into the church grounds and cemetery though thankfully this possibility had been anticipated with speakers set up to relay the service to those unable to fit within.

The tributes were touching. Robert and Rose as toddlers, holiday frivolities, pride in passing school exams, the high standards they set themselves, a love affair which glittered like the stars, the tenderness between them, marriage, parenthood.

By the end there was barely a dry eye in the church.

The family filed out feeling at peace. And they were sure Robert and Rose were at peace too.

Members of the congregation who chose to do so made their way to the family home where a spread of food, cups of tea and coffee had been laid on. No alcohol – it didn't seem appropriate when it was two young lives, different had it been, say, an elderly individual whose full span could be celebrated in all its elements.

Many people did go back, talked about the happy times, came up with amusing anecdotes, met up with friends and acquaintances, and expressed their deep condolences.

It was a release that so many cared.

There was no rush to depart. Languid and patient was the 'theme'.

Soon a lot of people were also having to be patient as Suzi entered pre-school and threatened to create chaos.

Paint would be splattered about, there would be screaming and spitting, kids were pushed and pinched and, while teacher was trying to read a story, balls would be thrown at other children.

Her first nursery school asked Suzi to leave, saying she was just too disruptive and destructive.

Sara and Jeb were upset. They knew her behaviour left much to be desired but it was surely harsh in the extreme to expel someone so vulnerable, someone with no mother or father to set an example.

They tried a second play group and she lasted longer there. However that came to an abrupt end when Suzi was caught trying to stab another child with a pair of scissors.

At home it was little better – the dog was still getting it in the neck and everywhere else on its body. Garden flowers would be pulled out. Creepy crawlies would be battered with stones. Crockery was being smashed.

Jeb and Sara tried kindness, they tried infinite good humour, they tried verbal discipline and, at their wits end, they tried corporal punishment. But smacking Suzi prompted even worse behaviour along with outright defiance.

They took her to a child psychiatrist but she switched on the charm and the woman struggled to find anything wrong with her.

Abby did her best to take the pressure off her parents whenever possible.

She would take Suzi on nature rambles, to parks, sit with her in front of the television, read books galore to her.

But it was hard going and not easy at all when abused in public and private by this little minx.

Poor Abby was constantly being told by Suzi that she was a 'cow' and she 'hated her'.

Of course, Suzi didn't always understand what she was saying, Abby accepted that, but it was nevertheless hurtful.

Yet there was clearly an intelligent child somewhere in there. If only her energies could be channelled correctly.

And all the time, regular as clockwork, the letters from Kevin kept arriving.

Jeb and Sara always read them – just in case there was some question or other they were expected to answer.

The letters detailed the experiences of a dysfunctional adult, abandoned in a world lacking in any sort of meaning – no ambition, no interest in achieving, divorced from those around him, out of kilter with society.

Sara was aware of the uncanny similarities between Suzi and her rescuer but revolted from going down that road – preferring to put this down to pure coincidence. Perhaps, thought Sara, she was making more of it than was really there. She certainly hoped so. Yet the two of them, Suzi and Kevin, in their own way seemed estranged from the rest of humanity.

Perhaps, thought Sara, things would get better when Suzi started proper school. Perhaps school routine and the development of young minds would shift Suzi onto the straight and narrow.

Sara didn't want to think about the alternative.

There were no such tantrums from Kevin – his parents sometimes thought it might be better if there were.

He was perfectly civilised and pulled his weight around the house – doing the dishes, making his bed, putting washing on the line. Yet he had become so subdued, introspective, almost reclusive.

He showed no signs of wanting to go back to work and no signs of returning to the flat they had bought him when he first got the sports agency job.

The first anniversary of the crash was looming and the worry was that this might set him back further.

If they could just persuade him to return to work – diverting his attention onto ordinary day-to-day existence, keeping him sufficiently busy that he could no longer spend his days analysing what might have been.

Indeed he really needed to make an effort as his boss had been incredibly generous, keeping open his job and continuing to pay his wages.

Everyone knew that couldn't continue indefinitely.

So when the office suggested that perhaps he attempt two days a week initially and see how it went, it was not to be dismissed lightly.

The family played it low key as they sought to tempt him into giving it a go,

His work colleagues who had been ever so encouraging despite little reciprocity, and who had previously sent get-well-soon cards and the like, mocked up a whacky video revolving around a spoof hunt for the missing Kevin.

Even Kevin could not but fail to find it a laugh.

At last he was talked into making a comeback.

But come the Monday in question the prospect found him a quivering wreck, cowering in his bedroom and unwilling to come out.

His mother phoned in, said there had been a setback to his recovery but expressed the hope it would be short-lived.

For the next month they worked on him, with the aim of putting him into situations where he had no alternative but to relate to people.

There was a surprise party for his birthday, Vicky dragged him out to bars and barbeques, they took him to their local church on Sundays hoping that the love emanating from the congregation would stimulate him to throw off the shackles.

And it worked to a degree.

He seemed to become less negative. There were spells of jocularity and joviality – not many but it was a beginning.

As for his part, Kevin acknowledged that the family were doing their utmost, pulling out all the stops. Their devotion was selfless. He was aware of where they were coming from and gradually he managed to accept that it might prove a way forward.

Somehow, nervous and frightened, he forced himself through the office door.

Years later he compared it to what it must have been like to 'go over the top' during World War I. The likes of Passchendaele where so many Australians lost their lives. Obviously that is a foolish analogy but it was indicative of how his mind was working at the time.

All the guys and girls made a fuss of him in what he realised was very much a genuine welcome – the lost sheep had returned.

That first day he didn't do much – made the tea, ploughed through a mountain of emails, tried to catch up. Much the same the next day.

They were being as tactile as they could while trying not to stress him in any way.

That was his week done – it hadn't been the catastrophe he had feared.

Naturally his colleagues had all been briefed on how best to play it sufficient that they had managed to conceal their shock at the state of someone who had been through such a torture.

He was gaunt, he was timid, there was no fun in him, he appeared careworn.

On the Friday there was a spontaneous meeting of management and staff to talk through what they might do to boost his spirits.

It was obvious to everyone that they couldn't just pitch him in to normal duties.

How to handle such a delicate situation?

Front-facing stuff was clearly out of the question while he built up his work capacity.

Perhaps purely office based for the first month, tidying up CVs, running errands, answering the phone when he felt able.

Maybe after that shadowing others at client events and marketing opportunities.

And all the time talking to him, asking his opinions, involving him in office banter, joshing with him over a pint after work.

They weren't social workers, they weren't psychiatrists, but Kevin was a great bloke and they felt for him. What he had gone through could have happened to any of them. It could have crippled any of them.

Should they try and set him up with a girl, suggested one optimist. That got laughed down amidst comments that the perpetrator should sort himself out first and gags about the sports agency morphing into a dating agency.

The meeting broke up with everyone in high spirits.

They would muddle through – Kevin would surely come round.

And indeed he did manage to adjust if somewhat tentatively.

Gradually they gave him extra bits and pieces to tackle and over a six month period he was doing more and more while graduating back to a full five day week.

So that was fine albeit the sparky, bouncy, full of ideas Kevin was not back.

It was a more plodding Kevin, a Kevin who was reactive rather than proactive, a Kevin who did not seem to have his heart in the job. The spirit was missing. Interaction with clients lacked a certain understanding. The final product was not quite there.

He moved back into his flat but gone was the happy-go-lucky guy whose love of life shone through.

Invited to some social occasion he would be first to make his excuses after a diffident couple of drinks. He was awkward interacting with the opposite sex when once he had been a magnet.

The improvement seemed to have stalled and, as he feared. it was impossible as the years rolled by ever to escape the plane crash entirely.

There was the one year anniversary, the five year anniversary, the inquiry itself seemed never ending.

The family was thankful that the depression and melancholy had been banished though they feared it could return. But concerning signs remained.

He was working with a sports agency yet his love of sport had virtually evaporated. He had never returned to playing rugby, no longer did he get along to cricket matches. He worked out in a gym when he felt the urge but that was about it.

This all spilled over into his employment. At best you would call his performance adequate. Consequently there were no promotions. He was stuck on the lower rungs of the ladder.

His 30th birthday passed with just a modest family celebration – mum, dad, Vicky and that was it. He had insisted he didn't want any fuss, no big party, no presents.

Old friends were fixing themselves up with partners, getting married, having children.

Some invited him to stag celebrations, at home and abroad. He told them it wasn't for him.

Since Becky nobody had touched him with star dust. Or rather he had never allowed them.

Nights in the flat with a book, watching TV, putting on the occasional film, writing to Suzi – that was the level of a typical week.

In short, he seemed to be missing out on much of what life offered.

Abby too feared life was passing her by.

Weeks turned into months, she was still in Normal and John was in Bali. Yes, they were in contact all the time but Abby was ready and eager to move to the next stage, to become a wife and hopefully a mother.

Sometimes to her dismay she became grumpy in her work, with the family and even with John.

So much so that she found herself picking faults in him – he wasn't exactly spontaneous, he didn't bring her flowers, there was a stultifying element to his nature, he did serious rather too well, was he trying hard enough to bring this enforced absence to a successful conclusion?

The doubts appalled her. She told herself she had the boy of her dreams, someone with a good job, who was supportive, caring, charming, and who loved her.

Pull yourself together, Abby, she told squirrel, the cuddly toy she took to bed with her as a child.

John too was frustrated. His superiors had taken on board the reasons for his transfer request but were reluctant to let him go and certainly without having a successor lined up.

The diplomatic machine grinded away interminably slowly.

There were days when he felt like screaming at them to get a bloody move on.

Not something of course a 'chap', in English public school parlance, put into practice – that would scupper everything.

To his regret, his conversations with Abby were sometimes a touch testy. Having to wait was in some ways a good examination of their suitability for each other. Not that he wanted it that way. He didn't do quarrels – that was not in his makeup. His inclination was always to avoid confrontation and he was aware this was both a strength and a weakness.

But there was nothing he could do to expedite things and there was nothing else for it but nose to the grindstone.

A future with Abby was for the meantime a wistful illusion.

Both of them were almost tearing their hair out when eight months on from when he had first raised the subject his boss called him aside one day.

Would he like to go to Toronto?

He almost leapt in the air – he knew it was probably the closest option he was going to get, and 'thank you, sir' but it sounded ideal.

The first thing he did was check the distances between Normal and Toronto – nine hours or so by car, one and a half hours by plane to Central Illinois Regional Airport at Bloomington-Normal.

The next thing he did was Skype Abby.

Abby was having a bad day. Stuff had gone wrong at work, Suzi had been frightful when she visited, and she was right in the middle of eating her tea.

She feared she looked a mess and she wasn't in the mood.

What did he want?

And instantly regretted her brusqueness.

He ignored the taunt knowing his news would transcend whatever she was upset about.

He almost shouted it out – a posting to Toronto.

She screamed, started madly blowing kisses to him, and couldn't get the stream of words out fast enough.

"Oh, John, I love you, I love you, I love you. When? What about the wedding? I'm going to have so much to do. Darling, that's wonderful."

They both agreed that Toronto was a splendid city and felt sure they would be happy there.

"You'd better go and eat your tea – it will be going cold," he suggested.

She couldn't care less about her tea. She only wanted to digest this fabulous news.

It meant they could at last be together and yet in easy travel distance of Normal so she could continue to play a role in Suzi's life. That remained important. She owed it to Robert and Rose. Suzi was hard work but that didn't matter. Keeping in touch was a matter of honour. Abby remained determined to do her best by her niece. She supposed that once she had children herself it would be tougher to maintain the same closeness, but it was incumbent on her to remain steadfast.

John didn't yet know the Toronto timeframe but was aware that once a decision had been taken there was a tendency to make it happen in quick time.

Abby wanted to know what was 'quick'.

Maybe three to four weeks.

She freaked out.

But what about the wedding, she asked again.

He laughed and told her haughtily: "Well, you'd better get on and organise it pronto."

She screamed again … and now they were both laughing.

On a high, buffeted by the prospect of being re-united at last, combined with the likelihood of a mad rush to get married, she was in a complete flap.

They broke off the call in happy raptures to enmesh themselves in the deep commitment they were about to make and all that revolved around it.

Abby went in search of her parents, dancing gaily as she went.

But she found them distracted and distressed.

Sure enough it was Suzi again.

It was the hurdle they knew was creeping up on them and they had no real idea how they were going to handle it.

Suzi was beginning to ask about what had become of her mummy and daddy. Everyone else seemed to have one so why not her?

The first time it came up Jeb and Sara had managed to dodge the question by persuading Suzi to take part in a game of hide and seek.

Subsequently she seemed to forget all about it.

It was weeks later that the topic was revisited.

"Granny?"

"Yes, dear."

"What's happened to my mummy and daddy? I can't find them anywhere. Are they lost?"

Sara was taken aback and, thinking on her feet, replied: "Well, Suzi, in a way they are lost."

But she wasn't ready for the response.

"Why can't we find them?" asked Suzi.

Then, she tugged at granny's arm.

"Come on Granny – let's look in the garden. They might be there."

Sara was completely stumped by this purest form of child logic, but thought she had better go along with it.

So they went out into the garden and began to search for Robert and Rose.

They looked behind bushes and trees, drew a blank when exploring the garden shed and there was no sign of them when they entered into the garage.

"I know," said Suzi. "Let's get Lady. Policemen always have dogs when they are looking for bad men."

Gosh, thought, Sara, how had she ever learned that? A troubled child but a bright child.

Suzi went into the house and began hunting out Lady. There was much calling of Lady's name and banging of doors.

No doubt Lady was trying not to be found as usual.

But eventually Lady burst out the back quickly followed by Suzi.

Lady ran to Sara as if for protection, her baleful eyes asking what all this was about.

But Suzi was giving the orders.

She pointed at Lady. "Go and find mummy and daddy."

Lady appeared bewildered and looked to Sara for guidance.

"Go and find mummy and daddy, you stupid dog," screeched Suzi, waving her arms.

A frightened Lady shot off all over the place, charging about aimlessly, darting here and sniffing there, with Suzi trying to keep up but completely failing.

Until Lady was back at square one with Sara.

Suzi was quickly becoming fed up.

"You hopeless dog," she berated the poor thing. "Shoo, shoo, find, find."

She aimed a swipe of her hand at Lady who yelped and sped away.

Another mad circle of the garden ensued.

Suzi fell over in the pursuit, picked herself up, shouted 'bad dog', and went chasing after.

Before Lady thrashed around in the plants and emerged with a smelly old tennis ball, depositing it at Suzi's feet with a 'perhaps this is what she wants' expression.

"Bad dog, bad dog."

She threw the tennis ball at Lady who caught it in mid-air thinking perhaps Suzi had decided to play a game.

But it just made Suzi even more hyper.

She picked up some soil from a flower bed and hurled it towards Lady.

Looking disgusted – what did this infuriating child-human want – Lady headed for the still open back door and bounded inside.

Sara had been watching this whole piece of theatre, chuckling to herself – surely something akin to an early Charlie Chaplin "talky".

Suzi didn't see the funny side. Indeed, she was almost apoplectic.

And then came the tears of fury.

Sara went to hold her and got short shrift.

"I hate you," shrieked Suzi. "I bet you've stolen mummy and daddy – you pig."

That set off Sara into another giggling fit which in turn infuriated Suzi even more.

She ran inside screaming and screaming and screaming, with Sara attempting to calm her down. It took many minutes and two bribes, a cartoon on the television accompanied by a Hershey bar.

Suzi relented, hands, face and top covered in chocolate, trying to take in the cartoon characters' antics.

However, Suzi's antics left Sara aware that she could not escape the big question for much longer.

Abby revealed her news about Toronto, her mother and father said they were so pleased for her, but it didn't come from the core as it normally would have done. She could see this whole Suzi thing was having an effect on them and she was no longer going to be on the doorstep. Now she was able to pop round when they needed her. Soon, she was going to have to plan her trips back carefully. She wondered if she was doing the right thing.

They assured her she was. And told her much as the link with Suzi was so vital to them all she could not compromise her happiness. John was made for her and they must grasp a future together. She would regret it for the rest of her days if she decided otherwise.

Her mum and dad were right, of course.

How she wanted to be wrapped in his arms once again.

But the imponderables were piling up. They had to provide some sort of explanation for Suzi, she would also have to break it to her that she was going away, and then there was the whole wedding and hardly any time to arrange it.

Abby feared it might destabilise Suzi yet again.

And all this coming as the youngster approached school age.

Emboldened to meet the challenges head on, she was fervently convinced that Suzi too could rise to the occasion. But would she?

It was decided if possible to do this in stages.

First they would get Robert and Rose's picture and wedding albums out and explain to Suzi that mummy and daddy had gone to heaven.

Next Abby would reveal to Suzi that marriage to Robert was imminent.

And at a later date they would discuss Toronto with her, hoping that Suzi could be coaxed into being happy for Abby rather than taking the view that she was about to be deserted.

There was no time to lose even though it was going to be a huge ask for the tot.

How much she would take in was the issue. Would she completely lose it? Certainly too it would be just the start. She was bound to get even more inquisitive as she got older.

Sara, Jeb, Abby and Suzi had been grocery shopping. Suzi had assisted in putting all the goodies away in cupboards, fridges and freezers.

"Wow," Sara told Suzi, "You have been busy. You've been a great help. I don't know what we would do without you. Let's get you a nice glass of juice and have a sit-down."

When everyone was sorted the subject was raised.

Sara took the lead.

"Suzi, you know we were talking the other day about mummies and daddies."

Suzi, who for some reason was unusually amenable, nodded her head.

"Well, sadly, very sadly, very very sadly, your mummy and daddy had a terrible accident and have gone to heaven. That's why Granny and Grandad look after you."

Sara had planned to say a lot more but, losing her nerve, ground to a halt.

Suzi looked at them quizzically, as expected struggling to comprehend.

There was one of those dreadful silences which last seconds but feel like hours.

When Suzi spoke it took them all by surprise.

"Can I visit them in heaven?" she asked.

For all three adults it was the same reaction – huge lump in throat and hearts melting for the little one and her bravery.

Sara racked her brains as to how to respond. Nothing instantaneous came to mind that would cover it.

So she said: "Heaven is where God lives, Suzi. He takes great care of all those who go to heaven, but I am afraid visitors are not allowed."

"Why not?" said Suzi, clearly puzzled.

There was another silence.

Abby came to the rescue.

"Suzi, we've got lots of photographs of mummy and daddy here."

She opened up a photographic album. "Would you like to see some of them?"

A curious Suzi got up and went to sit beside Abby. They began to go through the snaps.

She saw Robert and Rose as young children, playing, singing in the choir, as teenagers, university students and getting married.

Abby finished off with pictures of Suzi in the arms of her parents.

It had been a relatively fast spin through and missing loads out, but it had still taken some twenty or so minutes.

Abby had tried to make it fun, something of a game even ... the intention being to avoid over-burdening her niece and certainly avoiding it turning into some sort of lesson.

Abby closed the album.

"Wow, was that interesting?" she questioned.

"Yes," announced Suzi. "It was nice. I wish mummy and daddy could be here now."

Then she was off, skipping and jumping. "When's lunch ready – I'm hungry," she exclaimed.

They were all thankful for Suzi changing the subject and saving them the dubious task.

How amazing that children can seemingly compartmentalise these sorts of issues. Albeit for sure the topic had merely been parked while Suzi took in the mass of information.

She had done so well.

For Kevin, It began to sink in that the job at the sports agency wasn't really going anywhere.

He should have been mortified because this had been the role he coveted and he had been good at it. Now he was drifting along and to be honest wasn't really that bothered. He definitely wasn't getting the same satisfaction – it had turned into a chore.

Indeed, he sensed that he had become something of an embarrassment.

He was more or less bomb-proof because no company would want the public ignominy of sacking an Australian 'hero'.

And in a way that made it worse.

Kevin knew he wasn't pulling his full weight and he knew that his colleagues knew he wasn't pulling his full weight.

He was letting them down.

But he was frightened for the future if he decided to jack it in. What would he do? How would he pay the bills? Where would he go?

He was getting a reasonably salary and it was easy to keep taking the money.

Yet, if it ended tomorrow would it really matter? Something would surely come up. Perhaps it was time for a change.

By coincidence, as this was flying around his mind, it turned out to be the week for office annual appraisals.

Down the years Kevin had hardly met anyone who thought annual appraisals were worth the paper they were written on.

Lies, bullshit and appraisals – that was the general view.

It was a total charade, an annual word game, with only the vaguest connection between assessment criteria and the actual job in question.

Generally, people knew full well where things were going wrong, but these were forbidden subjects because it would inevitably point the finger at those over-promoted, useless pain-in-the-necks who frankly weren't up to it – the management lackeys and yes-men who had clambered up the greasy pole by keeping their nose clean, never querying anything, doing it by the book, and robotically imposing the official business creed. Creeps who never thought out of the box, showed no originality and abhorred individualism.

Management pretended it all had value but in reality it was a worthless, box-ticking, veneer which meant nothing, produced nothing and changed nothing.

Typically no-one believed in it, not even the management.

The sort of cosy set-up which once in a blue moon got blown apart by a whistle-blower or economic crisis.

Which normally resulted in savage cost-cutting, the departure of those who were good, damaged morale, and wholesale change introduced by 'consultants' and bean counters who knew nothing of the business concerned, were not interested in knowing about the business concerned, and operated through algorithms and computer predictions.

So much for appraisals, albeit in a relatively small set-up like the sports agency much looser ties tended to exist.

But then there are always exceptions to any rule of thumb.

Kevin was expecting little from the exercise apart from a largely wasted thirty minutes to an hour as both parties circled around facets which neither dared delve into for real.

The meeting was being conducted by deputy managing director Rick Ronda, one of those plastic-faced clones who played it straight down the middle. Didn't give praise; didn't give grief. Hard to like but nothing to dislike.

Yet for once the conversation stumbled into areas of mutual interest where neither party had intended to head.

Not caring much either way, Kevin admitted he wasn't getting as much out of the job as previously. Ronda said management felt he was perhaps not contributing to the extent he had before the plane crash. Kevin acknowledged he had lost a bit of enthusiasm. Ronda said Kevin was still on the ticket but perhaps there were other scenarios they could explore.

It took all of Kevin's will-power to keep a straight face. They both knew this was management-speak for 'do you want out'?

Kevin muttered the usual rubbish back along the lines of the only certainty being change.

And the meeting ground on with vague commitments towards exploring whether there might be "alternative roles".

If not, said Ronda, he wanted to absolutely emphasise that Kevin could remain with them as long as he wanted. No question about it. Nevertheless times were tight and the management had looked at whether there might be scope for staff interested in taking redundancy to put their names forward.

They both knew this was more management-speak, this time for 'we'll give you a decent pay-off to go'.

It was agreed to re-convene in due course when both parties had looked into it further.

Now, it so happened that Kevin had shortly before the appraisal meeting bumped into a one-time school friend, David Sako, who he had lost touch with some while previous. But there had been an amicable chat over a cup of coffee. Sako said he was working in the property world, selling houses. It was easy for anyone with a bit of flair and the gift of the gab. Lots of money to be made. They were always looking for good people – might Kevin be interested.

Kevin was wholly unfamiliar with the ins and outs of estate agency, flattered the fellow by saying it sounded enthralling, but in reality never gave it a second thought.

They parted on good terms, exchanged contact details, and promised to keep in touch – in that casual manner where neither of you has any intention of doing so.

However, in the wake of the appraisal it crossed Kevin's mind that he ought to give Sako a ring and explore matters further.

I mean – how hard could it be? An extensive trawl around the internet and Kevin was intrigued. It had its merits. Varied. Person to person. Sounded down his street.

They agreed to meet up again and a serious discussion ensued. Sako suggested Kevin give it a try on a probationary, nothing definite, basis and see how things developed.

Kevin said he thought he would like to take up the offer, explaining in general terms his situation at the sports agency and the likelihood of him moving on.

It was left in Kevin's hands to get back in touch. If his answer was 'yes' then he could start more or less immediately.

By the time the appraisal was resumed Kevin had pretty much decided to take the money and run.

He and Ronda sat down again – venue being the usual desolate meeting room where bars on the windows were the one missing accoutrement.

Kevin decided he might as well take the bull by the horns – had the company put together a package for anyone who might be inclined towards redundancy?

He sat back quite proud of such a contrived piece of back-to-front garbage – management-speak wasn't simply the preserve of management.

Ronda said the usual arrangement for anyone forced to step down through ill-health and the like was two weeks' pay for every year of service. It was the first time they had alluded to ill-health and Kevin got the message – they believed the crash had turned him into a nutter.

Yet he didn't much care what they thought. Perhaps he was a nutter – admittedly the whole crash thing still seemed to straight-jacket him like being trapped in rain and mist atop a mountain in winter, not that living in Australia he had ever found the need to be up a mountain in winter.

Well, fine, they could make him out to be a basket case, just as long as the package was so nuts it would be impossible to decline.

But Ronda still held the floor and continued to speak.

In the truly exceptional circumstances that were Kevin's the company would agree one month's pay for every year of service.

Now 32, Kevin had been there for 12 years – that meant he'd get a year's pay, plus recompense for any holiday entitlement not taken up by the due date.

Also there would be a goodwill bonus.

All in all the offer amounted to a highly appealing and hefty five figure sum. There would be no requirement on him to work his notice.

Ronda strongly suggested he go away and think about it. They would pay for him to speak to an employment lawyer should he wish to take that up.

Kevin agreed that a cooling off period was definitely a good idea.

"Take the rest of the week," said Ronda. "Come back on Monday and let me know your decision."

Kevin picked up his jacket and headed to the flat.

Perhaps, he concluded, Ronda wasn't quite the total twat devoid of sincerity he had him figured for at the outset. There was some compassion there after all. He was just another bloke trying to turn a dollar.

The deal, he decided, was pretty decent. To be fair, the company had overall been decent to him during his career there.

He went back to his parent's place for the weekend and told them he was thinking of leaving, outlining what was on the table.

His mother was against it – he was in a secure job, they had always looked after him, and it could be a big mistake.

His father was less sure. If Kevin felt he could handle it then perhaps it was time for a change. A new career; a new Kevin.

Sister sat firmly on the fence, saying only he could decide whether it felt right or not.

Kevin said he would sleep on it.

It was a lazy Sunday and nobody said anything about it until, while they were relaxing around the patio, drinking glasses of wine before lunch, Vicky could no longer resist.

Had he come to a conclusion?

Kevin said he had.

He would first try bluff, and tell them he would take the package so long as they threw in the office car he ran around in when he had to do outside meetings and client visits.

If they said 'no' then he would take the package anyway.

That produced a measure of scorn, with everyone talking at once, the thesis being that Kevin was a right chancer.

They'd never give him the car too, surely.

"Well, we'll see," quipped Kevin.

Nobody said anything but Kevin must surely be getting better if he could come up with a bare-faced wheeze like this.

The atmosphere lightened completely, there was laughter, merriment ... it was a good day. Such that Kevin hadn't really known with his loved-ones since before the crash.

The next morning he sat opposite Ronda like a poker player going for the big one. He'd never played poker but felt like a veteran.

He showed his card.

Ronda went away and consulted.

Ten minutes later he came back into the room. They would throw the car in.

But the tone of voice and the way he said it made it very clear that was it. They wouldn't be pushed any further.

But, hey, they wanted shot of him, for sure. It said something about how much of a burden they felt he had become.

It was agreed. They shook hands.

It would take a day or two to put the paperwork together and a week after that to pay the money over.

But, they noted, Kevin was free to take the car home that evening.

The office telegraph was at work – everyone knew something was up though they weren't sure what. After all, Kevin had hardly done a stroke of work for several days.

"Come on, tell us what's happening," questioned one of the brasher ones.

But Kevin said he was sworn to silence – they would find out soon enough.

He was elated … getting the car too was a coup. But he was also cautious – he was stepping out into the unknown and the crash had knocked his confidence when it came to going it alone.

In due course they got the paperwork together. He signed; they signed.

And, with what seemed slightly indecent haste, as though they felt they were ridding themselves of a millstone around their necks, it was his leaving day.

To do them justice, they gave him a decent send-off. The office ground to a halt for three quarters of an hour late afternoon, some wine and nibbles had been laid on, they presented him with a card signed by everyone complete with piss-takes, plus a laser measurer for working out the size of rooms instantly – it had got about that he was toying with estate agency.

The MD had the usual 'urgent meeting' to attend – not wishing to demean himself by supping with the plebs, it was presumed – but Ronda offered some pleasantries along the lines of long serving Mr Reliable, thank you for your important contribution, wish you well for the future … blah, blah, rubbish, rubbish.

Shouts of 'speech, speech' shamed Kevin into replying. He managed the usual platitudes – would miss them all, wished the company every good fortune, he was leaving with the best tea-making skills of anyone in Australia, and he bumbled to a halt amidst genuine bonhomie.

The wine was drunk, some tales were told and it was off to one of the local bars.

Most stayed a decent length of time before disappearing, a handful bantered on for an hour or so, a couple of mates kept him company in a minor pub crawl … and then it was off home.

He enjoyed the night. It was a reasonable way to go out.

He sat down in the flat and not for the first time dwelt on where he was headed – not a good idea. Beware over-philosophising – it can take you to dark places. Sometimes better to simply get on with life, accept there will be ups and downs, good and bad, success and failure, rich and poor.

Back in Normal it was the day of the wedding and Abby was in a panic.

Not all the flowers had turned up, the 1950's Lincoln they had booked had suffered a tyre blow-out which was being mended at the side of a road somewhere in the back of beyond, and rain was pouring down instead of the promised sunshine.

A dozen of John's side of the family were attending from various parts of the US and England and Abby was desperate to put on a good show for them every bit as much as she wanted it to be special for her and her fiancé.

Then someone knocked over a cup of coffee and it splashed onto one of the bridesmaid dresses.

Finally, Suzi was in frumpish mood, dancing in the rain outside before being hauled in, then refusing to have her hair tied in a bow.

"I don't want to go – it's yucky," she insisted for the umpteenth time.

People were rushing about but at least Jeb and Sara were stalwarts. There was still two hours to go and a lot could happen in two hours. They'd seen it all before – things had a way of working out.

They felt sure of getting her to the church on time.

Jeb was checking with the car hire company, Sara was working on getting coffee stain out of the dress, and, according to the local weather forecast, the rain would soon be replaced by a mix of sun and light cloud.

John was blissfully unaware of the tension.

He was just nervous, plenty nervous.

He'd been ready for ages. Easy for men of course, except slightly more complicated because he was resplendent in a kilt, dirk hanging ferociously from a belt around his waist, all in honour of the Scottish connection.

Now he was just hanging around, drinking cups of tea and praying nothing disastrous would happen, like having a coughing fit all of a sudden just as he was supposed to kiss the bride.

Take it steady, breathe in and breathe out, said best man Tommy. But Tommy had to make a speech at the wedding breakfast so he wasn't in great shakes either.

It was the only time John had ever been tempted to smoke, but resisted.

"Is my tie straight?" he asked for the fourth time in twenty minutes.

"Yes," insisted Tommy. "Relax."

One hour to go and Abby was afraid her hair still wasn't right. The florist had been rounded up and was supposedly on the way with a second drop of flowers. They hadn't arrived yet.

"Have the orders of service made it to the church?"

"Yes," said her dad.

Was he sure those black shoes he hadn't worn in years were going to hold up?

"I went out last week and bought new ones."

Where were the flight tickets for the honeymoon in Hawaii?

"They're safe – it's all arranged."

Half an hour to go and the missing flowers arrived.

The hire firm phoned to say the tyre was fixed and they were making good progress.

Twenty minutes to go and John and Tommy were walking into the church with an air of confidence which they certainly didn't feel.

Fifteen minutes to go and the rain had stopped.

Ten minutes to go and the cars arrived.

Carefully, ever so carefully, Abby, Jeb and the bridesmaids manoeuvred themselves into them.

Suzi tried to splash in a puddle and was bodily picked up by one of the chauffeurs and placed inside the requisite limousine, much to her chagrin.

The cavalcade left for the church and now a new panic emerged.

They needed to get a move on, Abby convinced herself, as the fleet took it sedately through the town.

Fashionably late by five or maybe ten minutes was one thing – all brides were fashionably late – but to be twenty or, God forbid, 30 minutes late would be mortifying. She could not do that to poor John – he would be a quivering wreck by the time she reached his side.

Nearly there, insisted her dad.

And right enough at that precise moment the church came into view.

They were bang on time.

Exiting the vehicles there was a lot more fussing as they sorted themselves out, checked dresses, made tiny adjustments.

And five minutes late Jeb was walking his radiant daughter down the aisle as the organ music rang out and shafts of sunlight danced through the stained glass windows.

John stuck out his chin, breathed a sigh of relief, and snuck a quick glance towards his oncoming bride. She was indeed looking radiant.

She arrived alongside him, they smiled, the minister offered brief reassurance, and then coaxed them through it.

For the two of them the service went past in a blur.

The minister extoled the vows they were exchanging, marriage was a wonderful institution beloved of God, marriages faced many obstacles, but he was sure theirs would be a loving and fulfilling union.

And for both, when he pronounced them husband and wife, it was the most beautiful feeling in the world.

John and Abby kissed, goose bumps running down her spine, cheers from the congregation.

Sara shed a tear – mothers were allowed to do that.

And so the di Matteos and the Munros were joined together on United States soil.

Definitely a touch of the American dream about it all.

The reception hit the button – everyone in high spirits, a multitude of congratulations for the happy couple, carefree dancing ...

The speeches were a mix of serious and frivolous, nothing too embarrassing.

Realising she could probably get away with just about anything for a day, Suzi hid under the table drapes, discovered she liked wedding cake and got all gooey, and took a sneaky taste of champagne from an abandoned glass when no-one was looking. It was nasty.

She jumped around the dance floor pretending to be a big person and eventually totally spent Sara carried her up to the room in which they were staying and put her to bed.

Another new experience came just a few days later when she started 'proper' school.

By and large she was OK.

Naturally, being an orphan, the teachers kept an eye on her to try and ensure she did not feel 'out of it'.

And they made a big effort to get her to respond in the classroom and say her piece.

When it came to reading and writing she got on with her learning, picking it up quicker than most.

But there appeared no great love for school. Indeed you would probably say she was inured to the whole situation.

You got the impression she was simply biding her time.

Meanwhile her interaction with other pupils could best be described as erratic.

There were times she looked as though she was playing happily. And other times when chairs were turned over, faces scratched and kids pushed and shoved.

To the extent that her classmates saw her as a loose cannon who could explode with no warning. It didn't help her make friends.

The staff sought to explain firmly that certain behaviour was unacceptable. You wouldn't say their interventions were treated with contempt but certainly disdain.

Suzi always knew best and she could be a right little madam.

You would see lads crying in corners, complaining their feet had been stamped on. Girls would be found howling, their pigtails pulled viciously. It was always Suzi and always she was nowhere to be seen. And when the reckoning came the 'charm tap' was turned on, allowing her to talk her way out of so much.

As for lessons, she liked history, particularly the building of America. Music interested her and she was quick at English language.

Yet overall she treated school as a bore which greatly frustrated both her teachers and Jeb and Sara.

They tried to get across how vital learning was but found Suzi impassive.

And when she discovered computer games, social media, mobile phones and the whole spread of what, far from counter culture, had become mainstream, then her road ahead was set.

Work and lessons were relegated down the list of priorities. Trolling and hip-hop music rose up the agenda.

It was the start of her disaffection for school and authority generally, a tragedy given her intelligence.

Meanwhile, bullying fellow pupils, the swots who did want to do well, became category one.

She had turned into one of the bad girls and she began to revere her hard nut image.

There were staff pow-wows about what to do with her and how to control her. There were discussions with Jeb and Sara who were equally at a loss. Nobody was able to come up with an answer.

At the age of ten she began playing truant,

Jeb and Sara would somehow get her to school and at the first break she would just walk out. She was picked up for shoplifting – it started with sweets, cola, jeans.

Then it moved on to stealing purses and wallets, pocketing the money and dumping the rest in lakes, creeks, bins, anywhere easy.

Which is when the local police started taking an interest.

Suzi and sidekick Molly Goodright were lifted from the streets, arcades … anywhere they could get up to no good.

It was something of a game for Suzi. There was the adrenalin thrill of stealing stuff and getting away with it. Running rings around grown-ups was fun. Not so nice getting caught but all you ever got was a smack on the wrist.

Appalled, riddled with embarrassment, horrified by what the neighbours must think, Sara and Jeb pleaded with Suzi, implored her to put a halt to this counter-productive behaviour, and warned her she would end up in prison. Did she want that?

That wasn't how Suzi saw it.

She had never known her parents – stolen from her by a harsh world. How unfair was that? Then Abby had dumped her by disappearing to Toronto. Suzi felt lonely. She felt betrayed. She felt rejected. School was akin to a prison camp. Nobody understood her. Nobody cared. So nobody should expect her to care. She would please herself. She had declared war on society.

Much older she would look back and appreciate the flaws in those arguments.

People did care. Sara and Jeb cared very much. Abby cared. The school cared. But you don't always see it that way when you are young and vulnerable.

Hard to reconcile that the underlying wounds from the plane crash and losing her parents in the process had left an imprint on Suzi which could never be erased.

Just like across the globe nobody could really relate to what Kevin was going through.

Suzi feeling harshly cheated; Kevin still mortified and scarred.

Abby was particularly shocked by the way Suzi was disintegrating.

Toronto had been a great success as had marriage.

Hawaii had been extraordinary. Neither of them had ever been there before. But, as the guidebooks state, the natural scenery, warm tropical climate, abundance of public beaches, oceanic surrounds, and active volcanoes make it a popular destination for tourists. That is why they had decided to honeymoon there and they were not disappointed.

They explored the islands, taking a number of trips, wrapped up in their beauty.

They also explored each other – their bodies, their hopes, their foibles and their love.

Setting up home in Toronto was a new chapter. The embassy had helped them find an apartment and they had invested a lot of themselves in the way they had decorated it and fitted it out.

Much of that had been down to Abby as John's duties meant extended hours.

She had given herself six months to make sure this marriage and the new home worked. There was the odd spat like all young couples had but they were very happy.

It was going so well she decided it was time to start applying for leisure/hospitality jobs – naturally distance had meant reluctantly she had given up her previous post.

And then she discovered she was pregnant.

They hadn't planned it but both of them were thrilled as were their families.

Gosh. They were going to be parents. Everything would be transformed – first marriage, now parenthood.

In a way not ideal – meeting, marriage, maternity. They had barely had time to get their bearings.

But, hey, there was no chance they were thinking that way. They were very much looking forward to all that the future held.

But there was one downside – Abby had been unable to get back to Normal and Suzi as much as she had wanted.

Just twice in the six months – morning sickness had latterly been a factor – it wasn't enough but circumstances dictated.

It hadn't sat well with Suzi and to be honest it hadn't sat well with Abby either.

It was back to being a "cow" and that was really hard to take.

She explained to Suzi that it wasn't nice to be called rude names and she wouldn't like it if it happened to her.

But that was just a sign of weakness.

So she got called a "cow" all the time.

She tried to ignore it but these things gradually wear you down.

Abby tried everything. Offered to go on walks with Suzi. She asked if she could accompany her on bike rides in the local park. She tried to cuddle up to her watching children's TV. She suggested going to the movies to watch a Disney film. Could she help with school work?

But the response was pretty much standard – "Go away, cow. I hate you."

She inquired as to why Suzi hated her. What had she done? Had she done something wrong? If she had, she was very sorry and would never do it again.

"Go away, cow. I hate you."

It was impossible.

Naturally, Abby went back home again on finding out she was expecting.

She wanted the reassurance of her mother. She wanted to share her excitement. She wanted to be part of the joy Sara and Jeb felt at the prospect of being grandparents for the second time.

This time John came with her for the weekend, leaving her in Normal to fly back to Toronto early on Monday morning for the start of the working week.

Sara and Jeb found both of them had changed already. Abby was blooming. John had a near permanent smile.

At one point the conversation swung back to Robert and Rose. Sara and Jeb reminisced – a bit like at the memorial service – about Rose as a little girl, the fun times, moments of heartache, getting through the terrible teens, her kindness and how she mellowed into a daughter of which they could be very proud, met Robert, got married, became a wonderful mother … and then … and then …

"Don't go there," said Abby softly. "Not on this day."

They went back to safer subjects – Normal's latest new buildings and roads, news about Abby's childhood friends, where they might go on holiday.

Suzi was out in the garden, unsuccessfully trying to throw stones at next door's conservatory.

Abby sat down on what had been her favourite patio chair.

"Suzi," she said. "Come here, darling, I've got something to tell you."

Suzi gave her one of those disbelieving looks.

This time there were no insults – John was around and Suzi was still trying to figure out his make-up and status in the family.

So she simply ignored Abby.

"Please Suzi," pleaded Abby. "It's really important."

This time there was something in the way she said it that caught Suzi's attention.

Intrigued now as to what it might be, she sauntered over.

Abby held her hands and asked: "What would you think if I said you were going to have a little cousin?"

Suzi rubbed her eyes. After all, it was a jolly hard question for an infant, even a precocious one.

Abby tried again.

"I'm going to have a baby," she told Suzi. "That will be nice, won't it?"

But Suzi still wasn't connecting.

"Where's the baby?" she asked, and spun around as if it should be behind her.

Abby needed to get on the same wavelength.

"We won't get the baby until near Christmas," said Abby.

"Christmas," stated Suzi dreamily. "I like Christmas."

Actually, Suzi had already worked out that Father Christmas was Grandad pretending. But she hadn't let on. That way you got more presents.

"Is Father Christmas bringing the baby?"

The question was a kind of test for Abby.

"Well, not quite, but sort of," said Abby.

Suzi wasn't at all sure what that meant.

She looked down at her shoes. She looked at a bird which was seeking grubs in the grass.

"Where's the baby now?"

"In my tummy," said Abby.

Suzi was at a complete loss at that.

There was a 'pregnant pause'.

"Why is it in your tummy – have you eaten it?"

Abby realised this was getting out of control – all too much for her niece to grasp.

How was she going to exit this bizarre exchange?

"No, I haven't eaten it. Babies are safe there when they are very tiny. And when they are a bit bigger they pop out into the world. I'll explain the whole thing to you when you are older."

Now bored of babies, Suzi left it there.

Instead, she chased the bird which flew off smartly.

Abby laughed. Suzi laughed.

Abby hoped it wouldn't be the last laugh as she knew that once the baby was born it would be hard to return to Normal with any consistency.

The baby arrived on time but not without incident.

The gestation was routine.

Lots to do – medical checks, parent classes, preparing a nursery, getting a cot, a pram, clothes, a pile of nappies. The list went on and on.

It kept Abby busy.

John did what he could to help – she teased him about changing nappies. A loving father for sure but most likely all fingers and thumbs when it came to babies' bottoms. She could not imagine that stinky nappies would ever be his thing.

He insisted he would do his share – she wasn't convinced.

When the day came and her waters broke he rushed back from work, got her to hospital and tried to be strong.

She had dreamt of one of these 'natural' deliveries you seem to constantly read about in women's magazine where celebrities emerge from childbirth with hardly a hair out of place and back to a svelte figure in a couple of weeks or so.

But it is rarely like that.

Time went by, baby wasn't showing, Abby's blood pressure started rising, there were signs of the baby becoming distressed in the womb … and it all ended in an emergency Caesarean.

A throng of doctors and nurses, tubes and medical equipment everywhere, all a bit scary, touch and go, but they got it out in time.

It was a boy and they had already agreed to call him Edward.

The aftermath wasn't easy as it isn't for many first time parents.

The baby always seemed to be crying, there were midnight feeds, sometimes it took ages to persuade him back to sleep. And all this on top of how much the operation – because it is a major operation – had taken out of her.

John sought to weigh in but there was only so far that went – men don't breastfeed!

It all became a bit too much for Abby who began acting more than strangely.

She started 'hearing things'. Then there were sudden panic attacks. Next came screaming fits that someone was attempting to kidnap the baby. She turned on John – he was a monster who was casting spells on Edward. She became hysterical.

She wouldn't go to the doctor – he managed to half cajole and half drag her there.

The medics were shocked at her anxious appearance – and instantly diagnosed a bad case of post-natal depression.

When a nurse tried to take Edward to be weighed a near tug-of-war developed.

Which ended with Abby sprawled on the floor. For a second John thought she was dead.

So many emotions flooded through him – shock, heartbreak, guilt, worry, fear.

Fear for his wife and her health, guilt that somehow he should have done more, shock at the unseemly and frankly disturbing struggle he had just witnessed, heartbreak at Abby's distress and fear for the baby not least that he might be taken into care while his mother was so ill – thankfully it didn't come to that.

But Abby spent ten days or so being treated by mental health services as an in-patient. Baby with her so he could be fed and she could re-establish the bond between them.

It was a grim time.

John visited as often as he was allowed. Work were very good – he had told them what they were going through.

She improved and they let her out, but not without concerns and not without monitoring. They wanted to be sure she was no longer uptight, was fully adjusting to motherhood, and caring for the baby appropriately. It was important there was no relapse. The great danger was that she might harm the baby – mothers, not knowing what they were doing, could be very devious in such situations.

Her own mother flew in from Normal to support her and bolster spirits.

Yet it took the best part of a year to get the real Abby back.

John bent over backwards, went the extra mile, did everything he could to help, be attentive, take some of the pressure off.

But he was rejected at every turn.

Nothing he did was right, she constantly snapped at him, she was always berating him.

By now he was as tired as her, the drama was eating away at him, their marriage was at times hanging by a thread.

He dug in and decided to just take it on the chin. Surely the fire and brimstone would subside.

And it did.

At length they were a proper family once more and they could put the wretchedness behind them.

Many things fell by the wayside during this oh so destructive period ... sadly, one of them was Suzi.

Abby's sole focus was Edward; there was no time for Suzi.

Abby theorised that Suzi had reached an age where she needed to be thinking in terms of helping herself – she couldn't look after both Edward and Suzi. She would pick up the pieces when she could; she hoped Rose would have understood.

When Jenny arrived three years later the birth scenario had been planned in advance.

This time it was an elective Caesarean – Abby had learned, there were no airs and graces now, she was an experienced mother, she knew the score.

All went straightforward and no post-natal depression.

The family slipped into a routine as soon as Jenny was home – they had by now moved to a bigger apartment.

Everything was good.

No longer did John and Abby ever take anything for granted about their partnership. They worked at marriage – that way you got the most out of it.

Suzi was still just about on the radar and, aware of how out of control she had become, Abby felt awful.

She had made those promises to herself to look after her sister's child.

What else could she have done, she asked herself? Edward's problem birth – no apparent long term health consequences when he could have ended up disabled – had turned her world upside down.

She didn't feel she could offer to look after Suzi in Toronto – they hadn't got the space and it would have been simply too much to take on someone who was fast becoming a juvenile delinquent.

Abby instead pledged to catch up with the Suzi enigma as soon as the demands on her own self lessened.

Now entering his mid-30s, Kevin's change of career was going well.

He found he had an aptitude for flogging houses and was glad that he had chosen to run with it.

So long as he could maintain a divide between his work and his shaky personal life then he would be able to hold things together.

It was a period where the housing market was going through the roof – not quite the correct terminology, but you get the picture. Sydney was progressive and much-admired, and who wouldn't want to live in a place which averaged seven hours of sunshine daily?

A magnet for migrants, demand exceeded supply.

Kevin discovered he could make some seriously decent dosh into the bargain and, while the ethos at the estate agency was competitive, everyone got on.

And with no mortgage on the flat, no wife and children to support, low outgoings, Kevin's bank balance shot up by leaps and bounds.

Life outside work could be trite – too often he found himself sitting in the flat on his own. His own fault of course. He had failed to maintain his network of friends, he had made no effort to mix, the whole sports thing had lapsed, he wasn't really one for hitting the bar or club scenes ... in short, he had grown used to closing the shutters.

Few folk are able to grasp how you can be lonely in a Greater Sydney conurbation of more than five million people, but isolation is not confined to remote regions. In our cities today it's actually far more common than you think.

And loneliness let in the old dark thoughts and depressive tendencies.

He would keep seeing the faces of those four dead chums from the plane crash. It was the same old bad dream – there was no way out, he was drowning, it was the end ... he would awake in a frenzy.

Sometimes he was shaking so much he was sick.

Work was a blessed relief.

Naturally, the estate agency knew nothing of his torment.

When I say nothing I mean they were completely aware that he was the plane crash survivor – all of Australia were aware of that.

But they did not know anything about the twisted memories which ensnared him.

They just saw someone working his socks off for the company – long hours and plenty of commitment.

And so impressed were they that after a year and a half Sako, who was a director, and executive chairman Mick Coff, called Kevin in, told him how pleased they were at his performance, and offered him a junior partnership, a stake in the business and hence a share in the profits.

He thanked them, said he wanted to remain at the sharp end, and his only reservation would be if he were to get bogged down in administration and paper work.

They assured him that wouldn't be the case – they employed accountants and others to handle that side.

So he accepted and felt good about it.

One day he bumped into Becky in the street – they probably hadn't spoken for five years or more.

They said hello, smiled, made small talk. He told her she was looking well; she expressed surprise at his career shift but said she was pleased for him that it had been successful.

It was a diffident, slightly reluctant, meeting.

Hands were trembling and neither spotted it.

Becky searched his face to see if there was any flicker of their old closeness. But Kevin was good at disguising his feelings these days.

He restrained a desire to kiss her – she looked sensational. He must have been out of his mind to have given her up – but then he probably was out of his mind at the time.

He asked if she was with anyone. She said she had got engaged but they broke up and there had been no-one serious since. And him? No, said Kevin, no-one.

"Right pair we are," she jested.

They went on their way – he hadn't even checked whether her mobile was still the same.

He went to a bench, sat down, held his head in his hands and bemoaned what might have been.

He should, he told himself, chase her down, invite her out and try and re-kindle their love. But he couldn't face it – he feared the nightmares would get worse, the pain would resurface.

He was a coward. No other word for it.

When he got back into the office they noticed how subdued he was for the rest of the day. But next morning he was himself again and they thought no more of it.

Kevin had jolted his way out of the 'downer' by writing to Suzi once more.

In it he again poured out his heartache – how his post-plane crash life had unravelled and how hard he was battling to turn things around.

His thought process turned to how old she would be. About 14, he reckoned. Surely not. He recalculated and it still came to 14. Time was flying past. Then found a mirror and looked hard at himself – the first grey hairs were brutal evidence that he was no spring chicken any more.

He wondered what she must look like, how she was getting on in school and whether she was into boys yet.

He had never received a reply yet from any of his letters. It didn't matter – it was his way of escaping from a day to day existence which gave him so much grief.

Having introduced Suzi, when the questions started, to why she was an orphan, the family had gradually expanded on it as they hoped the time was propitious.

When she was ten she knew there had been a terrible plane crash but not the full details.

From there, already highly computer savvy, she found out for herself exactly what had happened.

She felt deep sadness reading about how many had perished – her mother and father and all the others must have had an awful death.

She hoped they were unconscious as it hit the water and they were spared the worst.

The knowledge of what had taken place perhaps explained why she felt so alienated from everything and everybody. She had been shafted and it was all the fault of those rotten bastards, society, God, authority and all the rest.

"I hate them all," she ranted at her computer.

The one intriguing element was this guy Kevin who had saved her from drowning.

Suzi wondered what sort of individual he was – there was no getting away from the fact that she was in his debt.

But she did not dwell on it.

Here was someone else, like Abby, who had abandoned her.

Someone who had made no attempt to get in touch – she would have liked to have asked him things, many things, but he was just a name and a face.

She decided she couldn't hate the man – he did after all save her life – but she parked him in a folder named 'indifferent'.

Wherever he was, whatever he was doing, she was clearly not his concern … and why should she be?

By now her truancy from school had become more sophisticated – she would go in at the start of the school day, pay a certain meagre attention to teachers and work, have lunch and then do a disappearing act. Alternatively she might quit at some point in the morning and reappear mid-afternoon.

There were all sorts of excuses – stomach upset, sick relatives, migraines (she didn't suffer from them but could act like she did) and so on and so forth.

Naturally, she didn't shoot a line every day – some days she went to all her classes.

Her teachers were not fooled.

Here was a girl with known problems who could be as bright as a button when she wanted to be but whose grades were so poor. Because of her attitude issues.

But of course there were lots of other children who wanted to learn and you couldn't spend endless hours trying to motive those who didn't.

They tried remedial classes but being "locked up with the grots" simply made things worse.

Sending her to some sort of corrective centre for malcontents was assessed in outline but they were afraid of the bad publicity were it to leak out that the country's plane heroine was being treated so "shabbily".

So, in essence, she did virtually what she felt like.

Sara and Jeb couldn't control her, the school had lost patience, and the authorities were frightened to step in.

By now several of the school "awkward squad" had joined her on the street corners and down the amusement arcades.

Fags and booze nicked from local stores was now the norm. It offered a buzz, it was cool and it was a means of blotting out the scumbags.

One day someone produced cocaine – exchanged for rings knocked off from a jeweller – and Suzi tried a line. It brought her into a world where she felt anything was possible, heightening the senses, taking her to a different level of 'enlightenment'.

The crowd decided this was the place to be and soon various tablets – nobody quite knew what was in them – were being handed around.

They started getting zonked … and then zonked some more.

One day the state's Child Protective Services staff picked her off the floor and took her back home.

Sara and Jeb were appalled – it was the first time Suzi had seen grown-ups cry – but set firmly against accepting they could no longer cope for fear she might be taken away.

That would be admitting defeat and Robert and Rose would never forgive them.

Suzi was feeling woozy and sick, promised to turn over a new leaf, and crashed out.

The next night she walked out of the front door and disappeared for several hours. On her return she was stubbornly tight-lipped as to where she had been.

She simply laughed at her grandparents.

The pain on their faces zeroed into Suzi's conscience but, come on, she knew better than a couple of old codgers ignorant of today's youth culture.

A couple of days pretending to be a dutiful schoolgirl followed, interspersed with evenings spent in her bedroom listening to music and posting a picture of her tits on social media outlets.

She was delighted to see that her 'followers' multiplied hugely – she was getting inquiries from men promising all sorts of sexual thrills.

For now she didn't take them up – she wasn't quite there yet.

But that had to be the next step, she told herself.

So far her so-called sexual activity had been restricted to snogging sessions with blokes she half fancied along with the groping of body parts with lads older than herself from the other side of the tracks.

She knew soon some serious shagging was in order. She was looking forward to it big time.

Would it be all it was cracked up to be though? Would she be any good at it?

School had taught them about human sexuality, age of consent and the availability of contraception, and the danger of contracting sexually transmitted diseases.

Those were classes which Suzi made sure she did not skip.

So she was well aware of things like periods and the changing nature of her body.

Sara had made an effort to take Suzi through the whole process and had provided a book which, to be honest, she had found helpful.

Soon afterwards Suzi had plucked up the courage to go to a clinic and ask to be put on the pill.

She was given counselling, she was handed some concise literature to read, and she was asked whether she was sure.

She said she was sure and she started taking it.

Now she felt a proper 'tart' and when she was ready she determined she would have sex for the first time.

When it happened it was a bit of a fumble and a rumble.

She had agreed to go to a movie with Doug, who she occasionally knocked around with at school, though he was two years older than her.

It wasn't a great picture and the two had spent most of it delightfully down each other's throats.

They left arm in arm, stopped at a liquor store, where he went in and bought some shots and beer.

It was a hot, sultry, night and they went out into a local park and lay down under a tree.

They drank a bit, giggled, kissed lots, she took off her top and allowed him to unstrap her bra and fondle her breasts.

His T-shirt had long been abandoned and she basked in his strong, hot, toned body.

They had a couple more shots and she felt her desire for this boy rising.

He was good-looking, he wasn't pushy and he made her feel she mattered.

At length he pulled down her jeans – she didn't resist.

In no time they were just in pants and panties and absolutely hot for each other. Bring it on.

He felt inside her and stroked her gently. She held his erect penis, panting.

She opened her legs, he moved on top of her and, after a bit of prodding when it struck her that this was probably his first time too, he was there and they were both taking each other's virginity.

It was a bit rushed though she didn't know that, there was something lacking on both sides, but as he pumped his sperm inside her she had her own first 'real' orgasm.

Yes, yes, yes.

They clung to each other gasping for air in a eulogy of pollination.

And then it was over; they had done it. Ring out the bells; throw down the tickertape.

It was everything it was cracked up to be and she knew she would want more of it – lots more of it.

They broke off, gazed at each other, told each other they were magnificent and kissed loads and loads.

They got dressed, toasted each other's prowess in beer, and relaxed to take in the songs of the night, an insect choir which seemed to serenade their becoming one.

It had been a bit raw, a touch messy and she felt sore, but she was exhilarated.

She told herself next time would be better and the time after that better still.

He walked her home – that was decent of him.

She fell asleep almost immediately and next day luxuriated in the bath imagining she was doing it all over again as she wallowed and writhed.

When she next glimpsed him at school they each smiled that knowing smile which told of a dual connection for all time – you were my first. You always remember your first.

They left it a week and then did it again.

This time he spent a long time inside her and when it came it was like a volcanic eruption.

The time after he licked her fanny and she gave him a blow-job – they were learning about pleasure. And when it came to full sex she was on top of him dominating his thumping willy. It was glorious.

After that she lost count.

Time passed, it was still good, but she was ready to try someone else who might offer greater expertise and finesse.

When it happened it was very different – stark, brutal, absolutely no finesse, and life-changing.

Kevin used to be turned on by the prospect of sex.

He had always attracted girls. There were girls before Becky but that was more lust than love. And then there was Becky which was more love than lust.

Since Becky had been out of his life all interest had waned.

Sex seemed nothing in the greater scheme of things and with all his issues he didn't want the problems which girls brought.

They might claim to be concentrating on their career, they might insist they had no interest in a long-term relationship, but actually like the rest of the animal kingdom it was all about finding a mate.

Well, for 99 per cent of girls at any rate.

He couldn't face the responsibilities and hassles a new full-on girlfriend would bring.

Had virtually given up ogling women even when once upon a time he would be undressing them with his eyes.

True, there was this new bird, Alice, in the office.

She was, like him, a red-head. Delicate tits and legs to die for – a real looker.

And there were moments when he thought he was getting the come-on – she would drop a sheet of paper, reach down slowly to pick it up, thrusting her breasts forward as he sat at his desk. She would "accidentally" brush against him as they passed tight corners.

Unless he was imagining it – he had always found it hard to 'read' women.

Either way, he didn't let it bother him.

She was fun, she was clever and he guessed she knew she was having an effect on him.

But office romances were never a good idea and could cause headaches whenever they came to an end.

So there were plenty of reasons to keep his distance, and that's how it stayed.

Kevin concentrated on his work – it was continuing to go well and by now he was several years into it.

Women and sex – no.

Until one Friday when a popular member of the team was leaving for pastures new.

It was the end of the week, everyone was in a good mood and it was decided to take the farewell to the local pub where occasionally they gathered after work.

There was probably a dozen of them, it was a good laugh, a few drinks were downed and in great spirits it was decided to go on for a meal at a nearby curry house.

By then a handful had dropped out and it was down to about half a dozen.

Kevin had tried to make his excuses but the others had persuaded him, with Alice extolling somewhat ponderously how it was going to be a really 'hot' date.

It was a nice meal, lots of banter, more drink, no time pressure, a lazy scene-setter for the weekend.

Heading towards midnight, they split the bill and looked to go their separate ways.

At which point Alice was at Kevin's side and seemingly in a bit of a state.

She feared she had left her purse, with her money and keys inside it in the office – would he mind coming with her, and opening up, so she could hunt for it.

Being well brought-up you don't turn down a damsel in distress – he said that would be no bother.

Within a couple of minutes they were at the office and climbing the stairs when she appeared to trip and fell into him. He held her and they carried on to the first floor with her nestling into his side.

That should have set alarm bells ringing – it didn't.

He pumped in the code to gain entry and they stumbled inside together.

The lights went on in the hallway and she pushed open the door to the boardroom. What would her purse be doing there?

Then she put her arms around his head and pulled him towards her, snuggling into his neck and whispering how much she had long admired his body.

They kissed. At first he held back slightly but she was bringing him on and with the innate weakness of the typical male he responded in kind. She was a great kisser and he wondered what she would be like in the sack.

And then it finally dawned on him – there was no missing purse. This was a set-up.

Oh, blow the consequences, he was well into it. She was voracious.

Jacket, shirt, bra, panties were soon littering the boardroom floor.

They could not get enough of each other.

By now naked as the day she was born she coyly manoeuvred herself onto the boardroom table and told him to take her.

Primeval instinct kicked in and Kevin was on that table like an athlete responding to a starting gun.

She was as randy as a sow introduced to a boar; he was a gorilla on the rampage.

Rampant with each other, she proved a shouter.

"Screw me, screw me, more, more."

"Fuck me until I fart."

That inspired Kevin into even greater feats of manhood.

It was perhaps the best sex he had ever had. She was amazing. The satisfaction was monumental.

When it was done she told him he was astounding and she had wanted him from the first day she had set foot in the office.

They held each other, sweat and sex combining into a heady jungle aroma.

Then it was time to pick up the pieces, what would the board members have made of it, got their clothing back on, cleared anything up that needed clearing, laughed together at how naughty they had been.

And then they left, being careful to turn off the lights, endeavouring to ensure there could be no possible trace of what had taken place.

He managed to hail a taxi and took her home, close together, savouring her delicious perfume.

It pulled up outside a block of flats – a rotten cad would have waved her goodbye at that point but he would have been too ashamed.

And after such great sex he didn't need much persuading to join her.

He paid off the taxi, she took out her security pass, the front door clicked open, she stuck the card in the lift slot, and up they went. It stopped at the eighth floor and she led him hand in hand into the flat.

A one bedroom apartment, lounge, kitchen, bathroom. Bijou – the single girl's flat.

A coffee and to bed – both were too fulfilled for more hanky-panky.

She turned her back on him, he contemplated the delights of her pert breasts one more time, and then they fell asleep.

Sometime in the early hours of the morning he was having this delicious ever so sexual dream when he awoke to find it was no dream – she was caressing his dick in a manner sure to send any man into raptures. No red-blooded male could have held back.

The love-making started again and soon they were at it like donkeys.

God, she was good.

Afterwards they just held each other, and held each other, and held each other, overcome by the passion.

He must have drifted off because the next he knew was light pouring through the window and the sound of a shower being run – he checked her side of the bed. It was empty.

He lay there, trying to take in all that had happened in such a short space of time. It seemed surreal.

The shower cut out.

A few minutes later the door opened quietly and she walked in, towel around her head, dressing gown around her body.

"Oh, you're awake," she purred.

She sat on the bed, kissed him sensitively, then swayed away enticingly, took off the dressing gown and pulled on a pair of panties.

It sent him ravenous – there had to be a next-time, whatever the conflict with office politics.

She smiled at him – men were so easy to manipulate.

"The shower's free – make yourself at home."

So he did.

He wished in a way he could stay this horny and sticky for ever, but the warm water was reviving. He soaped himself all over.

She made him more coffee, buttered him some toast.

When they parted he went down the road feeling ten feet tall. In tune with the world in a way he hadn't been for a long time.

He suppressed a mad urge to sing to the birds and twirl with old ladies.

He knew he still had problems but it was good to be alive on such enchanted days.

That week he sought to maintain his professional dignity and she did too.

Hopefully it could stay a secret. Well, for as long as possible anyway.

So easy for colleagues to pick up on the tell-tale signs – over-familiar eye contact here; a whispered conversation beside the photocopier there.

They arranged via text to meet after work the following Friday.

Deliberately avoiding the office local, they headed to a bar in Darling Harbour hoping to get lost in the crowds.

They got themselves a drink – so serene looking out over the water. Sweeping views to take the breath away.

He was edgy, fearing 'discovery', but you couldn't be hung up for long in such a setting.

They clicked glasses, exchanged a pecked kiss, he stroked her knee.

She started on him. "Wait until I get you home tonight, big boy. I'm going to tear those tight trousers right off your ass."

He told her he was going to lick every inch of her body beautiful.

Then they burst out laughing and were soon scheming and giggling like teenagers, inhibitions cast aside.

He suggested a meal at a nearby fish restaurant.

There would be a twenty minute wait for a table – would that be a problem, sir?

No, that would be fine.

They got themselves another drink and pretended to be grown-ups.

"So, tell me all about yourself," he quipped, faking a serious tone.

It set her off into fits of giggles again which got him going too.

"What's wrong with that question?" he queried, feigning upset.

"That's a terrible chat-up line," she reposted. "I thought you were the great lover – great lovers don't come out with schoolkid rubbish. Besides I saw you reading my file the other day so you know all about me."

Now he was embarrassed – he thought he had been really sneaky.

"You're going red."

Then she moved closer to him, gave him a sultry look and surreptitiously squeezed his crown jewels ever so slightly.

He nearly fell off his stool – how dirty and dangerous she could be.

This was the slut from heaven … or was she from hell?

And before he could respond the waiter came up, asked them if they were ready, and showed them to their table.

"I'm ready for anything," she whispered, raising an eyebrow.

"I'm going to have the grouper," he told her suggestively.

She laughed at the feeble double-entendre and hid playfully behind the menu.

They ate a nice meal, washed down with a decent bottle of wine – Australian naturally.

Then left the restaurant arm-in-arm, walked out into the warm night, and stopped for a final view of the harbour front. He held her, she pushed erotically against him, and they kissed.

"Your place or mine?" he spluttered, the hots for her already building.

She placed a finger and ran it slowly along his lips.

"Well, you've seen mine," she smirked, throwing a double-entendre back at him.

Then she playfully dug him in the ribs. "Anyway, I want to get an idea of how the other half live!"

"OK," he said. "You might be disappointed."

"I already know there's no chance of that," she responded saucily.

They held hands and walked the ten minutes to his flat.

It was in a very pretty neighbourhood, had two bedrooms and a balcony.

She told him she was impressed. Nice things mattered in life.

They entered and she took in the ambience. It wasn't exactly neat, the bachelor's pile of cups and plates in the sink awaiting attention, but it was classy – leather suite, expensive lighting, and tasteful furniture.

Impulsively he picked her up and tossed her onto the couch as she squealed with delight at the same time as faking a protest.

She had absolutely no intention of faking anything else that night.

They were lying together kissing hungrily. She put a hand inside his trousers and massaged his tackle.

He nibbled her ear and caressed a breast.

They broke for a moment.

"Let's do it right here," she beseeched him.

"But you haven't seen the bedroom yet," he protested.

"We've got all night to arrive at the bedroom," she asserted, fondling his face.

And looked pleadingly into his eyes.

"I know," she announced, changing tack. "Let's do it on the balcony."

Her eyes sparkled. His dander was up.

He let her go.

"I'll get something to put on the floor."

And headed to a cloakroom cupboard, emerging with an old Li-lo and some towels which he suitably spread out.

She was already naked bar some spellbinding chiffon panties with jet black edging.

Draping herself provocatively, her tits seemed to shimmer under the glow of the moon above and street and car lights below.

Absolutely panting for this siren, he was on her in seconds.

Writhing together an errant foot of his knocked a pot plant which went sailing down to smash on the concrete several floors below.

He twitched in his ardour; she smiled to herself, holding him ever closer and wanting every possible inch of him inside her.

Savouring the enjoyment she moaned loud and long.

"The neighbours," he cautioned.

And then he came within her in an explosion of solar flares.

Her body saturated in the Milky Way.

A light came on somewhere below accompanied by a harsh-sounding voice in the blackness.

Neither of them stirred, still in raptures and utter contentment.

Until a door slammed shut outside just as hers closed inside.

It was time to investigate the bedroom she hadn't yet seen.

They fell into a deep sleep as if under the stars, he swimming in her feminine juices, she reeking of his earthy outpourings.

No early morning rendezvous this time – they had taken too much out of themselves.

Next day he sheepishly brushed up soil, shredded plant and broken pot and hoped nobody saw him.

In Normal, Suzi was feeling particularly belligerent.

There had been yet another row with Sara and Jeb and she had stormed out, hitting her mobile phone and rendezvousing with the 'awkward squad'.

She was sounding off about how shit it was living with grandparents when ear-splitting sounds of revving engines and screeching tyres scrambled their hearing.

Around the corner came perhaps 35 bikers – leathers, tattoos, gleaming machines, many with trophy girls holding tight onto their men.

It was intimidating, it was fierce, but it was strangely seductive.

This was the Bastards on Wheels motorcycle mob and for nothing more than a laugh they had headed into town, shooting up the city centre, intimidating drivers, touching up any female they could assault – from straight-laced executives to outraged housewives – and jousting with cops. Now they were pulling out.

They aspired to join the "Big Four" motorcycle clubs who have been competing for territory throughout the United States for years.

The Outlaws are the oldest, founded on the outskirts of Chicago in 1935, and still based in the Great Lakes region.

The Hell's Angels are the largest, with chapters in more than 50 countries. Their peak of infamy was arguably the 1969 Altamont Speedway Free Festival in California played by the Rolling Stones and other top bands where a concert-goer was stabbed to death and savage violence flared as the Angels decided to handle security in their own inimitable fashion.

The Pagans claim most of the eastern seaboard, and the Bandidos hold sway in the South, primarily in Texas.

All four are regarded as "outlaw motorcycle gangs" by the FBI, riddled with criminality, and associated with widespread drug and financial racketeering activities, extortion and prostitution.

The Bastards on Wheels weren't in this league ... but determined to make the big time.

Suzi may have been still a kid but you would have had to have been closeted away in a nunnery not to be aware of their reputation.

But on that day Suzi was up for a wild time.

One of the gang pulled his Harley Davidson alongside her and her chums.

"Ever been on a bike, honey?" he drawled.

He was big, he was bold and quite handsome in a ferocious sort of way.

"No," she croaked nervously.

And it was the truth – she had never been on a motorbike.

The Harley throbbed with raw energy; Suzi's loins started throbbing in tune.

"Well, get on the bike."

She wasn't sure. She put on what she hoped was a suitably mean expression and acted as if she was sizing him up.

"Don't do it," urged her pal Mitzy.

The biker's face splintered. "Ignore that slapper, we ain't bandits. What have you got to be afraid of?"

She was in two minds.

"I need to be dropped back here," she stuttered, naively hoping to lay down a red line which even she knew deep down was never going to be observed.

"Yeah, no problem. We're going to eat up some road – you're going to have fun. What's your name, sweetheart?"

"Suzi."

"Honcho," he replied, and patted the seat behind him in a gesture which questioned whether she had the bottle – was she the daring babe she thought she was?

What the heck …

She walked into the street, opened her legs to bestride the magnificent machine, and put her hands around his waist.

Up for the ride, there was every likelihood she would end up giving the guy a ride.

But that held a spell-binding anticipation in itself.

Then they were off and running, wheelies, whoops, a statement of being somebody, freedom.

Wind in her hair, power under her vagina, she was instantly in the zone.

They blasted the highways, sneered at the populace, cut up cars – they were the rulers.

She'd stepped up a notch – this was her time.

At length, the lead bike, ridden by a sun-burned tough nut with Gonz stitched across his jacket, turned off onto a side-track and soon they pulled up at what seemed a giant bomb shelter in the middle of nowhere. There were bars on the windows, roller blinds on the doors, spikes and barbed wire on the roof, security cameras on the corners.

Suzi felt apprehension for the first time but shook it off as quickly as it came.

After all, she was now a Bastard on Wheels.

They opened it all up and filed in.

Honcho had his hand on the back of her neck, part intended to show he was boss, part telling the rest that this was his property.

The first priority before all else was getting a beer.

He handed her one and took a long and thirsty slug. She was more particular with her mouthful – it had a kick to it all right.

He downed his, took another and then eased her into the inner warren away from the others.

He guided her into a tatty room – it was block concrete with just one high barred window, dimly lit, scruffy, an old armchair, a big bed, and that was about it.

He locked the door, pulled her to him and snogged her until she was gasping for air.

Next, her feet were no longer touching the ground and as she wrapped her legs around him and devoured his kisses she knew where this was headed.

He put her down, had a further swig from the beer bottle and told her to get undressed.

This was a man who knew what he wanted and, unlike with any of the others she had dallied over and rejected, she had an all-embracing urge to be dominated.

She stripped to her knickers as he slowly pulled off his heavy leathers.

He pointed to her pants.

"Off."

This was going to be basic sex. There was trepidation but also anticipation.

He cleared his underwear and she went goggle-eyed at this huge member.

She didn't wait for his order but lay on the bed and did her best to appear as if she wanted him – she half did and she half didn't.

He joined her on the bed – foreplay was at a premium as she held him, they kissed and he entered her, all at the same time.

Her instant reaction was euphoria as it seemed to fill her entire body.

She gasped, she panted, she groaned – this was sex in the raw.

When he came it was like nothing she had known before – a million miles away from fumbling about in the park.

And as soon as it had started it was over.

He got up, shook it around as if it was a trophy, and began getting dressed again.

She just lay there ravaged in wonder at this extraordinary happening. She had crossed a line into becoming a right-on sexual animal.

By now fully dressed, he gave her a half-smile, told her he had stuff to do but he would be back, unlocked the door and went out.

The key closed in the lock from the outside.

She stayed on the bed and struggled to compose herself.

She supposed Jeb and Sara would be getting worried about her but there was no point in getting worked up on that one. They would just have to stew.

This was biker life – no more school, no more nagging grandparents, no more inadequacies.

She had satisfied this man and she felt a sense of achievement.

Not only that, she wanted more of him.

Slowly, feeling slightly soiled, she collected her things and waited.

Half an hour later he was back.

There was no explanation as to where he had been.

"Time to eat," he grunted, with that same aura of total control.

She asked timidly whether she could wash first.

He took pity on her – she would have to understand that gang molls weren't expected to be particular.

Then he took hold of her firmly as if he somehow – goodness knows how – thought she might escape.

She recoiled from him, the first tiny sign that she had spirit.

"There's no need," she told him, fire in her eyes. "I'm not going anywhere."

He let her go – she was pleased that she had claimed a tiny victory – and he brought her through another part of the maze to some sort of communal block.

There was a line of showers – he probed in a cupboard and found her a towel.

Then motioned her on while holding his ground to ensure she was unmolested.

It appeared to be unisex. A biker was drying himself and a biker's girl was shampooing her hair.

Suzi took her clothes off, got a kick out of telling Honcho to watch over them, and let the water cover her.

The other girl offered her some shampoo. She washed her hair, she washed her body, and at last she felt clean.

Occasionally she sneaked a glance at him looking at her – pleased that her body was the centre of his attention.

Dry and dressed, she discovered an abandoned comb and slung it through her hair – it would have to do because he was agitating for food.

She was quite hungry herself.

Next she found herself entering something akin to a mess hall – almost a bit like school! Except there were no teachers here.

There were bikers on benches eating stolidly, bikers and birds on dilapidated armchairs in various degrees of clinches, the usual chatter you got in a typical canteen.

Honcho helped himself from a large bowl filled with a concoction which seemed to be rice and beans based, with a smattering of meat. He reached for some cutlery, picked it up in a big, brawny hand, and sat down at a bench to eat.

She took the hint and, though somewhat wary of this gruel, similarly helped herself, reasoning that there might be no knowing where the next meal might come from or when.

They ate in silence. He was obviously a man of few words notwithstanding his chat-up routine back in Normal.

He threw down the grub with alacrity. She found it adequate without being what you would call tasty. She wasn't sure she could eat it all. He told her to get it down her. No waste here, she decided.

He waited for her patiently, then indicated that you were expected to wash your own dishes, and that was definitely women's work. She wasn't about to complain of chauvinism in this setting.

She did as she was told while he liberated a beer, and slouched into a spare armchair.

She came over, curled into his body and gently kissed the side of his neck – she could sense his surprise, she was making an impression.

He passed her the beer and she drank from the bottle.

She felt relaxed and must have dozed off at some point because the next time she was aware of anything the light was fading away.

He smiled at her with what she interpreted as a degree of fondness.

It was time to leave the now much-diminished gathering and return to the room.

They got undressed matter-of-factly – this regular on-off of clothes was almost therapeutic, she decided.

He gave her space which she appreciated, and waited for her in the bed.

She shaped her hair, she attempted to freshen her face with her hands, she would have liked a dab of perfume but she hadn't got any.

He watched intrigued.

She didn't take long and came to him expectantly.

In complete contrast to what had gone before he turned into a true gentleman – well, of sorts.

They played it out, they cuddled, they kissed, his hands caressed the length of her body, she nibbled his neck and tugged at his penis.

And when they were both needing each other, she whispered 'wait' in his ear, rolled from under him and he gladly allowed her to mount him from above.

She wiggled her body to make it as sensual for both of them, he expanded in bounds, and they came together in mutual enjoyment and in mutual understanding.

It had taken less than a day but she felt she had already half-tamed this big, bad, Bastard.

Next day he allowed her to use the toilet and wash, he fed her, but then he led her back to the room.

He explained that there was some 'big shit' heading down that day and there was no way she was going with them. And anyway they only took fully fledged members of the gang and she had plenty to prove to be allowed membership – she would first need to get used to their ways.

"I'm going to lock you in – for your own safety."

She argued, said she could look after herself, but he was adamant.

"What about if I need the toilet?"

He pulled a large oil drum from out of the junk piling up in one of the corners.

"Use that," he said.

And was gone. They key turned in the lock. She was effectively a prisoner … and she was not pleased to say the least.

Apart from anything else it was going to be a very dreary few hours.

She thought once more about her grandparents – the balloon must surely have gone up by now. They were bound to have reported her missing to the police.

But, she figured, the police were probably inundated by run-aways, many of which often turned up again a few days later. She didn't think they would do much initially, routine inquiries at best.

Suzi tried not to think about it.

That lunchtime the 'big shit' hit the fan.

The Bastards on Wheels took on one of their local rivals in a violent brawl in a hick town 80 miles from Chicago.

Up to 75 bikers beating hell out of each other.

The Bastards on Wheels had come off worst – four left bleeding on the sidewalk, two arrested, and a lot of ego smashed.

When they got back to base Gonz was in a foul mood.

He ordered them into the mess hall and started ranting and raving at the 'fucking insult' they had just suffered. They were soft, they were weak, they were just "a load of fucking poofters".

His fists were smashing down on tables, cups were shattering on walls, anything that could be kicked was being kicked.

No-one said a word.

Eventually he had run out of obscenities and just stood there glaring at them.

Then, he singled out Honcho and snarled: "Give me the keys to that room – it's my turn to have the bitch."

Honcho recoiled.

"She's mine. I found her. You leave her be."

Gonz went ballistic at this challenge to his authority.

He ran at Honcho and tried to nut him.

Honcho pushed him off and pulled out a knife.

There was a giant intake of air around the mess hall – this was getting heavy.

"Right," hollered Gonz. "So you're the big hard man, are you Honcho? Well I'm going to see your knife and raise you …

He took a gun out from inside his jacket and aimed it at Honcho's head.

"… one gun."

Honcho shrivelled, backed off, threw his knife on the floor.

"Don't fire," he said. "You can have her."

He held out the keys. Gonz tore them from his hand, got him by the throat, put the gun to his temple.

He spoke slowly and menacingly. "Don't ever cross me again Honcho or you'll be a dead man. Do I make myself clear?"

"Absolutely," grimaced Honcho, shaking like a leaf. "You're the boss, Gonz."

"Say it again but louder."

"You're the boss, Gonz."

Honcho was hurled against a wall.

Gonz swung around 360 degrees. "Have you got the message?" he hollered.

There was general assent.

"Who's the leader of this fucking outfit?"

"You are Gonz."

"And don't ever fucking forget it."

Coldly he left the room.

Of course Suzi knew nothing of this so when the key clicked in the door a frisson of excitement ran through her – Honcho had returned.

Except it wasn't Honcho; it was Gonz.

"Get your clothes off," he bawled.

She shrank from him and did nothing.

"Get your clothes off, I ain't telling you again."

And he smashed her in the face with the back of his hand, sending her spinning to the ground.

Shaken, she rushed to take off her clothes.

But then made another big mistake.

"Where's Honcho?" she insisted. "I'm Honcho's – you know that."

She was lucky – the punch caught her a glancing blow but was still powerful enough to leave her in a heap by one of the walls to her 'cell'.

He picked her off the floor, flattened her against the concrete, pulled out his donger and rammed it up her.

Bang, her body thumped against the wall.

Thrust. He hammered into her.

Bang, her body thumped against the wall.

Thrust. He hammered into her.

The rape lasted no time but felt like for ever.

Weeping uncontrollably, finally realising how stupid she had been not to think a dalliance with bikers might come to this, she pleaded with the beast.

"Please, please, you're hurting me," she wailed. "You're hurting me."

"Hurting you," he repeated. "Hurting you. I'll show you what hurting is all about."

He exited her, reached for a truncheon, pinned to the wall as a prize following a previous altercation with the police, and rammed it up her.

The screams were so terrible they could hear them from the mess hall.

The place went instantly quiet. Nobody said anything. Nobody moved.

They sat there with their thoughts – if they hadn't been sure what sort of fate awaited them for angering Gonz, they knew now.

At length the screaming stopped.

He left her bloodied and in agony.

She was never sure how many hours she lay there, rolling in and out of consciousness.

Gonz was happy to see her suffer.

The inhabitants of the mess hall went about their normal business as if nothing had happened while Gonz's stare dared any of them to say anything.

When he had had enough perverse pleasure, he turned towards Honcho and muttered icily: "Go on, you can have her, what's left of her anyway."

And, leering, threw the keys at him and turned away.

Slowly, for fear of provoking him into another outburst, the biker moved towards the door, turned the handle and almost crept out.

He found her on all fours amidst a small but gradually extending pool of blood.

He reached down to her, horrified by the state she was in.

"I'm so sorry – it was never meant to happen like this."

His face a portrait of disgust, she grasped at the lifeline.

She was trying to say something and he strained to hear her muted words.

"Get … me … to … a … hospital … or … I'm … going … to … die …"

Her voice faded away – it had been a supreme effort.

A death, he was more than aware, had the potential to cause trouble from the authorities. But he also cared about this girl.

He hauled her up – she couldn't stand – and sat her on the old armchair while he found a towel which he wrapped and pinned round her in a primitive bid to stem the bleeding.

He gathered up what was left of her things and carried her in a fireman's lift to his Harley.

He placed her on the bike and let her drape across the front handlebars. The engine roared, he turned on the lights, and he drove as fast as sensible given the limitations towards Bloomington-Normal.

He turned the bike into the first hospital he came to, pulled up at the Trauma Center and Emergency Department, carried her as far as reception, leaving little blobs of blood in a trail along the corridor, and hollered for some action.

Appalled by Suzi's plight, gobsmacked at the presence of this hostile-looking biker in their midst, people came running, a trolley appeared out of nowhere, and he carefully deposited her on it – she was passed out.

He went back, returning to dump her stuff on the reception desk.

Then, amid the chaos, as they rushed about for drips, pads and goodness knows what, he slipped away into the night, turned the bike around, and was gone.

And he cursed himself for in effect running away.

She knew nothing of the first day as they pumped blood into her and fought to stabilise her condition.

The second day was a complete blank too as they took her to surgery and sought to patch up her insides.

Days three and four were equally lost as they kept her in an induced coma to give her body a chance to recover.

By then they had at last worked out who she was.

Hardened medics shocked at her injuries had called in the police at the outset.

They came up with a missing girl who seemed to match her description – a Suzanne Duthie, aged 16, from Normal.

The cops ran Jeb and Sara round to the hospital and asked them if they could identify the mystery female in the critical care ward.

Sara screamed at the sight – it was Suzi.

There were monitoring machines around the bed, tubes connected to different parts of her body, she looked like death.

It could yet come to that if infection set in, they were told.

Sara had been determined to stay strong whatever greeted them but that instantly went out of the window. She stood there sobbing, dabbing her eyes with a tissue, feeling more than a little faint, as Jeb held her and sought to console her. But he too was churning inside.

A thoughtful nurse brought a couple of chairs over.

But she was non-committal about Suzi's prospects. Officially her condition was 'stable'. Doctors would be around later to assess her again, after which it was hoped they would know more and might be able to brief the family in greater detail.

They asked if they could hold Suzi's hand.

Probably better err on the side of caution, said the nurse. But they could talk to Suzi as much as they liked.

Feeling both useless and self-conscious, they spoke of 'safe' subjects like how magnificent the garden flowers were looking, the bees buzzing as they collected nectar, a bird's nest in the fir tree. They told her everyone in the family was concerned for her and asking after her. And they promised they would take her on holiday once she got better.

Abby was stunned at the news and immediately packed a travel bag.

Edward and Jenny were now seven and four so Abby felt safe enough leaving them for what was clearly going to be several days if not longer. John took time off work – fortuitously his parents were on their way over from England and could step in. She hugged the children. Kissed John while at the same time ignoring Edward's cries of 'gross'. They waved her off in a taxi bound for Toronto Airport.

When she reached Normal and then the family home, she told the taxi to hold on while she dumped her suitcase.

She raced inside, dropped it in the hallway, locked the front door again, and then directed the man how to find the hospital.

Naturally, she had intended to embrace her mother and father, but when she arrived at Suzi's bedside Sara had nodded off in her chair and Jeb held a finger to his mouth indicating to her as not to wake mother. She noticed that they both looked drawn. She worried for them these days – handling someone as volatile as Suzi was hard enough but they were now in their 70s.

That evening, with Suzi still out of it, she persuaded them to head for a fast food restaurant and then bed.

Poor things were fast asleep the moment their heads hit the pillow.

But it was back soonest the next morning – they must be there when she first wakens, they insisted.

Day Five and doctors decided she was clear of danger and it was safe to gradually bring Suzi out of the coma.

It started with that half way house stage when your eyes don't function properly and you don't really understand where you are – a little like waking from concussion and wondering what planet you are on.

Her eyes flickered open and flickered shut, she felt extremely woozy, her insides were hurting so badly, she could just make out the family's presence.

She faded back into sleep.

Her inner self recalled the agony and the pain – she must be in hospital.

Her next perception was of a doctor being at her side.

"Hello Suzi," he cooed. "How are you feeling? You've been asleep a very long time."

She tried to smile – it was more of a grimace.

Terribly feeble, she managed a wavering hand as if to bring him closer.

He moved his head down to try and grasp what she was labouring to convey.

"Will ... I ... still ... be ... able ... to ... have ... children?"

He hesitated – you know, in the way you do when there are so many permutations of answering a question, you don't want to lie but neither do you want to set back a brave young girl's recovery. Be positive.

He pulled a chair up.

"It's too early to say Suzi – we need to get you better. Then we can see where we are. We can talk in detail when you are more yourself. Meantime, you must not worry. Let's be optimistic."

It was a clever answer, it was intended to be as genuine as possible, and it was also aimed at bringing calm to a troubled mind.

But Suzi was no fool.

She lay there quietly weeping.

That set Sara off, but Abby urged her niece to believe that everything would be fine.

"You've always been a fighter – if ever there was a time to fight then this is it. Listen to me, Suzi."

She held her hand. "You know we love you lots. Everything is forgiven. We just want you right. You must reach for a future that can be anything you want it to be – promise me you'll do that."

Abby felt her hand being ever so slightly squeezed.

Thank goodness, thought Abby. She didn't press the point. She felt confident that Suzi would be on the mend soon.

And she did indeed get better in stages – tubes out, sitting up in bed, starting to take normal food once more, far more alert, a tapering off of the pain relief.

She had cheated death for a second time.

They transferred her onto a normal ward, tucked her up for long spells in a seat beside the bed, got her walking slowly up and down.

It had taken so much out of her that she felt like an old woman.

But she had the bit between her teeth now and was determined to succeed.

The family were delighted at her progress and so was the hospital.

So were the police.

A sensitive, infinitely patient, female officer came in and asked to speak to her.

In half hour slots, with breaks between, they talked all through what had happened.

Others, afraid of reprisals, might have preferred keeping schtum. Not Suzi. This wasn't ratting on a pal. It wasn't even much to do with bikers per se. What had been meted out to her was so outrageous that she was prepared to be completely open, without restriction. Gonz had it coming. This was mutilation. He was an utter arsehole. He would have been an arsehole whatever the walk of life.

Her statement was detailed – she left Honcho out but otherwise spilled the beans.

It gave the police plenty to go on. They were talking rape, sexual assault or maybe even attempted murder against Gonz.

The police had long wanted to turn over the Bastards on Wheels headquarters. Now they could.

The officer left Suzi confident that action would be taken.

Yet revenge was not at the forefront of her mind – she wanted home.

And the day came when they decided she was well enough to continue her convalescence there – the bed was needed for others.

She was still sore, she felt fragile, but she walked to the car unaided.

It was a relief to be back at the house, her own bedroom, somewhere safe. Sara and Jeb were so solicitous.

Suzi felt terribly guilty for the abhorrent manner in which she had treated them – her obnoxious contempt for an elderly couple who only wanted the best for her.

They fussed about, building her up with home-made food, treats like chocolate and ice cream, refusing all help with the chores.

It left her plenty of time to think.

She got called back into hospital to see how the operation had healed and went with trepidation – Sara accompanied her to provide moral support.

A typical hospital appointment – you check in and then wait there with your anxieties and your inner turmoil until you are called through.

They gave her a thorough examination and deemed themselves to be pleased with the outcome.

But they could not or would not answer the million dollar question – would she be able to have babies in the future?

It depended on how her body adjusted.

It left her in limbo but what could she do?

Were she ever to meet the right man, someone special enough that, just like Abby and John, she would mark him out as the father she wanted for her kids, then it was crunch time.

Would she first tell him of her injury, admit children might not be possible, and risk him taking off?

That was a hard one to call. He was surely due an explanation. His right to know. If he then backed out that was his privilege and his loss.

She put it to the back of her mind.

The biker horror had left its mark. It had taught Suzi that there were consequences for being a wayward child and despising authority.

She span it around her head and decided that things needed to change. Getting shot of the chip on her shoulder would be a start. She wasn't unique in being an orphan, life wasn't always fair, there were no free lunches going – if she did not get a grip she would never make her mark.

Hopefully she could turn things around.

It was about then that the police hit the HQ of the Bastards on Wheels.

They went in mob-handed. They went in tooled up – explosive charges to blow entry, battering rams to break open doors, crowbars and monkey wrenches, super-sized cutters to bust apart padlocks. No messing and no concession to political correctness.

They turned the place over in a frenzy of evidence gathering.

There was plenty available – drugs, offensive weapons, an illicit still, stolen property.

Several guns were in the haul and they even found the truncheon Gonz had used on Suzi – proud of its capture he had put it back on the wall as a warning.

So confident was he in his own invincibility that he hadn't even bothered to wash the bloodstains off it.

The Bastards on Wheels had envisaged that were it to come to a raid then it would likely turn into an OK Corral shoot-out.

But so caught cold were they, and so well-planned was the raid, that it never happened.

With Gonz taken down before he could get a shot off, cuffed and thrown into a paddy wagon, the rest had little stomach for resistance.

Half got banged up, destined to head through the legal process.

The rest – how should we put this delicately – were 'encouraged' to seek pastures new.

The Pantagraph put it more explicitly – they'd been run out of the state, it asserted. And good riddance.

The paper gave the story big licks, billing it as a throwback to the 1880s Wild West, responsible citizens standing up to evil men, sheriffs and their deputies cleaning out the outlaw hideout.

Suzi soaked it up – Gonz was due everything he was going to get. The courts sent him down, plenty of years in the penitentiary.

No word of Honcho in the coverage – Suzi was secretly glad.

Had he got away? She never did find out. She assumed he must have done.

In fact it proved to be a stark lesson for him too.

It forced him to examine his lifestyle, and decide whether he really wanted to ride with tossers like Gonz.

He determined to break with motorcycle gangs, moved to the West Coast where nobody knew him from

Adam, found a job as a mechanic, got married, had kids, turned into the model family man.

Though he kept the Harley – couldn't face being parted from it, dusting it down on rare occasions, helmet on, the smell of leathers, a bit of a beat-up down the road.

It kept him sane when things were getting on top of him, a release valve, and just occasionally he wondered what had become of that pretty little girl from Normal who was forever on his conscience.

Back in Sydney the Kevin-Alice connection was getting even more frenetic.

Kevin had been forced to skip the after work meet-up – a family trip to Melbourne to see an ancient aunt who had notched up her 90th birthday.

It had turned out better than it sounded – nice meal, the old stick was on good form, change of scenery.

So when Kevin and Alice re-connected on the Friday after that they were once again ravenous for each other.

Unwisely, taking a gamble, they met up in the 'office pub' pretty sure none of the rest were heading there, fell into each other's arms and snogged their tonsils out – for the record, neither could care less who was watching.

And they were once more laughing and joking like a young couple in love – which they weren't.

He respected her; she lapped up the friendship and the fun. The sex was still all-pervading. They loved each other as friends but they were not yet in love and in truth neither expected to be albeit sometimes it seemed to be headed that way.

They ordered a second drink – he toasted her beauty; she toasted his virility.

"So," she said mysteriously … and he wasn't sure what was coming.

"We've done it on the boardroom table, your balcony has lost its virginity, where do you think we should make love tonight?"

They both knew this was a wind-up and they ended up in bits.

When at last they had half-composed themselves Kevin pretended to give it serious thought even as she tickled him and he snarled provocatively at her.

At length, as he sought to string her along and she told him wickedly that he had better match up to her expectations, he announced: "I know – we'll go to your place and make love in the lift!"

It wasn't a serious proposition – she smacked him in the chest purporting to be shocked while he held up his hands and claimed she should be grateful.

"It could put a whole new meaning on going up," he joked.

"Or a whole new meaning on going down," she taunted.

They were in stitches.

One or two of the tables around them glanced oddly at them.

"Shush," she cooed. "People are listening."

And once more faked offence.

They fell silent for two ticks, not quite sure who was going to take this on and where it was going to lead.

She spoke up first and deadpan asked: "So what are the rules for this shag-a-lift?"

He fell apart and almost losing it herself she hushed him into some sort of composure before the whole bar fixated on them.

They finally pupated into an impression of being proper.

At which point his estate agent persona took over.

"How many floors are there in your block of flats?"

She shook her head in disbelief.

"13," she said, playing him at his own game with not the hint of a smile.

"OK," he said, putting on his studious professional voice. "Right to the top, back down to eight, time up whether we manage to go all the way or not, and into your flat."

She desperately tried to hold it together without cracking up.

"Fine," she spluttered. "You're on."

Neither had any intention of doing anything of the sort.

They changed the subject but they could not have been more enthralled in each other's company and were very much enjoying themselves.

A bite to eat, a brandy each, and then a taxi to her place.

They got out of the cab in great good humour – they had been jesting about holidaying together and where they might go. The suggestions had got more expensive and outlandish by the moment.

Just a bit of tomfoolery.

They walked arm-in-arm to the block entrance and thence to the lift.

She pressed the 'up' button and their eyes met.

They could hear it rumbling down from whatever floor it had been on.

It came to a stop and the doors opened.

It was empty and they got in.

She looked at him, he looked at her, and spontaneously, almost as one, they started discarding clothing in all directions.

By floor four they were into each other in an upright position in all respects.

By flour seven they had sidled to the floor going for it as though an Olympic medal was dependent on the outcome.

Ding! The bell for floor 13 sounded.

The doors opened and suddenly she screamed, pulling out from him just as he was on countdown to launch.

She turned away and held her shame.

He looked to the open door and their stood a woman in her sixties, open-mouthed, jaw on the floor, unable to move, incapable of taking in the scene in front of her.

What was she doing there at this time of night?

His reaction was immediate.

"Sorry," he said. "Won't happen again. Have a good evening."

And pressed the button for floor 8.

The doors closed, she screamed again at the pornography of what they had done, clothes were frantically gathered together.

They burst out of the lift and raced for her flat.

Oh God, where were her keys?

Who had her handbag? It turned out he did.

She grabbed the bag, frantically fetched out the keys, dropped the keys, picked them up, stumbled with the lock, got the door open, and they fell into the front room.

Bundled together on the sofa, pieces of clothing like flotsam and jetsam along the hallway, they were half in hysterics and half riddled with guilt.

Creased up, they held each other before coming apart in a medley of claim and counter-claim.

"How could you? You're perverted."

She was trying hard to sound as if she meant it.

"What! It was your idea," he insisted.

"How dare you – I was brought up a nice girl," she exclaimed. "Anyway, it was your idea, don't pin that on me."

He burst out laughing once more. She purported to give him a smacking. Next they were on the floor again and thinking of making love.

Yet they held back.

"What if she calls the police?" said Alice.

"The police have better things to do than respond to some old granny who maintains she has seen two naked people having it off in a lift," he retorted. "At least I bloody well hope so."

"But what if there is some comeback with the property agents who look after the block?" she questioned.

"We will just say we know nothing about it," he said. "Will she remember what we look like – there's hardly going to be an identity parade! It sounds so fanciful. Who is likely to believe her?"

She decided there was logic in what he said, and her mood mellowed.

He pretended to be the presiding judge hearing the case. "Mrs Smith – was this knob, belonging to the defendant Kevin Jackson as before you naked in the dock, the knob in question you saw in the lift?"

It was back to laughter as she tried to visualise the revolting scene.

"How could you tell her to 'have a good evening'?" chortled Alice. "What are you?"

Now he was laughing too. "It just came into my head," he squirmed.

"I'm going to freak out if the doorbell rings," she chided.

That doubled him up.

"What's so funny?" she choked.

"No, it's nothing," he quipped.

"Tell me," she ordered.

"I just thought of ordering a pizza delivery and see how high you jump."

"Swine," she shrieked, hit him with a cushion, and jumped on top of him.

Giggling, he let his body go loose and 'take the punishment' until she ran out of energy.

The play-fight over, he feasted on her body, and then their lips met.

"Come on," she said. "Let's go to bed."

"This time, no hurry," he said.

"Definitely no hurry," she agreed.

Under the sheets they made it slow, deliberate, intimate, profound, meaningful and very much together.

It was as if their affair had gone to the next level as it were!

Yet it slightly frightened him and the next week in the office there was good reason to be frightened.

Within half an hour of arriving he sensed a different attitude and as the day went on he realised that he and Alice had been rumbled.

How had that happened?

They should never have gone to the office pub – someone must have spotted them there even though he had been pretty sure everyone was splitting. Somebody must have changed their minds and he and Alice, otherwise engaged, never noticed.

This was great gossip and it had clearly gone round the office in seconds.

There were little knowing glances and occasional titters in his direction.

Somebody asked him whether it had been a 'hot' weekend – they never normally said anything like that.

In the lunchtime queue at the sandwich shop the office wag Freddy ripped him to shreds.

"What's this about you and Alice – you dirty dog?"

And he nudged him in the ribs.

Kevin tried to look blank, but Freddy was on a roll.

"Wow, Alice is a stunner. How did you manage to pull her?"

Kevin feigned disinterest. "We're just friends – nothing to it."

Freddy was one of those guys who never knew when to let things go.

"Oh, the old just good friends line," he chirped. "Come on, Kev, spit it out – are you bonking her?"

Freddy knew Kevin hated being called Kev.

"That's very insulting," growled Kevin.

Now Freddy knew he was getting under Kev's skin.

"A long, sinuous French stick is it today?"

He was aware the symbolism would not be lost on his erstwhile colleague.

Kevin said nothing, took his sandwich, handed over the money, and was out of the door without another word.

But inside he was upset and furious.

He'd felt like punching the slime ball's lights out but that would have really put the cat among the pigeons.

As the afternoon wore on things didn't get any better even though Kevin and Alice were scrupulous to avoid looking at each other. Another giveaway? Or was that too Machiavellian?

Even senior partners Daniel and James – his friend Sako had moved on some while back – appeared to be frowning. Or maybe Kevin was imagining it.

That night he phoned Alice – what were they to do?

In great agitation he spelt out his fears – it was known that the bosses loathed office romances, it could jeopardise their careers, it would be easy to dream up some excuse to fire them, this was a disaster.

"Hold on," she said. "What's all the fuss about?"

That saw him hit the ceiling.

"How can you say 'what's all the fuss about'," he repeated, voice rising. "We're in big, big doo-dah land."

"Don't talk rot," she insisted, aware how men could act like babies in such situations.

She paused.

"Look I'll meet you tomorrow night after work and we'll talk it through."

"How can we do that," he gulped. "We can hardly walk out together and pretend nothing is going on."

She started to get angry.

"Well, if you want to play James Bond I'll turn left out of the office and you turn right. Is that dramatic enough for you?"

He began to feel a bit soppy. Perhaps he was over-reacting.

"OK," he mumbled unhappily. "Where shall we meet?"

"We'll meet in the Botanic Garden."

Not exactly an ultimatum but neither a suggestion.

"All right then," he groaned. "See you there."

The phone went dead.

It was a vexed night. He couldn't rid himself of anxious thoughts. How had he ended up in such a pickle? She had seduced him – that was what she had done. It wasn't acceptable.

Oh, God.

He was twitchy at work next day, found it hard to concentrate, and didn't know where to look, suspecting they were sniggering at him under their breath.

It was a relief to escape.

By Botanic Garden she had meant the historic Royal Botanic Garden Sydney.

For those who don't know it, it dates back to 1816 and holds a formidable position on Sydney Harbour immediately adjacent to the central business district and Opera House.

It is one of the most visited attractions in Sydney and covers 30 hectares (74 acres).

Flowers, shrubs, trees, lawn, ponds ... it is enchanting.

Except that evening its beauty was lost on Kevin.

He found her seated on a bench near the main entrance.

They greeted each other in a ridiculously formal manner and he sat down – there was no kissing.

"What are we going to do?" he gulped and instantly regretted an opening gambit which sounded so weak.

She went straight onto the offensive.

"I don't know what you are whining about," she charged. "What could be normal than two people going out with each other."

He groaned.

"It's the office – it could wreck everything I've built up there. You know I am quasi-management."

She wasn't having it.

"So?" she asserted. "If office romances were somehow banned half the country would never get themselves hooked up."

It was more serious than that, he told her. It was a relatively small office where colleagues had to get on together whether they liked each other or not, where small things could become big things, where work and private lives could rarely mingle without issues developing.

It was a mumbling thesis, he hadn't put it together well and it didn't sound convincing.

She wasn't impressed.

"If we are open and transparent about it there won't be a problem," she urged. "Only if we are devious and disruptive might they rightfully have concerns. We do our job, we show our commitment, and we go home together at night. You're building barriers where there don't need to be any."

He looked at her. It was a pretty good speech. He realised he was losing the argument.

"I just don't like the whole scenario," he insisted. "I mean … what happens if we break up and decide we can't stand the sight of each other? One way or another it's going to be bad news."

"Why would we break up?" she asked. "It's going pretty well, isn't it? I don't hear you complaining."

It put him in a spot.

"Well, yes," he acknowledged. "It has been good."

"Right then," she said. "Stop being so namby-pamby, pull yourself together and let's see how it pans out. I'll see you on Friday."

He'd been beaten.

"I suppose so," he whimpered, senses screwed.

"There," she said. "That wasn't so hard."

She kissed him gently, announced she had to be on her way, touched his leg as if to say everything would be all right, and, with a wave, was gone.

He sat there a long time, feeling thoroughly deflated, humiliated, insignificant in a vast park.

He'd gone into the conversation hoping he could ease himself out of what had become a suffocating relationship and had simply ended up in deeper.

She had twirled him around her little finger and he had had no answer.

He dragged himself home despondent, fearful that this could easily get on top of him, bringing the old doubts and depression back from the crash aftermath.

To be fair to her, the rest of the week turned out pretty routine. He wasn't actually in the office much which helped. Houses to inspect; clients to see.

Even so, he was jumpy and not himself.

The more he thought about it the more he convinced himself that Kevin-Alice had run its course and it was time to quit.

He had to steel himself, get back in control of the situation, and tell her it was over.

They went to the office bar, reasoning that, now it was out in the open, secrecy was neither here nor there.

He got them a couple of drinks and they found a quiet corner.

She sensed the tension and to his dismay jumped in first.

"Look, the week is over, freedom until Monday, I want to relax, let my hair down, and how am I going to do that if you are in a bloody mood. I thought we'd settled all this nonsense on Tuesday."

Her aggression put him on the defensive – must fight fire with fire he told himself.

He decided to state his case in no uncertain terms.

"I want out," he said. "I've had it. I've enjoyed it as far as it has gone. You're an outstanding girl, but I can't handle the office fall-out. We're done."

She flew into a fury.

"What fall-out." she yelled. "There has been no fucking fall-out."

"Keep your voice down," he pleaded.

She didn't.

"I've invested plenty in you," she charged. "You may be a fucking wimp but you're my fucking wimp. There is no way we are splitting up. Have you got that?"

He reeled back on his chair.

"I am sorry if this is upsetting for you," he said quietly. "But it takes two to tango and I am no longer tangoing."

He got up to leave. He had barely taken a sip of his drink.

"Sit down," she screamed at him.

The whole pub turned and looked in their direction. He sat down as he tried to hide from the disgrace and embarrassment.

But she was just getting going and with lethal venom.

"Now listen to me," she snarled. "It would be dreadfully unfortunate if Daniel and James were to find out that we did it on the boardroom table, wouldn't it?"

Rather like the granny in the lift, his jaw hit the floor and he sat their gob-smacked.

"You dump me and they are going to know how you raped me when all I was doing was innocently returning to the office to find my purse. Do I make myself clear?"

He sat their becalmed, unable to say anything, this was like out of a lurid novel.

"You wouldn't," he rambled. "That's not on – you know that's not the way it was."

"All I know," she stated vehemently and frostily. "Is that you took advantage of me – they are going to fire you on the spot … at the very least suspend you. Don't fuck me about, sunshine, or I will make sure you get fucked up big time."

His mind seemed to be on some sort of loop – he couldn't make it work properly.

"But that's blackmail," he gabbled.

"You bet," she said. "And don't ever forget it, hunk."

He sat there, trashed.

Both of them knew she had his goolies in a vice-like grip from which there was no escape if he wanted to keep working.

His thought patterns were all over the place. Surely she wouldn't tell the bosses – would she? If she did, he was finished.

He could make a clean breast of it but then he would be finished anyway.

She had sprung the trap.

What an ice cold, black-hearted, vicious witch.

He was to be her prized specimen, kept in a cage and let out once a week when she wanted to play.

Still speechless, he sat their mouth open like a dead fish.

"Oh come on," she chided, flicking an emotional switch. "Drink your drink. Now we've got our little misunderstanding straightened out it's time to have fun."

Her face broke into a wide smile. "You should be flattered. You've got a pretty girl who is mad for you. Sit back and enjoy the sex."

He sat back. But, as a performing sea lion from now on in, how was he going to enjoy the sex?

He took a long swig from his beer. He decided to do what many men do when hemmed into a corner – get drunk, it might go away, and, if not, put it off until the morrow.

Another swig – it would block out the bollocking.

"That's the way," she told him. "Lighten up. What about going to a club later – I feel like dancing."

What the fuck, he thought. In for a penny; in for a pound.

He smiled back at her, slid his hand up her dress, and kissed her – might as well make the most of it.

They started chatting away as if nothing had happened, he bought another couple of rounds, and the trademark giggling started.

They held hands, went round to a street café, ordered a Chinese, and sat at a table in the square. The food was delicious.

Then along to a club – she proved a great dancer, far better than he was.

It was hot, her gyrations were intoxicating – intoxication on top of intoxication – and the mix of sweat and perfume were like an aphrodisiac.

They danced lots until satiated they found a couple of stools at the far side where the dim light barely reached.

He held her close.

"You were great, you're a heavenly dancer."

She soaked up the compliment then soaked up his credentials with sensual caresses.

"Ready for some yet?"

He stroked her pussy.

"Balcony, lift ... let's do it here."

She smirked dirty at him and pumped up her boobs.

But, unlike the lift, they both knew this was not for real – the club was full and there were too many people around them.

They grabbed a taxi and left for her flat.

She joked that she was going to put him in chains and do what she wanted with him – it seemed an appropriate analogy given the way things had gone.

They may have had the row to end all rows but the sex was as tremendous as ever.

Given that had he had real balls it would not be happening, a bit of him hoped that his libido would disappoint her.

But she was so good at arousing him there was no chance of that.

He had to admit yet again, that office complications or not, she was a fantastic lay.

What is it the Poms say? Lie back and think of England.

It didn't happen very often but the Poms sometimes got things right.

And so, as the weeks and months ticked away, the connection spluttered along, driven primarily by pure sex albeit it had become more than that – knowing each other's likes, desires, temperaments and much more besides turned them into something of a girl/boy fixture.

Even the office, seemingly at first hostile, appeared willing to turn a blind eye. One or two even said they were happy for them.

The trouble was that Kevin began more and more to resent becoming her sex slave.

Gradually it began to eat him up.

He sought to hide his unhappiness from her.

Anyway, he reasoned, while the fling continued there was no point in cutting off his nose to spite his face by failing to take advantage of her voluptuous offerings to the full – the typical selfish male's take on these type of 'hard' choices.

But he found that letting things drift affected him at work – he was less driven, prone to day-dreaming, a touch tetchy.

And alone in his flat there were times he felt low and worthless. A danger sign.

What was he doing? Where was his life going?

At some point he had to escape from under Alice, however nice a position that was.

Maybe it was time for a complete break – from Alice, from Sydney, from Australia, from the whole cosy set-up.

Unlike most Australians he had never travelled outwith the south Pacific zone – Bali, Fiji, New Zealand was a terrific country, Tahiti … and that was about it.

Never had he been to the United States, England, or mainland Europe. Time to widen his horizons perhaps.

England sounded jolly. He could do the whole tourist bit, soak up the sights, explore the historic connection with the Mother Country, visit the Houses of Parliament.

He had vague memories of mum and dad checking out the family tree and discovering that some long-forgotten relatives had apparently emigrated from Tamworth back in the 19th century, some place near Birmingham. He wasn't quite sure where.

Might be a laugh to go and see what Tamworth was like today.

He took a while to mull all this around but gradually it became an increasingly attractive proposition.

Sydney was insular, he knew everything there was to know about it. He would miss it – that was for sure. Such a wonderful lifestyle.

He'd be exchanging that for the English weather – hardly a fair swop.

And the old jokes came flooding back – While Australians bathe in endless sunshine, the English are confounded by that mysterious yellow orb in the sky when it makes its annual cameo appearance each 'summer'; Australia boasts more than 10,000 golden strips of sand, meaning you could visit a new swimming spot every day for almost three decades – which is roughly how long it's been since the sun shone on one of England's pebbly excuses for a beach.

Ho, ho, ho.

But this was a turning point.

Australians of course usually go 'walk-about' in their early 20s – Kevin was now touching 40.

It might seem an odd move throwing everything up and taking a punt on a land he knew little about apart from what he had gleaned from books, lessons and the media.

However, you had to grasp the nettle on occasion.

And it would mean he could escape the clutches of Alice and the very real fear that the toxicity of their pairing was slowly, ever so slowly, tipping him back into what he referred to as 'crash mode' – the depression and negativity that had wrecked him in its aftermath.

At all costs he must avoid the shakes returning.

They hadn't been bad for a while – it was only on the rare occasion he still woke up in total terror. By and large it seemed under control.

So, a plan was formed but the next question was how to implement it.

He wasn't going to tell Alice – that was for sure. He hoped he could so arrange it that after sex on the Friday he simply wasn't there on the Monday.

He would tell his family a week or so before.

He first needed to outline his thinking to the estate agency. They had been exceptionally good to him. At the very least he owed them a proper explanation.

By strange coincidence, or maybe not a coincidence, just as Kevin was about to approach the bosses, they called him into a meeting.

There was the usual pleasantries, some tippy-tapping around whatever was to come, and then they broached the subject.

It has been noted that Kevin hadn't quite seemed his normal self of late, hard to put a finger on it, but distant, edgy, aloof. His business performance was still solid but had dropped off a tad. Was there something troubling him that they didn't know about? He was a valued member of the team – was there some way they could help?

The stance took Kevin aback.

They were right in their assessment but he was somewhat shocked that they had picked it up so quickly.

Still, better to get it out into the open before clients started being affected.

He had thought about what he was going to say.

He was definitely keeping all mention of Alice out of it, not only because he wanted a clean break but because he liked her and it would be absolutely out of order to tarnish her reputation.

So he told them he had become a little stale, was finding it difficult to motivate himself, was just beginning to take clients for granted, and believed a change of scene might be beneficial to all parties. He had loved working for the partnership, he had always tried to give of his best, but it was probably time to move on, seek pastures new.

Now, they were taken aback.

They had only ever intended using the meeting to bolster his spirits, gee him up and nip in the bud any issues.

His resignation was not on the agenda.

So they sought to persuade him otherwise. They did not want to lose him. He was a vital player. His contribution would be greatly missed. If money was a problem then they would look to incentivise him further. If it was greater responsibility he wanted then they had been assessing the commercial prospects of opening up in Brisbane – they would put him in charge of launching and running the new office.

He said he very much appreciated the confidence they showed in him. It wasn't money or responsibility, the remuneration was good and they had always allowed him his say.

It was more that the job had run its course, he wanted to travel, and then consider whether he should return to estate agency or look at alternatives. It was in the firm's own interest to bring in new blood. He had stayed longer than he ever envisaged – seven years. He feared he would stultify if he remained. They would get fed up with his face, he joked.

Don't do anything rash, they urged. Think about it. Take a week off. He'd perhaps been over-doing things. Had they been putting too much on him?

He felt like saying he had been over-doing Alice, but obviously didn't.

Instead, he promised he would definitely think through what they had put to him, the Brisbane job, and, thank you, he would take a couple of days off.

He didn't tell them he had already applied for a visa that would allow him to live and work in the UK – it helped that his grandfather on his mother's side had been born there.

He would let them know his decision on the Monday.

It was convenient because it would allow him to break the news to the family and no doubt another grilling on what was best for him.

So he did take two days off, and drove up into the Blue Mountains.

He loved the Blue Mountains and, if he was headed to the other side of the world for an extended period, he wanted to savour their delights one more time. Do some walking on one of the many trails.

A World Heritage Site covering more than a million hectares, the Blue Mountains get their name from the natural blue haze created by eucalypt forests. Tiny droplets of oil released from the trees mix with water vapour and sunlight to produce the distinctive colour.

Marvel at this wilderness region from cliff top lookouts. Explore waterfalls, valleys and rugged sandstone tablelands, the Jenolan Caves, see the Three Sisters Hanging Rock. Diverse flora and fauna; ancient Aboriginal culture.

It felt so pure, it re-invigorated the soul. He was so glad he had gone.

When he got back he decided it would be wise to savour the delights of Alice in case she was suspecting something was up.

She did indeed wonder why he had suddenly disappeared – the bosses had been in generous mood, he told her.

She sighed and said she wished she had been able to go with him.

It made her sound clingy and dependant. Definitely time to knock it on the head.

When he told his parents he was giving up the job to tour England and wider frontiers, he got a mixed reaction.

His mother was almost in bits – when would she ever see her 'baby' again? How could it be wise to throw away such a solid and rewarding job? He seemed so happy at last – where had all this come from?

Dad was more measured. He had travelled in his youth.

He cautioned Kevin that he was doing this as a middle-aged man. It might prove hard to fit in. It wasn't always greener on the other side.

Vicky who had done a couple of years backpacking around the world told him simply to 'go for it'.

All in all he felt he had their blessing – mum would come round.

Anyway they could all visit him. It wasn't like he was blasting off to Mars.

Kevin went in on the Monday and told his superiors that his mind was made up.

They said they were very sorry to hear it. He would be a huge loss.

There was a discussion about his shares in the business – they were willing to buy them back at a premium which was good of them.

They set a date – the end of the month which was three weeks away.

He told them he specifically did not want anyone to know he was off, there was to be no leaving party, he would simply walk out on the Friday and not re-appear on the Monday when they were then at liberty to reveal all.

They said that was most irregular.

He said that for personal reasons it was best done that way … wouldn't want there to be any upset.

At which point they cottoned on – so the rumours about Kevin and Alice were true.

And they reluctantly agreed to his request.

He worked hard in those last few weeks not wishing anyone to accuse him of winding down or slacking.

The visa came through, his plane tickets booked, he had arranged with Vicky to take over the flat and checked she was geared up, and he got all packed to go.

And so it came to the final Friday.

He spoke to the partners one last time, they shook hands, wished him well, told him to keep in touch, and if he ever came back and was needing a job to give them a call.

He thanked them once more for all they had done for him and thanked them in particular for keeping his departure secret.

That evening he took Alice out as usual. As far as he was aware she remained completely in the dark.

Whatever their differences she was a great girl and he wanted to treat her with dignity.

He wrote a long letter which he planned to post on the day he flew out. It told her she was gorgeous. He had had a wonderful time. He was extremely fond of her but that was as far as it went. He felt claustrophobic being unable to take the relationship forward or backwards. He apologised for not saying this to her face but wanted to keep it civilised. He trusted she would understand. He wished her well and hoped she would find happiness.

It was the best he could do.

But he had also decided to buy her a 'farewell' present to in effect say thank you for their time together.

It was a silver chalice and deliberately he had spent a decent amount of money on it.

It was important to do things right by her.

Disgracefully he had never given her a present in all the time they had been going out together.

He took her to the office pub, they quaffed a couple of drinks and then they carried on to what would be their Last Supper.

It was a 'posh' restaurant because he wanted to put on a show for her.

She was in her element.

When they got back to her flat he brought out the chalice.

He knew it wasn't her birthday but it was grossly remiss that he had never bought her anything, so he had decided to rectify that. He hoped she would like it.

She was made-up by the gesture.

She removed the wrapping, opened the little presentation box, said it was absolutely beautiful, tried it on, admired it in a mirror, took it off, thanked him and said she would always cherish it.

She put her arms around his neck, and kissed him slow and smutty.

So much so that his knees began to shake.

Part of his inner self told him he was crazy to give up this woman. She was beautiful. Any self-respecting man would desire her. When she wasn't threatening him with rape, she was a stimulating playmate. She was intelligent. She was wonderful under the sheets. He was very much wanted. Maybe he should stick with Alice. It wasn't too late to abandon the plot.

He teetered on the edge.

No, he had to go through with it. He had to be free.

The love-making was out of this world and he left the next day sucked dry, shagged out and glad that he had known her.

Finally, there was conclusion.

When Alice went into work on the Monday she was puzzled – there was no Kevin.

But mid-morning the bosses drew them all together and explained that Kevin had left. He had wanted to go travelling for a long while and they were sad to part company. He hadn't wanted a fuss, a going away party, nothing ... there was an apology for keeping it from them but Kevin was insistent.

And that was it. They went back to their desks and got on with it.

Alice was wounded but she was tough. There were no tears – she held it together.

When she got back to the flat that evening there was the letter on the mat.

She read it and this time there were tears.

There were many emotions – she was furious at having been duped, she was heartbroken to have lost him, she would have liked to have given him a piece of her mind, she would have liked to have taken him home for a spanking session.

For ten days or so she was unusually self-absorbed – until Kevin's replacement Rikki turned up in the office.

He had French origins, he was tall, athletic, blue eyes, handsome, a neat dresser.

Rikki never stood a chance.

And so Kevin was forgotten and erased from the history books.

In Normal, Suzi took things steady, no need to rush her recovery, simply try and do a bit more as each day passed.

She helped her Gran around the house, took an interest in cooking, pottered about the garden, made it up with old dog Lady.

She went for walks, having promised Sara that this was exactly what was going to happen – no bunking off. She began jogging, read books, worked on her suntan, tried to solve the newspaper crossword.

Determined this was going to be the new Suzi.

At length she discussed going back to school – that's if they would have her back – and subsequently she, Sara and Jeb met with the principal.

Suzi told her that the penny had dropped … and she meant it.

Finally she realised how important it was to study – it was probably too late to salvage all that she had missed from her truant past, but it would be good to start somewhere.

They talked about her dropping a year and seeing how she got on. She agreed that sounded a wise move.

The next week she went back to school and from the outset she started grafting, much to the teachers' gratification.

The new Suzi was applying herself.

She was determined – in particular boys were off limits until she had got herself sorted.

She grafted at home too – decrying television, computer games and social media for long hours in her bedroom looking to catch up on the many missing gaps in her education.

Months went by and Suzi kept at it.

She had turned into the model pupil – the school were pleased and her family were thrilled.

And she herself felt much the better for it.

In a way dropping the year had helped because her new classmates were mostly unknown quantities and in turn knew little about Suzi's chequered background. So she had something of a clean slate. Children tend to take people as they find them and there was no problem fitting in. Indeed she discovered she was quite popular.

Rarely coming into contact with her old friends was probably for the best – kept her out of temptation.

But being streetwise was on occasion an advantage – bizarrely she had turned into a bit of an agony aunt. Younger kids making their own mistakes increasingly used her as a sounding board.

You couldn't have made it up.

Yet she knew that inside, rather like a dormant volcano, the old destructive Suzi had not gone away. She had just put a lid on her.

Would something set her off?

The cynics would have said it was a question of not if but when.

And when it did happen it was so dreadfully disappointing for all concerned and so avoidable.

Her resolve withered on the vine one Saturday as she returned from window shopping – T-shirts, jeans, shoes.

Yes, she had become fashion conscious.

Pity then she was not more conscious of the dangers of being led astray when one-time "awkward squad" member Emma strode into view.

"What ya, Suzi," hailed Emma. "Heard you'd had a bit of bovver with them bikers. Awful that. Back on the scene now though, are you?"

"Actually, no," replied Suzi. "Turned over a new leaf. Trying to keep out of it."

"What?" sneered Emma. "You haven't gone all boring on us, have you?"

Suzi bristled. "No, Just other stuff to do."

Emma cackled.

"Never thought you'd be one to sell out."

Suzi blushed. "It's not like that."

She felt tongue-tied and defensive.

"Well," responded Emma. "You go off and play with your dolls – we're going to the race."

"What race?" asked Suzi.

"Baz and Mickey are lifting a couple of motors," said Emma. "There's a place a few miles outside of town where they're going to have a face-off. Should be a right hoot."

Suzi felt the adrenalin rising.

"Na, don't want to fall foul of the cops."

"Don't be a baby," snorted Emma. "Smokey know nothing about it."

She could see Suzi was torn.

"Come on," she insisted. "We're only going to watch – what's wrong with that?"

"OK," said Suzi. "But if there's trouble I'm out of it."

Emma flicked her eyes back with disdain.

She was wearing a T-Shirt emblazoned with the words "Hot Chick" and strategically ripped to expose a bra strap. The top button was open on old jeans which had been cut down into shorts complete with a badge provocatively stating "Press to Enter". She had leather boots rising to her thigh.

All for one thing – to pull good-looking fellows.

Emma had arranged to meet Joy and Joy's boyfriend Jez in a bar for a couple of drinks first.

Half the blokes nearly fell off their stools when the pair walked in.

Joy and Jez were already there seated at a table.

Every eye turned as Emma flounced over.

"You two up for it then?"

"Yeah," said Joy. "Half the kids in Normal will be there. It's going to be awesome."

Jez ordered a couple more bottles of lager for the newcomers.

They sunk them slowly, basking delightedly in the attention from burning eyes.

Emma liked making a statement.

Jez ran a battered Chevrolet Impala and they all piled in.

When they got to the meet there were already a host of folks there.

Horns honking, engines blasting, music blaring. It was a cool, bright evening. Just right for showing off.

"Cheers," said Suzi, exiting the Impala.

"Magic," said Emma.

They mingled with the crowd as they waited for the action to start. Every type of outfit. Every type of hair style. Baby-faced teenagers pretending to be hard men. A host of Sandys out of Grease.

At last a ripple ran through the 120-plus gathering.

Arriving at a rudimentary starting grid were the two protagonists.

Baz was in a Ford Mustang, his mate Joey in the passenger seat, and two glamorous girls in the back sending out 'look who I ride with' boasts.

Mickey was in a Porsche 911 with pal Ben. That meant there were vacancies.

They were sizing up the girls in the crowd. And didn't the girls in the crowd know it, pouting and flaunting as if in a beauty contest.

Mickey's eyes alighted on Emma and Suzi.

"You two – get in the car," he drawled.

Legs alluring, tits titillating, Emma strutted her way to the Porsche, stuck out her bum, and squeezed herself on the back seat.

Suzi nearly fainted. Timid, frightened, but excited and revelling in being a sex object again, there was no turning back. She would have lost too much face. This was like out of the movies – power, thrills, studs, let's get racing.

It was like walking on air, she never seemed to move a muscle but there she was beside Emma on the back seat, hair thrown back, chin out and her 'this is for big girls' face on.

Mickey turned to look at Baz, and nodded.

Baz nodded back.

A lad with a Ferrari flag had been designated as starter and was milking it for all it was worth.

Finally, engines revving, dust flying, screeching tyres, screams from the crowd, the flag came down.

They were off.

Instinctively Suzi reached across and put on her seatbelt – nobody else did.

Sixth sense? Premonition? It was to save her.

Occupying both sides of the road the cars were racing wheel-to-wheel at over 100 miles per hour.

It was quiet at the best of times this out-of-the-way stretch and they had reasoned that, it being late evening, it would be clear.

Wrong call.

Two hundred yards up a pick-up edged out onto its correct side of the road, right into the path of the Porsche.

Mickey had two seconds, maybe three, to do something about it.

The farmer who was driving the pick-up surveyed death bearing down on him and brought his vehicle to a shuddering halt.

Mickey, he said later, had, like he, terror etched across his face.

The Porsche swerved to avoid a collision, but the roadside gravel destabilised the speeding sports car, it clipped the pick-up's wing, and that sent it out of control.

It bounced over and over perhaps five times, hit a tree, bounced perhaps another three revolutions, all the time metal fragments being chucked about like confetti, and crunched to a halt hissing fury and threatening to explode.

It was carnage.

Lucky for him, Mickey died instantly – so mangled was the corpse that his parents couldn't recognise their own son.

When they found Ben they discovered the branch of a tree had gone straight through his brain and out the other side.

Emma's torso was spotted 12ft off the ground – it took them three hours to find her head buried deep in foliage.

Suzi came round, at first not knowing where she was, beyond bewilderment at what had happened.

She seemed to be in a trance-like state. She was having trouble seeing. She was hurting. She couldn't remember how she had come to be there.

There was only an eerie silence.

A tiny flame danced in front of her eyes and suddenly the threat of fire galvanised her into action.

She had to get out of this car – had to get out.

Uncoupling the seat belt, she realised that the door no longer existed.

She fell out onto the dirt and began to crawl ever so slowly away from the vehicle, every movement an agony.

Maybe she managed fifteen feet before the Porsche exploded in a fire ball.

It burned her eyebrows away, seared her face, frazzled what was left of her clothes and left her unable to hear properly.

Somehow she had to get back to the road – sheer willpower pulled her through.

When they found her passed out she had nearly made it.

It was Baz who raised the alarm.

He had watched appalled, the girls were screaming and screaming and screaming, Joey was ashen.

The farmer had survived but was clearly badly shocked, sat in the roadway, head hunched, completely out of it.

Baz began thinking fast.

He turned round and told the girls in no uncertain terms to shut it. Red eyed and shaking, they obeyed.

Then he took his phone out and dialled 911.

When it answered he provided the basics – road traffic accident, location, multiple injuries, and then he turned his mobile off.

It was time to save himself from possibly a hefty prison sentence for his part in the affair.

Aware there was a deep lake about three miles away he turned the car, and ordered Joey to check out the best route.

Yet more screaming from the back seat.

Joey managed to get a sat nav fix.

Baz put his foot down and sped towards the lake.

When he got there he manoeuvred the Mustang onto a slope close to the water.

The other three bailed out.

"Right," said Baz to Joey. "She's going under – get ready to push."

He got himself half clear, let off the handbrake, and the two of them gave the thing a shove. Seemingly reluctant, it began to move, gathered pace and plunged into the lake. Spray everywhere, it sunk fast, bubbles peppering the surface, one last gasp, and it was gone.

They had got rid of the evidence.

One of the girls was slobbering.

The other was all over the place, wailing that she needed her mother but so distraught she kept on hitting the wrong button on her phone.

"No way," screeched Baz and smacked her full in the face. Leaving her crumpled on the grass.

He tore the mobile out of her hands and hurled it into the water.

"What I say goes, or you follow your fucking phone into the lake."

His victim cowered; her pal, intimidated by a Baz stare, cut the racket.

This was the date from hell.

He took hold of the girls.

"The first thing we're going to do is get out of the fucking view from the road – now move it, slags."

He part pushed, part kicked and part dragged them into the cover of trees.

"Now listen to me all of you."

He threw the girls onto the floor.

"I ain't going down for no fucking road race. We was never in a road race – have you got that?"

They looked petrified.

"We ain't going anywhere tonight – we stay here, hunker down and make sure nobody finds us. I'll arrange for someone to pick us up in the morning so long as the police heat has cooled."

Frightened eyes stared back at him.

He pointed at the girls.

"Behave and you won't get hurt. Normally, you being attractive babes, I would happily get into your knickers but not tonight, you'll no doubt be relieved to know. I've got enough hassle."

Both looked terrified.

He eyed the one who had been in hysterics.

"You tell your fucking mother when you get back that you was out camping with friends."

He gave her another slap though not quite so hard as the first. "You fucking sort it, or I'll come looking for you and when I'm finished that pretty face won't be pretty no more."

She whimpered miserably, a weal already coming up on the side of one cheek.

Her friend tried to console her.

They went deeper into the woods.

Nobody slept much that night, particularly the girls. It was unpleasant, it was scary and they kept on being bitten by insects.

The next day Baz made some calls and at length around mid-day a Toyota Sequoia sports utility vehicle hove into view.

They all got in – nobody spoke much as they continued to get to grips with the enormity of what had happened.

And they made it back to Normal without attracting suspicion.

Back at the shocking crash scene police, fire and ambulance had all descended, battle-hardened emergency workers grim-faced at the gruesome sight.

Straight-away a team of medics were around Suzi.

She was unconscious, bloodied, pulse and heartbeat steady, but breathing laboured.

They took their time for fear of neck, spinal or internal injuries, packed protective padding around her, eased her onto a stretcher and into an ambulance,

Oxygen mask on, drip set-up and it was onwards to hospital, lights flashing, siren blaring.

Other medics were already assessing the farmer.

His vital signs were fine, he was speaking in a rambling fashion, he was still very shocked.

They helped him to a second ambulance and took him to hospital for further checks.

The fire brigade had been hosing down what remained of the Porsche as a precaution.

It was obvious to all that nothing could be done for the other victims.

From there it was a long haul for the emergency services – removing the bodies and body parts and investigating what had caused the accident.

It appeared at first glance to be a one-on-one car crash, but the farmer had spoken of two cars bearing down on him.

Could there have been two cars? Or had the man, in his hazy state, got himself muddled?

At the hospital trauma department staff were working hard on Suzi to ascertain the extent of her injuries.

Collapsed lung, broken ribs, broken arm, smashed cheek bone, severe concussion, superficial second degree burns, but nothing internal and nothing life threatening.

She had been fortunate.

Sedated, she was transferred to critical care.

Sara and Jeb were worried and anxious – Suzi hadn't come home.

They were also deeply disappointed because they thought she was over all the disappearing acts and let-downs.

With heavy hearts they phoned the police and reported her missing.

The police took down her details, asked for a description, promised to keep a lookout, and said they would get back in due course.

Probably just another runaway.

Until someone suggested that the description matched the kid in the car wreck.

They ran a check on Suzanne Elizabeth Duthie and of course discovered they already had an extensive file on her.

They put two and two together.

An officer was sent round to see Sara and Jeb to inform them there was a strong possibility their grandchild had been in a car accident.

He ran them round to the hospital.

They were taken to the girl's bedside – Sara started sobbing, Jeb looked shot.

There was no doubt. It was Suzi.

And so began another family vigil at Suzi's bedside though thankfully buoyed by the knowledge that she should make a full recovery.

Suzi woke up on day two – she was lying in a bed, with white sheets, white ceilings, white walls, white curtains around her bed.

She knew what that meant – she must be in a hospital.

And then it all came back to her – oh, yes, the race.

She grimaced, what a foolish thing to do, why was she such an idiot, how did she allow others to persuade her into such pranks.

At which point she noticed Sara and Jeb.

"I'm so sorry, Granny, I've let you down again."

"Never mind that, we need to get you better," said Sara.

Suzi smiled.

Her whole body hurt, she felt weak, she knew what it meant, she had been there before.

"What have I done to myself this time?" she whispered.

Sara tried to be matter-of-fact. "Oh, you've broken a few things, nothing too serious, but the doctors and nurses are looking after you, you're going to be fine."

It was a relief to hear. She had cheated death for a third time.

A nurse appeared and asked them to pop to the waiting room while she changed a tube. They could return as soon as she was finished.

When they did so Suzi had dozed off.

Abby flew in on day three and went straight to the hospital.

"What have you done to yourself this time?" chided Abby playfully.

Suzi tried to laugh but couldn't.

"It's good to see you," she responded, which brought a tear to Abby's eye.

After all the times when she had been called a 'cow' and more beside.

They stuck to safe subjects and talked about Normal, Toronto, the family, the weather.

Until Suzi's mood changed slightly and she became earnest.

"I tried so hard not to get into that car," she stuttered. "What's wrong with me, Abby? Trouble seems to follow me around."

She clasped Suzi's hand.

"You were doing so well. We were all monitoring your progress. This is just a blip – an aberration. Nobody is annoyed. We know there is so much good in you. You're a wonderful human being and we love you lots. We're going to get you better. We're going to get over this as a family. We got the real Suzi back once and we're going to get the real Suzi back again. You'll see."

Suzi began to cry. "I'm such a weak person. I am forever having regrets. But I promise you that one day I will make it up to you."

On an ordinary ward now, she was picking up by the day.

And then the police came round looking to take a statement from her.

Cooperate by all means, advised Abby, but don't say anything that might incriminate yourself.

Suzi felt she had little choice – she owed that to the dead.

She had to take her medicine.

Confirming the respective identities, she admitted there was a second car, Baz was driving, she didn't really know the other three with him.

Were they racing?

Yes, they were racing.

She could remember a vehicle pulling out in front but had no recollection of the crash itself. She could dimly recall crawling from the mangled heap.

What was the make of the second car?

She thought it was a Ford Mustang.

They were still trying to locate it – a Mustang had been reported stolen that day. Did she have any information as to its whereabouts?

No, she hadn't.

Was money being bet on the race?

Not that she was aware.

How fast were they going?

Bending the truth a touch, she replied: "I honestly wouldn't know – maybe 80/85 miles per hour."

Could the cars have been going even faster than that?

They could, she acknowledged.

The questioning went on.

It really must be the last time I get myself into this situation, she thought to herself. Never again.

And that applied to the newspapers too where she was now being termed a 'wild child' and "the plane crash survivor who keeps trying to kill herself'.

The ignominy she was heaping on the family cut deep.

She wasn't the only one to identify Baz – there had after all been more than 100 witnesses. And despite Baz's threats the girl who had seen her mobile hurled into the lake was virtually forced-marched along by her parents to voluntarily cough to the crime.

The police did Baz for aggravated reckless driving and motor theft, his hopes of staying out of jail dashed.

The funerals for the victims were chilling – a dreadful waste of three young lives.

Suzi was released from hospital to recuperate at home.

It was back to helping around the house, smartening up the garden, watching television and, when she felt up to it, walks around the local neighbourhood.

There was also the poser of – what next?

Another break in her schooling. This time they probably wouldn't want her back. She didn't think she could face going back anyhow.

As her strength returned, Abby suggested she headed for Toronto for a bit of a break.

That seemed a good idea and once she was cleared to fly she ran with it.

Spending time with her cousins and being generally spoiled by Abby was not to be sneezed at.

They did the tourist thing – boat trip around the harbour, went up the CN Tower, walked the Toronto Islands.

But the highlight was a day trip to Niagara Falls.

A scenic drive there, cruise to the base of the falls, mist in your face – it was unforgettable.

It brought back so many happy memories for Abby – she and her John and that quaint little motel …

Naturally, Abby and Suzi talked, but Abby wanted to avoid anything heavy or upsetting. So no discussions around sorting herself out; no deep conversation of where her life was headed.

The closest it came saw her simply advise Suzi to lay down some moral standards but otherwise to go with the flow. She pointed out how insane it was that she should fall in love with a man in a country she had never dreamed she would ever visit – and it was all down to Suzi. Someone had surely been watching over her. So, you never knew what twists and turns life would bring. She was sure Suzi would find herself.

Wise words deserving of proper contemplation at the right time.

When the holiday was over she thanked Abby and John profusely for their kindness and hospitality. It had been brilliant.

She didn't deserve an aunt like Abby. It had taken her time to understand. Abby had done so much for her – thrown up her career in Dubai, gone all that way to Bali to look after her, brought her to Normal so the family could care for her, never failed to try and support her despite her own trials and responsibilities.

And for so long she had been so beastly to Abby. She could never repay her.

Suzi flew back to Normal and normality.

The trip had been greatly beneficial. It had enabled her to find an equilibrium, it had taken her out of the goldfish bowl that was Normal, it had opened her eyes to the huge possibilities that the world offered.

It set her thinking that perhaps the time had come to quit Normal – she was not in a rush, there would be no hasty decisions but it had to be an option.

Normal was home and would always be home, but it was small, it was hard to keep a low profile, and she was now one of its most notorious citizens.

Could she ever escape her chaotic lifestyle while still living in Normal?

Probably not.

But where would she go? What would she do? How would she put food on the table?

Questions she wasn't about to delve too deeply into for now, but matters she would have to confront in due course.

Perhaps Abby was right – play it by ear, don't over-complicate the future.

No doubt something would kick in.

All these thoughts were bubbling about in her head as she settled herself back into the tranquillity of Sara and Jeb's.

Mundane and domestic.

Yet everything was about to be thrown high in the air and it came about in the most innocuous manner.

On this particular afternoon Suzi was in her bedroom reading when Sara shouted to her from downstairs.

Winter had come, it was cold outside … Sara and Jeb were heading out. Could Suzi find her black gloves and drop them down please.

"Go into our room – they're in the chest of drawers. Try the second one down."

Suzi did as asked.

Hard to shift the second down, took a yank and a heave, and she discovered why. It was jammed full of letters. Heavy as a rock.

She opened the third. Ah, there were the gloves granny wanted.

She picked them out and tipped them over the banisters.

"Thank you," said Sara. "That's excellent. See you later. We won't be that long."

The front door opened and clicked shut again.

Suzi returned to the bedroom and first pushed shut the glove drawer.

Next she shaped up to the heavy second one.

But as it shifted something caught her eye – one of the letters was addressed to her, Suzanne Duthie.

Intrigued, she opened the drawer out wide again.

She probably shouldn't be doing this because this was her grandparents' room and their private domain.

But Suzi being Suzi could not resist.

She turned over some of the other letters, all still in their envelopes.

And she got quite a shock.

It wasn't just the one that was addressed to her – they all appeared to be.

Who could they be from? What were they all doing bundled up in the drawer?

She felt like a burglar, but she had to open a letter up and ascertain who had sent it.

Delicately she did so and spread the letter out on the bed.

It began 'Dear Hope'.

Well, that was bizarre for starters – who was Hope?

She looked at the envelope again.

Yes, the addressee was definitely Suzanne Duthie. So who was this Hope?

Somewhat baffled, she read on.

It was a long letter and the tone was definitely adult to adult rather than adult to child. The author, she quickly deduced was male, and it spoke of all that he had been doing in the period, the people, the setbacks, the successes, his inner-most anxieties poured out onto the page.

At the bottom it was signed Kevin.

Kevin? She didn't know a Kevin. Oh, but hang on, wasn't that bloke who rescued her from the plane crash called Kevin? That could be it.

She looked at the date – it was ten years previous.

How very strange. It was hard to take in.

She re-read the letter – what was she to do about all this?

Feeling guilty at 'ransacking' her grandparents' room, she decided it was only right to play this straight down the line.

She determined she would read no more of the letters … and she shut the drawer.

When propitious, she would reveal to Sara and Jeb that she had accidentally stumbled on the hoard when searching for the gloves – that, after all, was the exact truth.

Then she would quiz them on what it meant and ask that she be able to read them all.

She wasn't sure why, but it felt that this was something very important.

Half an hour later Sara and Jeb had returned.

"Hi, we're back," shouted Sara. "Everything OK?"

"Yes, fine," said Suzi.

She said nothing about her letter discovery.

They had a nice tea – home-made burger, with lettuce, tomato, cheese and fries.

Suzi cleared the dish washer and then stacked it with the dirty plates and cutlery.

Jeb went into the computer room – said he wanted to catch up on emails. Sara sat down in the lounge, reading a magazine.

Suzi asked if she would like a cup of coffee.

"Yes, that would be nice, sweetie. I could do with a warm coffee."

Suzi made the coffee and took the two cups through, giving one to her grandmother and holding hers by her chest as she levered herself into an armchair.

She took a sip of her coffee.

Sara seemed relaxed – it was surely as good a time as any to bring the subject up.

"Granny."

"Yes, dear."

"You know when I threw you down the gloves when you were going out earlier."

"Yes, dear."

"And you said to open the second drawer."

"Yes, dear."

"Well, they weren't there – they were in one of the other drawers."

"Is that right, dear?"

Sara was engrossed in a magazine article and was only half listening.

"Yes," said Suzi. "And it was impossible to miss noticing that the wrong drawer was stuffed full of lots and lots of letters."

Sara glanced away from the magazine and towards Suzi.

"And, by accident, I noticed that all the letters were addressed to me."

She now had Sara's full attention.

"I'm a bit flummoxed," said Suzi. "I was wondering whether you could tell me about them."

Sara sighed and hummed to herself.

"There's no great mystery," she began. "We told you about the plane crash, didn't we?"

"Yes," agreed Suzi.

"And we told you about the man in the water who helped save your life."

"Yes," said Suzi.

"Well, ever since you were tiny, he has been writing these long letters to you. We read them just in case there is some question or whatever posed within them. Then we put them away in the drawer. To be honest they seem pretty odd and we did not want you upset by them given the other problems you have faced. They have I am afraid just piled up – out of sight out of mind. They come as regular as clockwork every two months or so."

Suzi chewed over this for a second.

Her irascible side wanted to know why, if they were addressed to her, Sara had taken it upon herself to open them and never revealed their existence. Fair enough when she was a child but surely that no longer held true.

Instead, she bit her lip – she had upset her grandmother enough. She was learning that you picked your fights carefully, standing fast only when it really counted and letting the rest go. This was not a battle worth taking on.

"I am afraid I couldn't resist reading one of them," admitted Suzi. "What I can't figure is why the letter begins 'Dear Hope'."

"Well, neither can we," replied Sara. "They all begin 'Dear Hope'. I can only assume that it is some sort of nickname for you. That was another element we thought dubious."

"It does seem strange," admitted Suzi.

She paused.

"What else do you find odd about them, Granny?"

"Goodness me, the questions you ask," chided Sara. "It is more the general tone. First, they all constructed as if you were an adult which of course you aren't, or rather you weren't. Second, they are almost obsessive. Thirdly, they are starkly confessional. Fourth, you could argue that they are unduly forward – the sort of material you might find in someone's personal journal.

"It is hard to exactly put a finger on it and maybe I am being too harsh. This is not fair but he sort of comes across as a stalker. In that vein if you know what I mean.

"I hesitate to be too judgemental but one might suspect he is slightly unhinged."

She took a breath. "Do you understand where I am coming from?"

"Yes," said Suzi. "I understand how that perception could arise."

It prompted Sara to take a step back, concerned that she might have painted too bleak a picture.

"On the other hand," she said. "You wouldn't be here without him. He clearly holds you dear in his heart. Having said that, these are not love letters or even akin to love letters. Yet they predicate some sort of glue binding you together. Maybe there is; maybe there isn't. But, in a way that is hard to describe, we just felt the whole thing was unhealthy. You may think otherwise but for better or worse we decided your welfare must be paramount. I apologise if you believe you have been hoodwinked. That was never our intention."

Suzi took that on board. Her grandparents had obviously sought to shelter her and believed they were doing the right thing, acting in her best interest or what they thought to be her best interest.

The room fell silent for a few seconds.

Then, in danger of seriously irritating her grandmother, Suzi returned to the 'fray'.

"I hesitate to raise this, Granny, and I don't want to upset you, that's the last thing I want to do, but would you have any objection to me reading the letters and making my own judgement in due course?"

What a mature question, thought Sara.

"Not at all," she said. "That is your right."

She went on: "It will take you weeks to get through them all if that is what you want to do, but by all means feel free.

"And you know we are here for you if, as I mentioned before, you find something upsetting. We may be able to put it into context; we may not. But we are here for you."

Suzi got out of her chair, kissed Sara on the cheek and gave her a hug.

"That's really good of you, Granny," she said. "I know you and Grandad mean well. I love you both very much."

Which brought a tear to Sara's eye.

"If it's OK, Granny," said Suzi. "I'll remove them from the drawer, put them in date order and then start working my way through them.

"It will give me something to do. I feel a need to work out what motivates this man, Kevin. I'd like to try and picture where he is coming from."

"That's fine, dear," said Sara. "You do what you want."

"Thanks, Granny."

Sara returned to her magazine. Suzi pretended to fiddle with her mobile phone, but her thoughts revolved around the gold mine of letters.

She felt it incumbent upon her to crack the puzzle.

Next day Suzi collected them all up out of the drawer and – it took her several trips – transferred them to her bedroom.

She dumped them on the bed.

Then began the task of getting them in date order – it took her the better part of an hour to do so.

She stacked them neatly across the top of a table in the corner.

She began reading and quickly picked up the tenor of the letters.

They were in turns compelling, banal, shocking, and tragic. As Sara had indicated, they were certainly from the heart and she found her own heart going out to a brave but complex individual.

Obviously he had been torn asunder by the plane crash – he was carrying an enormous burden of guilt.

And her thoughts turned to the mess in which her own life had descended. Perhaps it too was all to do with the crash and its aftermath.

Maybe they were both searching for answers which weren't there, trying to find outcomes where none existed.

The letters were in part narration of events – Bali, Sydney, the sports agency, estate agency.

But they were far more than that, taking her along with him on the rollercoaster of depressive lows and small but defining victories.

The description of his break-up with Becky, his detachment from the opposite sex, and the extraordinary Alice saga mined deep feminine urges.

His inability to fully re-connect with the world after the pulverising of his very being in the confluence of the Indian and Pacific oceans gave her a connection to his despair.

As Sara had predicted it took Suzi a long, long time to get through all the letters.

But she read them religiously from start to finish.

It was, she decided, a remarkable pulling together of events and emotions which cried out to be turned into a book … and it was all written to her.

She had neither the energy nor the desire to take on such a task but perhaps she could go one better and meet this victim whose prose was like poetry.

She had been bitten with a craving and a curiosity to find out more about Kevin, what sparked him, and what over and above the manner of their sheer survival they might have in common.

Would they click, and by that she definitely meant platonically. She didn't entirely rule out anything, though getting physical across the age gap certainly wasn't in the script.

Put him on a plinth as her guardian angel maybe… but no more than that.

She would take her time and think this through. Was she building a mountain out of a molehill?

Would this be a disastrous wild goose chase or could the two of them prove cathartic saviours of each other?

The one thing she determined she must not do was put her grandparents through the mill once again.

Kevin got off the long and arduous Sydney-London flight, having spent much of it reading through a guidebook to the capital city.

He had already booked ahead bed and breakfast at a reasonable budget hotel for a week – enough to charge round the tourist sights while assessing whether he could hack living in the midst of ten million people.

Transport would not be a problem – his own two feet and extensive use of the Tube.

He had his bucket list worked out – Houses of Parliament and Big Ben, Buckingham Palace, the London Eye, the Tower of London, British Museum, Tower Bridge, Hyde Park, Trafalgar Square, St Paul's Cathedral, Piccadilly Circus, Harrods, Soho, Portobello Road.

That should do for starters and he was itching to get going.

Taxi to the hotel first, wonder what the bedroom will be like, take a shower, dying to brush his teeth and eradicate the taste of airline catering, a quick nap, three beers – no more, put the phone on charge, crash out and hope the jetlag isn't too excruciating.

Must remember to text his parents to let them know he had arrived safely.

And so began the great English adventure.

The tourist bit went well even if he was somewhat flaked out – you're there in body but in mind you are somewhere over the Bay of Bengal.

Buckingham Palace was impressive; wonderful views from the London Eye.

The Tower of London was great – from the Crown Jewels to the Tower Ravens, tales of lost princes, World

War I spies, daring escapes and the tragic story of Anne Boleyn, one of Henry VIII's many wives, through her imprisonment, trial and execution.

Trafalgar Square and Nelson's Column certainly lived up to the hype.

He was like a kid in a candy shop at Harrods – not that he bought much. Jaw-dropping what you could purchase there and in many cases jaw-dropping prices to match.

He could have eaten dinner in his hotel but deliberately took himself out to sample the nightlife, check out the scene and reach for the buzz.

There were so many bars, restaurants and clubs it was hard to know where to start.

So much so that he felt somewhat inhibited.

He had beers in various different bars – mostly nobody spoke to him though he did share the crack with a couple of Irishmen and talked Down Under with an Aussie barman. He ate in restaurants without knowing what he was doing there. He tried a couple of nightclubs, danced with girls, but never quite felt he belonged.

Now, you had to work at these things – hard to go to somewhere you had never been before and make instant friends.

But equally he could vision how lonely London could be despite all its inhabitants. After all, he had felt exactly the same in Sydney.

There were other doubts.

It was hard to walk on pavements without bumping into folk, everyone seemed to be in a perpetual hurry, there were hustlers all over the place. Would anyone stop and help if you collapsed to the floor or would they assume you were simply a dosser/druggie/waster and walk on by? He wasn't at all sure.

He made some desultory inquiries about jobs with estate agencies, handed in his CV, got some polite responses, but felt age was against him – this was a young man's game.

So, towards the end of his week he wandered into Regent's Park, had a walk around, it was so pretty, sat down on a bench, watched the bird life ... and gave thought to the next step.

London was a truly magnificent city.

He could probably pick up a job of some sort easy enough but then accommodation was incredibly expensive.

Could he cope with buildings, buildings, buildings, stretching mile upon mile? Could he cope with the constant traffic? Could he cope with people, people, people at every turn?

His instinct said London would crush him.

Anyway, there was more to England than London however much Londoners believed otherwise.

Might as well take in the bigger picture. Birmingham billed itself as the nation's Second City – worth exploring whether the title fitted or not.

So, he packed his bags, checked out of the hotel, got a taxi to Euston station and bought a one-way ticket to Birmingham New Street.

The busiest station outside London, New Street, he discovered had been 'done up', had millions spent on it and was now surrounded by a quality shopping centre.

The locals were helpful, the atmosphere was relaxed, it was a strong first impression.

At around one million people, nowhere near the size of London. It almost had the sense of being a village – it appealed to him.

First stop was Birmingham's tourist information centre not far off the main drag.

He needed to fix himself up with a hotel – there proved to be lots of them – obtain a map of the city centre, inquire as to what were the main sights and generally find his bearings.

They sorted him without any fuss and he followed his London approach by booking a week's bed and breakfast.

It was important to get a feel for the place, what it was trying to do, how serious it took itself.

He found it a curious ebb and flow – a mix of ethnic origins, a mix of manufacturing and professional, a mix of low paid retail and leisure jobs and yet seams of hidden wealth.

As for the sights, he hadn't realised how highly connected Birmingham was to JRR Tolkien, of Lord of the Rings fame, and how little it made of that connection in terms of tourism.

The Jewellery Quarter was fascinating as was Birmingham's leading role in the Industrial Revolution.

About as far from the sea as you can get in England, its restored canals are a magnet for walkers, cyclists, the young and the old. He ambled along them – what history there must be beneath his feet.

Pity then that it let itself down with a dearth of tender loving care – too many selfish types whereby it was completely acceptable to litter the streets and expect someone else to sweep up.

Stuck between a massively dominant London, which treated it like a mat to wipe its feet on, and jealousy for Manchester – better bands, better football teams – Birmingham seemed to be struggling to find a new identity.

Not at all confident, weak at grasping the nettle ... perhaps as a result of being defined by the grotesque Spaghetti Junction and the permanent traffic jam which is the M6 motorway.

However, warts and all, he would take it because friendly and welcoming transcended its flaws. Plus he sensed that it was slowly getting its act together.

From Birmingham, he took a train ride to Tamworth in the footsteps of his ancestors.

A market town on the River Tame, it was once the capital of the Anglo-Saxon Kingdom of Mercia.

In its day far bigger than Birmingham, it is now a satellite to the regional capital.

Kevin wandered into a couple of estate agents' offices to check out job opportunities but worryingly discovered that the regional market was going through one of its very few dodgy spells and nobody was taking people on.

But they did put in front of him a good offer for a six month lease on a pleasant enough two bedroom furnished town house in a decent location, and after checking it out he decided he might as well take it – something more permanent and cost-effective than a hotel room.

He was optimistic, he had plenty of savings to fall back on, but everyone needs a purpose in life.

And that is where it all began to unravel.

Initially, it didn't matter. He bought a second hand car, drove to a supermarket to stock up, and took trips out into the beautiful countryside which surrounds Tamworth.

There was a fun day out at nearby Drayton Manor, a theme park covering 280 acres which hosts about 1.5 million people each year.

A visit to Twycross Zoo – billed the largest collection of monkeys and apes in the Western World. It brought back the times had had visited zoos as a child – lots of goofing around and making faces like a chimpanzee.

Fascinated, he toured the site of the Battle of Bosworth Field, the last major battle of the Wars of the Roses, the civil war between the Houses of Lancaster and York that extended across England in the latter half of the 15th century. Fought on 22 August 1485, it was won by the Lancastrians. Their leader Henry Tudor, Earl of Richmond, supplanted Richard III, the last king of the House of York, who was killed.

Then what?

At a loss for what to do next, he toured the Tamworth estate agents again – still no openings.

He hit a whole load of Birmingham estate agents – nothing doing.

Back at the house, over three days he composed letters to estate agents all over the West Midlands, inserted his CV, posted them off, and awaited replies – none arrived.

In the evenings he tried several different pubs, went to the cinema, had a first attempt at skiing at Tamworth SnowDome, but found integration almost impossible.

He watched the television, he read a book, he stared at the four walls.

With his interest in sport, he had always been aware of the old adage that you could turn up at a rugby club anywhere in the world and instantly you would be among chums.

And he found that to be the case as he took himself along to a couple of Tamworth Rugby Club games, cheering them on from the touchline. People did speak to him and the jars of ale went down a treat. It was certainly a novelty having an Australian around, provoking the usual banter. But he felt a bit of a fraud – too old to pull on the jersey and something of a square peg in a round hole.

He was frustrated, the solitude was getting to him … this was not how it was supposed to be.

And alarmingly he discovered the plane crash yips returning.

Maybe it had not been such a good idea to take the Tamworth house after all. Something of a spur of the moment decision, he should have been more circumspect.

Had he been young, thrusting and driven, like he once was, maybe he would be making a better fist of England. As his Dad had warned, there was a hill to climb if you were middle aged.

He should have held his nerve, told himself that for most people it took two years to 'smash' living in a new place, stayed confident that his persistence would pay off.

Instead, he began drinking over lunch, at the house, in the boozers at night until it all merged into savage benders.

Next day he couldn't remember where he had been or what he had done.

Sometimes he discovered cuts and scrapes on his face, bruises down his body, hangovers like no tomorrow – must have fallen over but had no recollection.

Eating junk food or no food at all.

He knew it was dragging him down, he was aware the old depression was ensnaring him, there was just no reason to do anything about it.

Getting out of bed about 12 noon, brunch was the liquid variety down one of the cheap pub chains.

It was all getting out of control.

It culminated in the bender to end all benders – a ten hour session and he wasn't done then.

As drunk as a skunk, and pretty much out of it, for some reason, he knew not what, he asked to be taken to the rugby club.

Paying off the driver, he stumbled out, fell over, got up, and wobbled as far as the main door. It was way after midnight and unsurprisingly the place was shut.

Firmly locked; not a light in sight.

Empty.

He thumped on the door to no avail, he shouted for attention … he cursed the club, he cursed the world, he cursed his rotten life.

Slumping onto some steps, he tried to clear his brain, failed, held his head in his hands, and felt total despair.

He reached for his mobile but couldn't find it.

Had he left it at the house? Had he lost it on the pub crawl? Had it fallen out in the taxi?

He let out another vast array of expletives, prompting hooting from an owl hidden somewhere in the trees.

It sounded as though it were mocking Kevin.

And well it might. The rugby club is in an out of the way location – a long walk back to civilisation beckoned.

Then it all got dangerous – very dangerous.

Tamworth Rugby Club play on Wigginton Park, next to the clubhouse.

Totalling 45 acres, the park is small but popular – with dog walkers all year round, with children, sledging in winter, footballers, cricketers too.

One side of the park is bordered by the fast West Coast Main Line railway.

Trains thunder past along a line of track parallel to the rugby club's pitches.

In his inebriated state, the solution came to Kevin in a moment of madness. He would end it all there and then.

Bye, bye, cruel world.

While watching games he had observed how easy it would be. All he had to do was step onto the track and it would be over.

He probably wouldn't feel a thing as his body was smashed to pulp.

To his sozzled mind it appeared the logical answer to his troubles.

Exit stage left.

The owl, he decided, must surely be a sign.

Somewhere he had read that in most Native American tribes, owls were regarded as a symbol of death.

Hearing owls hooting was an unlucky omen among other peoples too, with numerous 'bogeyman' stories told to warn children to stay inside at night or the owl might carry them away.

Probably codswallop but a sinister thought.

Bugger the owl – time to act.

He lurched to his feet and weaved his way down the grass slope into the park proper.

But he had forgotten how slippy it could be and pitched forward into the mud as he lost his footing.

He got himself back upright, plodded onwards, fell again. There was mud on his face, his hands, his clothes. Somehow he had lost a shoe. But, hey, what did any of it matter. Where he was going there would be no need of clothes and shoes.

He stumbled on, patted the rugby posts one last time for posterity, trees eerie in the night air, a fox padding across the grass in search of prey.

At last he was almost there, but had never realised how strong and substantial was the perimeter fence which barred his way to the rail lines.

This was a worthy obstacle and it flummoxed him.

Had he been stone cold sober it would have represented a major barrier. In his exceedingly well-oiled state, it was virtually an impassable one.

He could not bring himself to concede the possibility that he might be thwarted.

But there it was looming as large that night to Kevin as the Berlin Wall at the height of the Cold War.

Heading left, he wandered alongside it, hoping he might find a weak spot, perhaps a tree trunk where he could lever himself over … to no avail. He turned on himself and tried to the right, walking, walking, walking, and still couldn't see any way of scaling it.

Until finally he admitted defeat, fell to his knees and began sobbing his heart out.

What a useless, pathetic human being – so useless and pathetic that he couldn't even kill himself.

As if goading him a high-speed train sped on its way, casting further disapprobation.

So near yet so far.

Hunched, despairing, he lost track of time but must at some point have drifted off into a sodden sleep.

Whatever, dawn was poking through next he regained some sense of what was going on.

Cold, bedraggled, covered in gunge, looking like a tramp, there was nothing left but to re-trace his steps and begin the long slog home.

Much later he realised that Wigginton Park represented some sort of watershed.

But caught up in his wretchedness he could only regard it as the most God-forsaken place on earth.

He never found the missing shoe and it was agony limping along as stones tortured the sole of his foot.

He never found the mobile phone ... until hours later he arrived back at the house. It was sitting on the kitchen table.

A passing workman stopped his van and took pity on him – "whatever happened to you, mate?"

He was a decent sort and gave him a lift most of the way.

But by the time Kevin turned the key in the lock the commute was underway and kids were headed to school.

He lost count of the strange looks he received – half of him recoiled in embarrassment and the other half was too tired to care.

Almost falling into the house, he managed to remain upright, kicked off the remaining shoe and with the last of his energy mounted the stairs and collapsed onto the bed, fully clothed – oblivious to the mud, oblivious to the dank and damp, and oblivious to the ignominy.

It made a pitiful sight had anybody been there to witness it.

Back in Normal, Suzi had been building up to breaking the news to Sara and Jeb that it was time for her to move on.

Researching the internet, she entered 'Kevin Jackson' in the search engine and for a second thought the computer was going to blow up.

Doh! She should have twigged that there would be many, many people with the same name.

Inputting 'Kevin Jackson air crash survivor' produced a more sifted response.

She was after any in-depth pieces purporting to explain his background and character. However, with thousands of articles out there, it was difficult to identify ones offering some sort of insight. Perhaps because there were very few of them. Clearly he was a man who liked to preserve his privacy where possible. She got a few pointers but actually not that many. Indeed, she felt she knew far more about him from his letters.

She also sought to bone up on England – her ignorance about the country was manifest.

The American War of Independence had been against the English; World War II had been in alliance with the English.

London was the capital.

The place still had a monarch.

The Beatles came from England, didn't they?

Er, that was about it.

Once again, she reflected how playing truant from school had left gaping holes in her knowledge.

When next Suzi found herself alone with Sara she once more turned the conversation round.

She told her grandmother that two things were coalescing in her mind.

First, she believed she must at least meet Kevin face to face and get to know him. She had found the letters fascinating, he had saved her life, the very least she could do was thank him personally. Letters or emails would never cover it.

Second, she had come to the conclusion that she needed to step out of the goldfish bowl that was Normal. She was a marked woman in her home town – everyone had an opinion of her. In addition it was too easy to be tempted, like with the road race, by remaining in Normal. She had blown the trust of good people and was still a focus of the baddies. She had to get out or one way or another she would be dragged down once more.

Sara poured over the words – she didn't want to lose Suzi albeit there was an argument that they lost her mentally in that appalling plane crash, in body in Normal but in mind with Robert and Rose.

Suzi was her own person, her travails had in some ways taught her more about life than school ever could, ultimately she deserved to find the answers to whatever it was that was eating her.

Sara would have liked to have gone backpacking abroad when she was young but it never happened.

As for Kevin, if it would put Suzi's mind at rest then do it.

A week in his company and the two of them would have run out of conversation, she speculated. Their story would have come full circle and hopefully both could move on.

She and Jeb gave Suzi their blessing.

There was one proviso – before Suzi did anything else they wanted to talk finances with her.

Finances had been the next item Suzi had on her agenda so such a discussion would be very welcome.

All three sat around the dining room table on which Jeb had spread what appeared to be documents and bank statements.

Jeb explained that in the aftermath of the plane crash people around the world had been touched by the heartache of this orphaned baby.

The family had been so appreciative for the outpouring of love and, while reticent to do so, had fallen in with the clamour that a trust fund be set up to safeguard Suzi's future. Years on they were still uneasy at having allowed themselves to be swept along with the flow ... but there it was, money matters but you cannot buy happiness.

It was decreed that the huge sum which had been amassed would be kept safe for Suzi until she was 21 when she would gain access to it and do what she wanted with the cash.

An absolute fortune, sufficient that after years of compound interest Suzi was an exceedingly rich young heiress.

With Suzi going off the rails so badly they had never seen fit before to explain all this to her. Now she seemed to be on the cusp of turning her life around it was time she found out. After all, it would be hers to do with as she pleased in a couple of years anyway.

On top of this donated money, Robert and Rose's savings had been kept for her including the proceeds of the house – it had been sold when Abby and John moved to Canada.

They accepted that if she was bound for England she would need ready cash.

They strongly suggested the trust fund be left intact – it would be too difficult to unravel and there could be tax implications.

Jeb said he and Sara would pay her air fare – money from Robert and Rose could be utilised for living expenses.

They would all go down to the bank, fix for her to open an account, put in place an arrangement with an English counterpart, sort debit and credit cards, and generally regularise any financial loose ends.

Did she think she could take on such a responsibility? Managing your financial affairs was a serious matter. At one extreme you heard of kids blowing their inheritance on drugs; at the other extreme every variety of crook and internet shark was out there and would try and find ways of fleecing you.

She should never reveal her worth to anyone.

Suzi ran with it and, as over several weeks matters came together, she did take it seriously – very seriously.

The revelations had left her flabbergasted. The trust money, stated Jeb, was meant for capital purposes – to purchase a house or establish a business. He asked that she try and respect this.

And that made sense. She gave her word.

The next task would be to get in touch with Kevin.

While she knew he was in England because that was from where the latest two letters had been sent, detailing the trip and his hopes for it, she didn't have address, phone numbers or email for him.

Maybe Abby would – she had once told Suzi they had exchanged such details when meeting all those years ago in Bali. Perhaps he had updated them since.

She spoke to Abby on the phone.

Abby was intrigued and supportive.

Of course, given John's parents lived there, she had visited England most years at least once since their marriage.

She filled in some of the gaps for Suzi and stressed the Munros would be very keen for her to call by. No pressure to commit, but Abby promised to brief them just in case.

She expounded all she knew of Kevin's character and personality, adding that he was a good person.

A man of principle, a man who had standards, but someone who had been badly warped by his plane crash wounds.

Abby said she was glad Suzi intended to meet him – the two of them might find they had a lot in common.

She did not explain exactly what she meant by that, but she didn't need to.

Suzi appreciated that it was made with the best of intentions.

As it happened, Abby did have up-to-date phone numbers for Kevin – she had absolutely kept her pledge to keep him in touch with the family, and it had been reciprocated.

Suzi wrote them down.

"I want lots of postcards," quipped Abby. "And, if you go native and put down roots, I want an invitation to Buckingham Palace to meet the Royals."

They both laughed.

"But seriously," noted Abby. "Keep me posted – it sounds very exciting and I am envious. A great age to be doing it too – I wish I was 18 again."

"Nineteen," said Suzi. "You sent me a birthday card the other week – don't you remember?"

"Golly, yes," said Abby, and pretended that maths was not her strongest suit.

"Have a great time."

"I'm sure I will."

They said their goodbyes.

Bolstered by Abby's enthusiasm, Suzi told Sara and Jeb she would make the call to England the following day when the time difference was more favourable.

She gave some thought to what she was going to say to him. He would be caught on the hop. She didn't want to startle him.

She came up with various ways of attempting to break the ice but wasn't entirely happy with any of them. Maybe best to play it off the cuff. She decided she would sleep on the predicament – hopefully the morning would bring greater clarity.

Except it didn't and she began to suspect she was digging a bigger and bigger hole for herself.

Just relax, Suzi. You'll find the words even if they are not quite the right ones. A crabby, wooden conversation was the last either of them needed.

Making the phone call was what it was about – they would find middle ground. It was bound to be testing for both of them.

She dialled the number, and it began ringing out.

Kevin was awake but far from recovered from the shambles of trying to do himself in, and still not up and about.

Filthy, not even got round to a shower, hadn't eaten for two days, hated himself.

"Brrr, brrr."

Initially it didn't register.

"Brrr, brrr."

The land line was ringing.

Fuck, probably another of those scam callers who needed their heads punching in.

He picked up the receiver and, summoning every ounce of venom he could find: "Yes."

There was silence, usually a giveaway and he nearly slammed the phone down.

He checked himself – the woman who had begun to speak wasn't the typical foreigner with only a basic command of English. Nor was there the fake background noise purporting to be a call centre.

"Is that Kevin Jackson," she enquired.

A more cautious 'yes' this time.

"My name's Suzanne Duthie."

He almost fell over. He had long given up on hearing those words.

There was silence from his end – he was simply tongue-tied.

"Hello," she queried, unsure whether they had been accidentally cut off.

"The Suzanne Duthie?"

It was all he could come up with and it sounded lame.

She laughed hesitantly.

"Well, I'm not sure about that," she jested. "This is the Suzi Duthie you rescued from the water all those years ago. Don't tell me you've forgotten."

It was now his turn to feel chastened.

"No, no, no," he mumbled. "I remember it like it was yesterday. It's just … it's just … it's just hard after all these years to take in that it is really you."

The thick American accent should surely have given him a clue.

Then he began getting jumpy. What was she doing calling now? What did she want off him? Was this some sort of trap?

She sensed his reticence – she had been well aware it might prove a shock.

Clearly she must disarm his fears before springing the news that she was intent on flying to England to see him.

"Don't worry," she declared. "I understand you being cautious. But this is purely a social call – no more and no less.

"I recently read your letters, they spoke volumes, and I felt I had to contact you. I know it has been a long time. Forgive me."

It shook him, but in a nice way.

Berating himself for being rude and mean-minded, he blurted his apologies.

It was wonderful to hear her voice. Fantastic that she had thought to get in touch.

Then a flood of questions streamed forth. How old was she? Was she still living in Normal? What news of Abby?

Another one of those slightly hesitant laughs and he realised he must have sounded like a chattering machine gun.

More apologies.

She was nineteen, she was still living in Normal, though maybe not for too much longer, and Abby was fine.

As she had intended, he picked up on the 'not for too much longer'.

And painlessly she was able to reveal that she was looking for a change of scene, was keen to do some travelling, and was coming to England. It would be nice to look him up while she was there.

She didn't mention that meeting him was the prime reason for making the journey.

His response was perhaps more wary and defensive than she had hoped.

He said it would be fantastic to see her but the tone of voice suggested that he had his doubts as to whether she would really make it over. These things are easier said than done.

She told him she was yet to finalise dates or book airline tickets but it would be certainly happening within the next three months. He was in the middle of the country – right? Some village outside Birmingham?

Not so much a village, he told her – nearly 80,000 people.

There was more small talk as they fenced around trying to get the measure of each other. However, in conclusion both were ebullient at the possibility of meeting up.

She pledged to ring him again when she arrived in London.

He explained that the house was rented, was small but nice – she could take the spare room. Stay as long as she liked.

"There is a vacuum cleaner – if I can find it," he joked.

"I want fresh sheets and clean towels," she told him gleefully.

By the time they broke off the call they were almost bosom buddies.

She blew out her cheeks and breathed deeply – it had gone well, certainly as well as she could ever have hoped.

Now to get on with organising the visit. Regularising US passport status – she assumed there must have been documentation of some description covering a child to enable her parents to take her on the ill-fated Bali trip – booking her flights, sorting a tourist visa.

Go to a store and purchase a large backpack.

Make a list of everything that had to go in it, ruthlessly culling anything that was non-essential. She could buy stuff like jeans and tops in the UK as and when required.

Thank goodness she had told him three months. It might take even longer to get all her ducks in a row.

He meanwhile was seated on his favourite chair, astounded.

That had to be the most unexpected phone call he had ever received. Wow, how that little baby had grown up. She sounded very adult.

He tried to visualise her – Abby had sent the odd photograph but nothing recent.

Next, he turned the computer on and looked to see if she had a social media presence. There he found the new Hope – he hadn't called her Hope on the phone for fear of spooking her but would definitely do so if she made it over.

The woman who looked back at him was pretty if careworn. Lots of earlier shots too of a teenage rebel.

Well, doesn't everyone rebel to a greater or lesser degree in their youth?

He could only guess at how much the plane crash and everything surrounding it might have taken out of her. He knew how much it had taken out of him.

He would have to tread warily at first but he would love to ask her about it.

Kevin was day-dreaming away, detouring here and there in his thoughts, lazy and leisurely.

Come on – snap out of it.

He looked himself up and down.

His clothes were filthy, he needed to shower and wash his hair, his bedroom was a pig sty, there were piles of clothes to wash, piles of dishes in the kitchen, the flat required cleaning from top to bottom – what would she think being introduced into such a dump?

Mortified, he promised himself he would get cracking ASAP.

As host it was down to him to make her stay as accommodating as possible. Essentially a nice property, he promised himself it would be spotless long before she arrived.

He had let things slip; he had let his personal standards and hygiene slip.

Daily shaving, monthly haircuts, deodorant, nails short, shirts which hadn't been worn for a week, shoes that hadn't gone into holes.

Jogging every day, no more junk food, a ban on binge drinking, checking his weight and waist measurement.

He would get back to the Kevin who could do sleek and handsome so well.

She would come with expectations that her rescuer was somebody of stature and that's what she would get.

No more shabby tramp. A transformation was underway.

First stop the shower. He stripped out of his clothes and indulged himself under the warm water, shampooing vigorously, soaping himself thoroughly.

Once dry, he searched cupboards for clean clothes – hardly any existed.

Dressed in what you might call remnants, he gave himself another verbal kicking for letting that side slide.

So, the next day he really went to work – three loads in the washing machine and drier. Every utensil in the kitchen cleaned. An initial vacuum of the entire house.

The day after that – wipe clear grease from the kitchen while putting in the elbow grease in making the bathroom and toilet fit for purpose, eradicating disgusting man smells in the process.

Phew! She was still weeks away from turning up yet he couldn't be more highly motivated.

He felt better for having a purpose again.

It took a week to get the flat up to the required standard.

Just call me Mrs Mop, he told his diary.

Time to upgrade his wardrobe too – a train into Birmingham and a shopping spree around the big stores.

He came away with much-needed new shirts, three pairs of shoes, handkerchiefs to replace what were now rags, and some colourful sweaters.

His old brown leather jacket was staying – he couldn't bear to be parted from it. But it was sent to the dry cleaners to remove years of dirt and alcohol stains.

OK, what next?

Time for a breather surely. What was all the rush about? Stop getting into such a tizzy. She was just a visitor. There was nothing big shot about it … except there was.

Got to get fit.

To supplement the jogging he joined a gym even though he hated gyms. Mindless, robotic treadmills where you tried to block out the pain by listening to the latest music on headphones. Weights – but no longer the justification of a new rugby season ahead. The stink of perspiration.

Gyms were both putrid and soulless.

He reasoned that he was improving himself on behalf of himself when he knew full well it was a vanity project for her.

Middle aged man meets nubile young woman. God, he was a disgrace.

Not wanting her to perceive him to be a slacker, he determined that he would have another go at finding work.

He would hit that other treadmill again, the estate agency circuit.

Determination, confidence, make himself out to be an ace Aussie salesman, give them the full treatment.

And, Hallelujah, he pulled it off.

There was an element of good fortune – some poor kid had been sacked for failing to hit his numbers and Kevin happened by the next day.

It took the better part of three weeks to sort it – the boss had done a professional job, two interviews, tough questions about his CV, even phoned up Oz to check references.

Thankfully he never twigged about Kevin and the plane crash but then he was the sort who probably wouldn't have cared anyway. So, no baggage; level playing field. Perform and the three month trial would be made permanent.

He walked out of the interview, bought a bottle of Champagne, took it home, toasted Hope, and drank the lot.

It was the first alcohol to pass his lips since Suicide Night.

The weekend was coming up and he would be starting on the Monday. He was in employment and it would keep him occupied.

He'd turned it around – no more self-doubt.

Suzi too was trying to banish self-doubt.

She was looking forward to England with trepidation but genuine awe.

Sorting the red tape was a pain, but it had to be done.

John, Abby and the children came over from Toronto – rather than flying they decided to drive, stopping off on the way.

And where were they bound to make their first stop? Why, Niagara Falls of course. Had to be.

The children thought it was fabulous; Abby and John knew it was fabulous.

While there they stocked up on some bottles from the famous wineries. More than 20 nestle below the Niagara Escarpment amidst a landscape of vineyards and orchards.

Naturally, the family celebration to mark Suzi's great leap into the unknown saw her toasted in Niagara's best.

It was a moving occasion – Suzi realised how much she would miss Normal.

Never mind, she was going to make Sara, Jeb and Abby proud.

She was going to make a success of England.

Looking at how to play it on arrival, she decided to head straight for Tamworth via Birmingham rather than sight-see around the London hot spots. Might get sucked into wicked ways! She wanted a base from which she could find her feet, and initially, though he didn't know it yet, Kevin's place would be that base. Later she could figure out what parts of England would be fun to see.

It seemed most sensible to fly Normal to Chicago and then Chicago to London Heathrow. From Heathrow she could grab a National Express coach to Birmingham without ever needing to fight her way into the capital's centre.

Kevin had promised to meet her in 'Brum' – picking up the slang already, she joked.

She texted him the tentative arrangements and later the definitive dates.

Both times she got an effusive reply saying he was very much looking forward to seeing her.

There was just the one factor to bear in mind – he had got himself a job so she needed to arrive either in the evening or at the weekend.

No problem, she replied. And passed on her congratulations.

And so it was decided.

She got a bit jittery ahead of her departure and in a bizarre sort of way was already homesick when she hadn't even left home yet.

But on the morning in question she was up for it, determined to master what lay ahead.

Sure, there were bound to be setbacks, disappointments and hurdles to jump. But if things went well these would pale into insignificance as new doors opened and new vistas stretched in front of her. It would be her own fault, nobody else's, if she failed to take advantage of them.

Sara and Jeb ran her to the airport in plenty of time.

There were tears, hugs, make sure you phone, we're going to miss you terribly, don't let the Limeys grind you down. Cups of coffee. More tears and hugs.

It was very emotional.

Again and again, she could only say 'thank you for all you have done for me'.

Two generations removed but family counts for everything.

So to check in, a final wave goodbye, on to security and then the gate. The comparative short hop and then the big flight, Chicago to London.

It was at that point, leaving the United States proper – Canada didn't count – for the first time since the baby trip, the enormity of it all struck her, and she nearly lost her nerve. Far too late to do anything about it. At 30,000 ft over the Atlantic the die was well and truly cast.

The vast US offered certainty; there was nothing certain where she was headed.

England might once have been the Mother Country, but, still in her teens, it was all a little intimidating. What if it went wrong? What if this bloke Kevin did turn out to be unhinged?

Come on. Be strong. You can do it.

Well used to snatching sleep at odd times and in odd situations, she spent much of the flight snoozing.

A routine flight, a routine landing at Heathrow, nothing else was likely to be routine.

Heathrow is so large that getting to and from gates is seriously time-consuming. But the signage is good. So exiting was straight forward. To be on the safe side she had factored in being delayed when booking the bus, but touch down had been on the money. She found the National Express office and inquired as to whether there was anything any earlier. There wasn't, and anyway they would have charged her extra to switch and she would have had to mess Kevin around.

She bought a sandwich and a cup of English tea, the first of many she supposed, then wiled away an hour or so watching the world go round.

The bus was prompt and soon she was devouring the English countryside. Very green and she discovered why when a hefty twenty minute rain storm struck.

Quite a few stops on the way so plenty of time to prepare.

Relaxed, her only mild concern was recognising Kevin when she got to journey's end. She was pretty sure she would be able to pick him out, but it kept nibbling away at her guts.

It was mid-evening and the motorway wasn't too congested.

The route in past Birmingham Airport gave her a first view of the outskirts. Interesting.

And at last they were turning into Birmingham coach station.

Wearily, she negotiated the steps down, collected her backpack, put it on her shoulders and headed through the gate into the main complex.

She looked about her and spotted a well-dressed man with the lean look of your typical Australian. But the kangaroo T-shirt – presumably deliberate on his part – was the giveaway.

They exchanged a tentative acknowledgement.

Kevin?

Hope?

They smiled broadly at each other – it broke the ice.

He relieved her of the backpack. That was nice of him.

"You must be bushed?"

"I am, to be honest. It's a long haul. Hope I'm not looking too dishevelled."

"No way – it's magic to meet you again. You've grown a bit!"

More smiles.

Did she need the rest room? No, she was fine, there had been facilities on the coach. Was she desperate for food? No, she had grabbed a sandwich at Heathrow.

Anyway she didn't want to hold him up – coming to Birmingham to meet her was a decent effort.

He'd driven in – wasn't sure how much luggage she might have.

The car park was round the corner.

"Ready to go?"

"Yes," she said, putting on a carefree air she didn't really feel.

"This way," he indicated.

Backpack on the rear seat, safely ensconced in the front, she was soon getting a spin around the inner city.

Wow! A bigger place than she had thought. And industrial. A bit like the Rust Belt back home. She felt sure she was doing Birmingham a dis-service.

Onto the motorway network, he told her they were now negotiating the famous Spaghetti Junction. She'd never heard of it.

Next stop Tamworth. Too dark now to see much other than the lights of the cars and lorries.

"If you are peckish when we get there then there is likely to be a few fish and chip shops open. Don't suppose you have ever come across a fish supper before, but it's something of a local delicacy in these parts."

She professed that the only thing she really needed was her bed.

"No worries."

Someone had told her that this was the catch-phrase of Australians the world over – she expected to hear it plenty more … and she wasn't to be disappointed!

They turned off for Tamworth, meandered through the town, and pulled up beside a modern-looking semi-detached.

For sure, far smaller than Sara and Jeb's place in Normal.

But, she guessed, he didn't need a whole lot of space.

He turned the key in the lock, inserted the code to shut off the bleeping burglar alarm, and ushered her into the lounge area.

"Have a seat – I'll just get your backpack. Here, let me take your coat – there are pegs in the hallway."

He disappeared back out to the car.

She surveyed her surroundings. It was pretty basic but it was clean. He must have been sprucing it up, she surmised.

And her first impressions of him? Polite, a gentleman, open and surprisingly good-looking for someone in their forties.

He returned with the backpack, temporarily abandoned it by the stairs, and re-entered the room.

Would she like a drink?

"Just a glass of milk, if you've got enough to spare."

"No worries."

There it was again!

He'd taken the precaution of stocking up at the supermarket, with two four-litre containers of milk on the shopping list.

He handed her the glass.

She was cute, she looked even better in real life than in her photos, she was certainly all-American and, he supposed, would probably be bossing him about in no time, but he was intrigued.

Feel free to sleep in as long as she liked in the morning – he would be out at work and back around 6pm. He found her a spare set of house keys and quickly double-checked that they worked. He took her into the kitchen, indicated the main food cupboard, opened the fridge and told her to help herself. Finally he briefed her on the number for the alarm.

"Ring me on the mobile if you need anything," he said. "I'm sure you'll find your way about."

He suggested he show her the room, picked up the backpack and headed up the stairs as she followed.

It was functional.

He promised he had laid down on the bed and it seemed agreeable enough. If not, he would see what he could do about it the following evening.

She said she was sure it would be fine.

There was a chest of drawers and a wardrobe for her clothes.

"The sheets and the towels are all clean and spotless, madam."

It was her own bit of fun being thrown back at her.

They laughed together.

He showed her the bathroom.

Not exactly spacious but it would do, and again he had clearly spruced it up too. She was taken aback by his dedication to housework. If this was all for her, then she was impressed. She doubted he could keep it up, and nor should he. She must do her bit too, and, as a guest, more than her bit.

He suggested she might like to get washed and dressed first, so she could hit the sack.

He had a few things to finish off downstairs.

She thanked him for his facilitations.

He left her to her own devices.

She got her wash things out of the backpack and her makeup bag for morning. Removed a night dress. Everything else could wait for the next day.

Dumping the backpack in a corner, she got undressed then locked the bathroom door. Did her teeth, splashed water over her face, too exhausted for a shower – that too could wait until morning. Looked in the mirror. Scowled. Determined she would be at her best for when he returned the next evening. After all, she needed to make her presence felt.

Called down to him that the bathroom was now free.

Got into bed and was soon fast asleep.

He gave it five minutes then went to bed himself. Already the bathroom had a slight smell of woman about it.

Women ruled bathrooms and no doubt it would soon be transformed. He felt easy at the prospect.

The house was generally a bit ordinary – a woman's touch would make it more homely.

He dozed off thinking about perfume bottles, nail varnish, hair spray and being lassoed in the bath by discarded tentacle-like hairs.

She woke with a start – sun streaming in through the window. She looked at her watch and was startled to see that it was past 11am.

Yet she felt threadbare – must be the jetlag and the travelling.

The bed was warm and snug – it was so tempting to just lie back and drift into oblivion,

She forced herself to her feet and headed for the bathroom.

A much needed shower was definitely going to be the highlight.

She eyed it suspiciously. When you weren't acquainted with the knobs and gizmos, it sometimes took an engineering degree to get the things going.

She fiddled around and was promptly hit by a jet of cold water.

Squealing, in that distinctive manner only girlies can squeal, then cursing like a trooper, she diverted the flow away from her body.

It then promptly started to warm up.

Her mood improved and soon she was luxuriating.

Now, much more herself, she turned the tap off and stepped onto the mat.

She opened up the towel he had provided for her – clearly he had picked it out in the dark because it said on it Big Boys Do It Better.

Hmmm.

She finished drying herself and determined to start off on the right footing looked around for a cloth and bath cleaner.

Nowhere to be seen.

Men! He was going to need sorting out.

She swilled the ceramic down as best she could – one of those shower and bath combination jobs.

Then went to the bedroom, got herself presentable, put on her make-up.

If he was at work all day there was plenty of time to beautify herself later.

Next she spent twenty minutes emptying her backpack, putting her things neatly away. The backpack itself went on top of the wardrobe.

She smoothed the bed out and edged open the window to provide some air.

Thence downstairs.

The letterbox clanged as some post tumbled through – what a fright she got.

How silly she could be. She collected it up, gave it a cursory examination out of being nosy, and left it on the side for him.

Through in the kitchen, she had a good trawl to see what was what. Many of the plates and utensils had seen better days, but, hey, it was a rented house. There had to be a limit on expectations.

She uncovered some breakfast cereal, poured on the milk from the fridge, and tucked in.

Spotting one of those ghastly cork boards where you pin 'to do' notices as conscience salvers, she noticed there was an item with her name on it.

It rambled about her not bothering to fix tea – there was loads of salad items in the fridge, meat, cheese ... could all be decided when he got back. Then it apologised for not asking about her likes and dislikes.

Sweet of him if a bit nannying.

She discovered the back door key in the lock and wandered out into the garden.

Early spring and a bit chilly, he'd had a go at cutting the weed-ridden lawn but the flowers and flower beds left much to be desired.

The forced garden tutelage of Jeb during her early teenage hissy fit years now came into its own.

Nothing that a good chop back wouldn't sort. Many plants and bushes thrived on some harsh treatment to bloom and be of their best.

If she could find some garden implements, and once she had established herself, she might give it a go, she thought.

There was a small shed at the bottom – might they be in there.

The door creaked open and she was confronted by a mass of cobwebs in what was clearly spider heaven.

Yikes, she hated spiders.

What was it Sara used to say? Women only ever got married so there was someone to remove spiders from the bath.

Something else on her man-list.

Shivering slightly, she headed back indoors.

Wiped her feet – that was clever of her – and surveyed the lounge cum dining area in rather greater detail than she had managed in her half-awake state the night before.

She turned the television on and played around with the channels – but it was mostly the afternoon dross programmes. She did find the 24-hour news and caught up with what she had missed – it felt very odd to have this English take on everything and barely a mention of anything going on in the US.

After a while, she switched off.

At a loss about what to do next she decided that despite only being on a tourist visa she would need a part-time job or go stark staring mad.

He'd been here longer so one to ask his thoughts about … this man-list was expanding by the hour!

She went upstairs, tweaked the make-up, ran a comb through her hair, checked that her boobs were prominent.

Then waited for him in the lounge.

It wasn't long before the front door opened and in he walked. They greeted each other like old friends.

He was in excellent humour having agreed a couple of house sales – the job was going well and he was getting on fine with the team.

How had her day been?

She told him she had been a sleepy head but felt much better for taking things easy.

"Good for you," he told her. "Travelling takes so much out of you."

He pretended to look her up and down.

"You scrub up well."

She put on her haughty expression. But at least he had noticed.

Had she eaten?

She explained about breakfast. Lunch had just never happened.

"You must be famished then."

The question prompted hunger pangs.

"I should have asked, and forgot, as to whether you have any dietary requirements – vegan, gluten-free, nut allergies … that sort of thing."

She didn't.

Was she all right on salad – lettuce, tomato, hard-boiled egg, onions, beetroot, cottage cheese, cold potato, a couple of choices of meats.

"Sounds yummy."

She offered to help.

Why not, he thought.

She shelled the hard-boiled eggs and sliced up the onions and beetroot. He put a portion each of chicken breast and ham on plates, plenty of lettuce, washed the tomatoes, took the potatoes from the fridge, and prised open the cottage cheese.

He poured a couple of glasses of milk and they took their meal through to the dining area.

He offered a toast – to her safe arrival. Not exactly quality crystal but the glasses made an acceptable clinking noise.

They made small talk as they ate.

She couldn't find any sign of a cloth or bath cleaner. He made a stuttering apology – the cloth had disintegrated in his spring clean and the last of the cleaner had been used up. He had made a note to get both when next at the shops.

The towel was nice and large though the wording was a bit rude.

He gaped, and then it dawned. "Oh Jeez, was that the one with the Big Boys motif?"

It was, she confirmed.

"Sorry," he confessed. "I never noticed. I'll find you a different one."

Amused at his embarrassment, she said there was no need but perhaps she could change it when next it needed a wash.

"No worries."

She burst out laughing.

He looked astonished. "What have I done now?" he groaned.

How long had he had the catchphrase and had he attempted to copyright it, she jibed cynically. Oh, of course, he couldn't – every Australian owned it!

"Go on, make fun of a poor Aussie becalmed in a foreign land," he complained.

More banter followed until they were in such a state that their stomach muscles were twitching and eating became impossible.

"I can see I'm going to have to watch you," he teased.

Yet more broad smiles.

The jocularity was put to one side as they concentrated on finishing their salad – it was plain, but then she had been brought up on plain food.

At length they brought the dirty dishes through to the kitchen – he washed and she dried.

Then they settled down in the lounge with a cup of coffee.

"What, no English tea – I thought it was compulsory."

"I'm not English," he quipped.

She changed the subject.

"Your letters gave me an insight into how tough it must have been after the plane crash – it really opened my eyes."

She then explained how they had all been stacked up because her grandparents hadn't wanted to upset her.

He clasped his fingers together, his face hardened.

Probably a bit early to talk it through in any depth, but he was pleased she had discovered them. She shouldn't take them too literally – he hadn't been entirely himself when a lot of them were written.

She silently kicked herself for probing too hard too fast.

"Hope, I'm happy to discuss it with you, but it's been a busy day."

"No worries." Goodness, now she was saying it.

And they were both laughing again.

Once more she changed the subject.

"I'm thinking of having a walk around the local area tomorrow just to get my bearings," she said.

"Absolutely fine."

"I appreciate your time off work is limited but at some point could we go through to Birmingham city centre – I could do with picking up a few extra items for my wardrobe."

It was unintentional but came out terribly pretentious. She held her breath but he didn't pick up on it.

"We'll definitely do that. Do you like walking in the countryside – there are some beautiful parts quite close?"

She said she loved walking in the countryside.

"Great," he said. "I'll hold you to it."

"And sorry," she said. "I know I'm rabbiting on but I do want to make my contribution to the house – help with the shopping, cooking the dinner, tidying up the garden. Don't think I am going to be sponging off you."

"You're hired," he announced. "Just don't expect to be paid!"

She looked at him with dancing eyes – he was a right meanie, she declared.

Of course she wasn't being serious – both of them knew that.

She parked the part-time job idea. That would be for another day.

It felt good between them.

They liked one another. It had only been 36 hours but they were already friends.

Yet there was also an acceptance that both had so much baggage in tow that there was a steep learning curve before they could properly relax in each other's company.

Things between them continued to blossom as the days passed.

She walked around the block, discovered a convenience shop, got her hair done at a local salon.

He took her in the car to the supermarket and allowed her to pick and choose what she wanted. She cooked her first meal – pork chops, potatoes and peas. Best to keep it simple – poisoning him at the outset would not have been a good idea!

Kevin often worked Saturdays but managed one off and took her through to Birmingham on the train.

He was very patient as she tried on jeans and T-shirts. She was in her element. Feeling sexy, she chose to flaunt her curves in front of him as she asked his opinion.

Lots more fun and banter between them.

She purchased various new items but also took in some charity shops – amazing how you could sometimes get cool stuff in charity shops.

With summer coming on she discovered a pair of shorts which didn't leave much to the imagination. And she picked out a long, more formal dress – it was bound to come in handy.

She had forgotten to pack an anorak but there was one screaming 'buy me' on one of the racks.

On to a shop selling soaps and smellies. She could not resist.

It was a great haul and she was well pleased.

Except Kevin was looking as though he couldn't manage another step.

She faked concern, stroked his face and promised him no more.

It was the first time she had touched him in a womanly manner. He held her ever so slightly and garbled about watching paint drying.

She gave him one of her playful slaps in the chest,

He looked desperately handsome, she decided.

She was for sure one heck of a girl, he reckoned.

"I need a drink," he declared. "Don't you see, you're driving me to drink?"

She slapped him again.

"Stop hitting me, woman."

And, as though upset, added: "Anyone would think I'm a battered husband."

Now he was being melodramatic, she asserted, twiddling a button on his shirt and playing the innocent.

He took hold of her hand. Gosh, he was masculine.

"Fancy a pub lunch?"

"That would be lovely."

They spotted a place called the Old Contemptibles,

And discovered that the name honoured World War I servicemen. High ceilings, oak panelling, it was a classy watering hole and must have been really something in its Victorian heyday.

There had been money spent on it, it had appeal, and the staff seemed on the ball.

They ordered drinks – there was a choice of real ales and ciders. He went for a pint of cider; she had a half of shandy.

They surveyed the food menu. He picked steak and kidney pie – another English staple. She opted for fish.

Found a table and took in the ambience. Very pleasant. Lots of chatter – punters enjoying themselves.

They looked at each other but eye contact was shattered instantly as she clumsily knocked over her drink. It slopped across the table – he just managed to jump out of the way of a stream of beer.

"Oh, God, I'm sorry," she wailed. "Did it get you? Are you OK?"

He smiled wanly. "It's fine."

Examined his trousers. Just the odd drop. He wiped it off with a serviette.

Then went to get a cloth from the bar. One of the staff grabbed a mop and bucket and came to the rescue.

She apologised profusely once more.

"Same again ... or are you going to throw this one at me too."

Once more she groaned inwardly. He meant nothing by it but there was a tiny bit of edge.

"I'm not safe to be let out of the house, really I'm not."

"Forget it," he said. "You're allowed – it's just nice chatting away to a pretty girl."

She blushed. It was the first time he had given any real indication that he might fancy her. She quite fancied him.

The food came. It was hot, it was wholesome, it wasn't cheap but it was worth the money.

When they left to catch the train back to Tamworth they were definitely full.

She stuck her bags on a spare seat and sat back as it trundled along the tracks.

To walk to the house would probably have taken 30 minutes or so – not feasible with all they had to carry. So they got a taxi.

She insisted on paying for it – he had got lunch.

Back inside she feigned weakness and deposited the pile higgledy-piggledy on the lounge floor, dropped into a chair and surveyed them guiltily.

He watched amused.

She got up from the chair, went over to him, held his hands and thanked him for a smashing trip into town.

For a second she thought he might kiss her. But he held back.

There was that other baggage again – the plane crash variety. They were definitely going to have to do something about it when they were ready.

They had time on their side. She could wait.

For his part, he felt confused. Her influence on him was growing – where was this headed, he wondered.

But he was glad to have her around the place. The weeks were slipping by and she was now one of the fixtures. With every passing day she was growing on him.

Their walks in the countryside were a great success.

Wind in her hair, birds flitting to and fro, farm animals in the fields.

They ambled through woods, became kids again playing hide and seek. She claimed to have won. No way, he maintained.

He gently tossed a fir cone and it rebounded off her back.

It sparked a pretend chase, she was quickly after him and as she caught up he tripped and they landed on top of each other in the leaf litter, giggling outrageously.

This time he did kiss her. At last.

The sultry clinch zinged all the way to her toes but was over as quickly as it had begun.

"I'm sorry – that was wrong."

And rose to his feet as she remained on the floor.

"No," she said. "I shall treasure it … and I hope it is the first of many."

He reached down and pulled her upright.

Looking serious, he told her: "We need to talk when we get home."

Good, she thought.

But they finished the walk in silence.

They arrived home in silence.

She brewed a couple of mugs of tea – in silence.

They sat in the lounge … and there was silence.

Finally, he couldn't stand it any longer.

"Look," he said. "Forget about the kiss. It should never have happened. I was bang out of order. After all, I'm old enough to be your father."

Her blood boiled. Couldn't he have come up with anything better than the 'old enough to be your father' drivel?

She flew at him without ever moving from her seat.

"I'm a big girl now and I don't allow any Tom, Dick or Harry to kiss me. You should be bloody grateful I find you attractive and if nothing else that kiss was clear evidence that you find me attractive. Don't patronise me ever again. I go with who I want. Age doesn't mean a damned thing."

There – she had said it.

The outburst subsided as quickly as he had fired her fury.

She waited for a response. There was none.

The last time he had been spoken to like that it was Alice. He hadn't figured Suzi for a hissing alley-cat.

Struck dumb, words simply wouldn't come.

Instead, it was she who spoke, softly but lucidly.

"This isn't what it is about, Kevin."

She took a breath. "This is about the plane crash baggage we are both carrying on our backs. It is coming between us and it mustn't come between us. I want to talk it all through, I want to clear the decks, I want to tell you about the rotten times and I want to hear from your lips how it was for you. Letters can only tell half the story. I want us to be completely open with each other – nothing kept back."

She paused. "Are you up for it, Kevin?"

He looked at her like a little boy chastised.

"Yes," he said, to her utter relief.

"I tell you what," she said. "I'll start."

She gathered her thoughts.

"I have no idea how much the plane crash, losing my parents, has harmed my life but I suspect a significant amount. So much has gone array. I have been so ghastly to others. Most of the time I have been absolutely horrible to my wonderful grandparents who have only ever wanted the best for me. I have treated my aunt Abby dreadfully too."

He interrupted. "I met Abby on Bali – she was very nice. She cared deeply about you ... a beacon of light amidst hellish darkness. Bali was so, so, hard."

She looked at him as if scales were falling from her eyes.

"Abby has always been a saint," she said. "Yet I've called her names, I've screamed at her, I've treated her with contempt. Sometimes I think I am pure evil."

"You're not evil," he said. "You're a fantastic individual."

She smiled at him. His support was what she needed.

She started running through her catalogue of sins. Being thrown out of nursery, causing trouble in school, playing truant, dabbling in alcohol and drugs, falling in with a very bad crowd ... and then the motorcycle outrage.

He watched horrified as she outlined what had been done to her.

And then the big one – would she ever be able to have children?

At that, she broke down

Immediately he was kneeling besides her, holding her, telling her to let it all come out. Her sobs seemed to go on such a long time, but perhaps just a minute or so.

At length the convulsions came to a halt. He released her. She thanked him and tried to compose herself.

He reached for some paper tissues and dried her face. She took a few herself and blew her nose loudly.

"Not very lady-like," she submitted.

"I'm sorry about that – the thought is just so upsetting. The doctors aren't sure."

"Oh, Hope," his face full of concern for her vulnerability. "You mustn't. Bad things happen. Hold onto me. I'm here to look after you."

He kissed her delicately.

"Now," he said. "On you go."

And sat back in his chair.

"Nearly finished," she sniffed.

And then she went into the stolen car race, agonising over why after trying so hard to get back on the straight and narrow she had allowed herself to be talked into it. Sometimes she was just so weak and easily led. She wouldn't even be here had she not on the spur of the moment put that seatbelt on. The families of those who died would never get over it. The foolishness of youth.

She told him how recovering at home she had found the letters – there were so many of them in that drawer. And she had subsequently read every one.

Having not thought that much about him before, the discovery had greatly affected her. It had sunk in how much she owed to him. She had decided it was incumbent on her to meet face-to-face and thank him – the least she could do.

"And here I am formally thanking you for saving my life," she told him.

He got up and they embraced.

When he released her she thought she detected a tear in his eye.

He sat back down.

"Is that it?" he said.

"That's it."

"Right," he said. "My turn."

They both knew this was very important for her.

"First of all, I am formally thanking you for saving my life."

She sat back – what was coming next.

"I was gone," he said. "I had given up. Had it not been for you popping up in the sea beside me, it was Davy Jones' Locker. You were the impetus which made me fight."

He told her how lonely and frightened he had been.

"I think until now and you … that loneliness has stayed with me and in some ways blighted my life."

She could see how much it was hurting him. She reached over and held his hand. He had been there for her; she must be there for him.

He ran through as much of the rescue as he could recall, almost losing his hold on her, the pain in his arm, the whole thing had taken so much out of him mentally.

He had so wanted to keep her alive and when they told him she was indeed alive he wanted to get up and celebrate. Of course he was in no state to do so. But if that was the highlight of his life, it would do him. He could go up to the Pearly Gates and say – 'Let me in, I deserve it'.

Everything about the hospital was hard, he told her.

"Don't get me wrong – the medical care was excellent. The doctors and nurses were top draw.

"As I mentioned, I was mentally shot. I was in the middle of a whirlpool – this was a huge international story. It seemed everyone wanted a piece of me. Everything was closing in – I had been slung into a dungeon. I was in a prison called a plane crash – to some extent I am still a prisoner."

She squeezed his hand. This was tough.

His parents were round his bedside with his sister Vicky. And then Becky was there.

"I treated Becky so badly," he admitted.

He was back there now – the memories swirling.

"She tried so hard and I gave her nothing back. I was a brute."

"You're not a brute," she assured him. "You're kind, caring, supportive – what more could anyone want?"

His eyes twinkled.

"Oh, but I behaved so badly to her. Had it not been for the crash I think we would have got married. But nothing was the same after the crash. I couldn't think straight, I didn't want the burden, it was all too much."

He gulped as if he too was about to break down.

She held his hand more firmly. "I'm here Kevin. You're not alone. You're never going to be alone again."

They hugged.

"When I got home I was just not myself," he said. "Again, it was the mental thing. I couldn't concentrate. I couldn't come to terms with all those who had died. Why had I survived and so many others hadn't? It just seemed wrong. I suppose it was then that I started writing those long and rambling letters to you. Possibly a mistake. I'm sure your grandparents must have thought I was loopy, but it really helped. I had to tell someone about my true feelings. The rest of the world was on a different pathway. You were the only other survivor. I knew I could confide in you. Now I know I still can."

He paused.

"Does that make any sense?"

"It makes every sense, Kevin."

It gave him the strength to go on.

"Then they had that memorial service – oh, my God."

He held his hands over his eyes.

"I couldn't face it. Then Dad banged me up against the wall and lost his rag. It was just awful, awful. I felt so low."

Now he was quietly sobbing and reaching for a handkerchief.

She held him as the tears splashed onto her face.

"Sorry," he said.

"You can stop if you like," she said.

"No, I've got to do this. If you can manage it then I can too."

She desperately wanted to mother him.

"The service was beautiful but it broke my heart. I couldn't react, I couldn't empathise, there was nothing left inside me. Those poor people and I gave them so little of myself when they most needed it. I beat myself up about it all the time.

"I don't know how I got through – I suppose that was the bottom though I didn't realise it at the time."

The Becky thing had just drifted away on the wind.

And gradually the pain eased and he began to think clearer.

He meandered through the sports agency return. They had been more than good to him. But it seemed so inconsequential in the light of all that had happened. Sport was essentially just frivolity. He felt he was going nowhere.

Estate agency was different – a new ball game, nothing to lose. He didn't think he would take to it, but he had.

He wouldn't say he was exactly happy there but it was palliative, a degree of healing, restorative.

He had made money – lots of money.

Then came Alice – she was looking forward to this part.

He told her straight out, nothing held back as promised ... Alice was different class in bed. The sex was incredible.

She blanched somewhat – how could she match Alice – and he noticed.

He gave her a reassuring kiss.

"It was different," he said. "She was a great girl, it was tremendous, but I wasn't in love with her."

This was the moment.

"Are you in love with me?"

"I am in love with you."

She beamed. "Because I'm madly in love with you."

They embraced again, kissed again, she would have liked to have been swept up in his arms and taken to his bed, but that would come.

He told her about the blackmail – she was outraged – how he should have been strong but wasn't, and the way it had gradually started cutting him up.

To the point he decided to chuck it all in – Alice, the job, Sydney – and escape abroad.

But initially England had been a disaster. The loneliness returned, the plane crash depression re-appeared, no friends, no job.

Would he tell her about the suicide attempt? He had signed up to no secrets. He had to go through with it.

It got to the stage where it all overcame him.

She wondered where this was headed.

"I decided to end it all on a train line – wouldn't feel a thing, I told myself. But I couldn't even get that right."

His voice broke.

She was shocked.

But he wasn't quite finished.

"And then, thank God, the phone rang, I picked it up and it was you."

He smiled happily. "So, you see, you have saved my life twice – you're one up!"

Both of them were laughing.

"I'm not keeping score," she jibed.

They looked at each other. Both were worn out. To their astonishment, it had been a three hour session.

It was ten past eleven at night.

It was too late to take anything further, but now there was an understanding.

It had all come out, everything had been said, a new day had dawned early.

They went to their separate beds.

The next few days she wanted him so much but it wasn't happening and she couldn't understand why.

They cuddled, they kissed, but there was something missing … and there was definitely no sex.

She couldn't understand it. If she wanted a guy she snapped her fingers and they came running. She was throwing herself at this man but couldn't seem to engage.

He sensed her unhappiness.

"It's not what it seems," he pledged. "And I really thought I had cleared all the baggage."

"Tell me."

"I'll get over this hurdle – just allow me space to do it in my own way."

"What hurdle?"

"Please don't shout at me."

She promised she wouldn't.

"This is completely irrational but I've got to rid myself of the notion that when we sleep together – because it is when and not if – it is a form of incest. Obviously not in its dictionary definition. But when we were in the sea and you were crying and I thought maybe your nappy was the problem and I got rid of it … and there you were naked in the water. And now you will be naked in an entirely different way in my bed. I'm having trouble separating the two."

This time it was her who didn't know what to say.

She started to tell him that this was off the wall and far-fetched. It wasn't comparable – this was the two of them nearly twenty years on and they loved each other.

"I know," he said. "You're right – it is far-fetched. But I want to do you justice when it happens. I'm working on it. I'll be over it soon. Bear with me."

She said she would. She wanted to do him justice too. When he was ready she would take him to heights he never knew existed.

So she backed off.

Three days later and still nothing, she decided she had better bring some feminine intuition to the party.

The next night she went upstairs first, washed, called to him, went into her room, and closed the door.

She dabbed on her most expensive perfume, checked her lipstick and hair, admired her bare nipples and put on the polka dot panties which had always sent men potty.

Then she waited.

Now his footsteps were on the stairs, he didn't take long in the bathroom, the door to his bedroom closed, and she heard the click as he turned out the light.

She counted sixty long seconds, then she left, cautiously opened his bedroom door, slunk inside and tip-toed to his side.

She slipped under the downy, he was ready for her, she curled into his welcoming arms – it was like coming home.

They held each other, stroked each other's bodies, kissed madly.

He breathed in her beguiling scent; she inhaled the deep odours of his manliness.

She wanted him more than she had ever wanted anyone before; he was mesmerised by the sweeping curves of her restless body.

But this was going to be no rushed affair, no fumbling's in that park in Normal, no wham bam thank you maam with Honcho.

They were going to savour this first time.

He spent ages kissing nearly every part of her body until she almost came. In turn she nibbled his neck, licked his tummy button and taught his erect penis what was meant by ecstasy.

When he pulled down her panties he did so with all the charisma of a mime artist – it made her feel like a princess.

He slid his fingers through her pubic hair and explored her wetness.

She squirmed deeper into his body as if to say 'now, I'm yours'.

She opened her legs, he moved on top of her.

And when he entered her the satisfaction went off the gauge.

It seemed to last for ever, she came first, then a whoosh and his sperm surged into her in a raging torrent.

She had never thought that being in love could make such a difference.

So this, he discovered, was what it felt like when you met the woman who was right for you – Alice wasn't even close.

As at last they eased down she told him she would want him for ever. He told her he had found the girl who would make him happy.

Their minds and bodies enriched, still wrapped together, they slept the sleep of the angels.

He woke up with a start, and trained his head to see the alarm clock.

"Oh my giddy aunt, I'm late."

Panic in his voice.

"Late for what?"

"Late for work."

"It's Sunday."

He sank back.

"It's Sunday," he repeated. "What a prat."

He sighed.

She looked at him with bleary eyes and an eyebrow raised as if to say 'yes, you are a prat'.

He wasn't having that, and he tried to tickle her.

She screamed in mock disarray and beat him off.

And the love-making started again.

This time it was frenetic, it was rowdy, him grunting like a top tennis star, she urging him on.

When they had enjoyed themselves enough they lay there panting for air, hot, sweaty, but complete.

She was the first to speak.

"You rotter," she gasped. "You've taken advantage of me twice – poor, innocent, me."

He tossed a pillow at her.

She hit him with hers.

And, now knees on the bed, it was a full on pillow fight which only finished when they had no more strength in their arms.

He half pinned her down.

"I'll bite you," she shrieked.

It saw them chuckling away like kids.

"I love you."

"I love you too."

This was how they were determined to categorise their commitment – fun, laughter, play, love.

There had been too much darkness; they only wanted light.

He let her go and they paused.

Then, in bits and pieces of mirth, he burst out with the banal. "I bags the bathroom first."

She hadn't come across the expression before, not that she cared.

"You can bags off!" she told him forthrightly.

He nearly fell off the bed.

"OK darling," he said. "I give in – ladies first."

She searched in the bed and recovered the polka dot panties – they had done their job. Now she slipped them on to cover her modesty.

Then, on cloud nine, headed for the bathroom, his lover and his darling.

She had her man and she wanted to tell the world.

He lay back on the bed and tried to take it all in.

They were so good for each other. There were no reservations. Their coming together felt so right. They were extricating their plane crash straight-jacket in harmony – no flight of fancy this. He was convinced it would last.

For the rest of the day he could hardly keep his hands off her – she similarly with him.

And when they went to bed that night – always his 'place' now – they were tying each other in sex knots.

Except that this time he did have to get up in the morning and go to work.

"You're a spoilsport," she moaned, as he threw on clothes and tried to appear vaguely respectable.

He put his tongue out at her.

"See you tonight, Hope."

The words were erotica. It was like she couldn't wait. He was addictive.

The fun, laughter, play and love manifested itself in all kinds of obscure ways.

One weekend they decided finally to attack the garden.

He fought his way through the spider webs guarding the shed – he had only previously investigated its innards once.

She was wearing a favourite top and adamant she didn't want to get it all mucky.

Aware of a scruffy old sweater hanging on a nail, he gave it a good shake and suggested it might do the trick.

She looked at this moth-eaten man garment dismissively – catwalk it was not.

"Well, come on, give it a go," he entreated mischievously, knowing how ill-fitting it would likely prove to be.

Unwillingly she tried it on

He nearly wet himself at her doleful expression.

The sleeves hung over her hands in swathes and you could have fitted two of her inside the main bulk of it.

She looked dejected.

In stiches, arms wide, he spluttered: "Come here my scarecrow baby doll."

She pushed him so hard that they fell over, rolling around the grass, him telling her it was today's fashion chic, she telling him that as soon as his back was turned he was going head first into a bed of nettles.

With a wicked smile, he undid the top button of her jeans and twirled a finger in the direction of her sweet spot.

Her turn for the wicked smile.

She allowed him to suppose that he just might get away with taking this further … and then cut him off at the knees (or should that have been balls).

"I'm very happy to do it in the great outdoors," she said. "But it is probably not a good idea to put on a peep show for the neighbours."

They shared amused glances. That was him told.

He went inside and discovered a light sweater he had shrunk in the wash. It more or less fitted her.

And then they got stuck into several hours of hard graft, cutting, trimming, weeding, hacking … until they could hack it no more.

He made the tea; she produced the biscuit jar.

And then there was the occasion when walking beside a children's play area which they passed regularly that she suddenly had an irresistible urge to regress.

"Last to the swings is a scaredy cat," she cried, and took off in fine style.

To his dismay he couldn't catch up with her in time.

Thankfully there were no kids there to observe his disgrace.

She was on one of the swings and sailing through the air with the greatest of ease.

He looked to follow suit but the sides were too tight to his hips and he had to write it off as a bad job, much to her glee.

"Ha," she gloated. "The trouble with you is that you're far too fat."

He let the insult pass as she swung past his nose yet again.

Knowing he was beaten, he ogled that slinky waist which looked so glorious whether it be on a swing or in polka dot panties.

She had to be a contender for Rear of the Year too.

Now she was waving to him and blowing raspberries.

What a bundle of magnetic energy she was.

Mesmerised, he blessed his good fortune that this stunning woman should have set her sights on him.

But she wasn't finished.

As she allowed the swing to slow, she jumped off spectacularly, did a cartwheel, and sprung into his arms smothering him in kisses.

It was quite a finale.

He swung her round until her head was spinning.

All he knew was that he was as dizzy for her as any man could be.

They had taken too to going down their local pub a couple of times a week and were becoming familiar faces there.

It made them feel they were part of the community.

He had discovered Somerset cider and she had become partial to a gin and tonic.

One evening they noticed the landlord had a sign up – 'part-time bar staff required'.

She inquired as to how many hours were on offer and the shift arrangements. It transpired he wanted someone three days a week, mostly at lunch times and afternoons, but it varied.

"That's a job down my street," she told Kevin. "It would give me something to do while you are out at work."

He was fine with the idea but claimed tongue in cheek that she hadn't got big enough boobs to be a barmaid, which got him a 24-hour sex ban.

She explained to the landlord that she was only on a tourist visa and wasn't supposed to work, but he wasn't bothered. Said he would pay her out of the till – it wouldn't go through the books. Clearly, the black economy was thriving.

They started her off under the supervision of one of the regular bar staff, but she quickly picked it up – fill pints of cider to the brim but put a head on the lager, how to change a barrel, that sort of stuff.

She found it good fun, flirted with the punters, laughed at their jokes, however tame.

From time to time she got called in to work in the evening if they had a busy night on – a big football match on the television, a party in the back room.

Then, Kevin might turn up to keep her company.

And they developed a 'comedy' routine – pretending they were complete strangers he would chat her up outrageously and she would be dead cheeky back.

When they got home there would inevitably be plenty of banter around his suggestive naughtiness and her saucy put-downs.

Usually a prelude to rumpy pumpy later.

It was now four months or so since she had turned up on his doorstep, they were effectively living as man and wife, and it was all good. No, much better than good, absolutely sensational.

The demons had been driven away, hopefully for ever. And they were both fully aware that only they could have achieved the turnaround because only they knew what agonies the plane crash had wrought.

What could possibly go wrong?

One thing he in particular was fearful of was the media somehow stumbling across the pair of them.

Here were the only two survivors of a terrible plane crash, and he was 'shacked up' with the baby he had saved from drowning.

It wasn't hard to see that it was one hell of a story.

And he might come in for a lot of stick, with suggestions he had taken advantage of the situation, even groomed a child – the letters being the so-called evidence.

She was far more sanguine about it, seeing no reason why anyone should discover their secret and she thought they could handle it even if somebody did.

They both knew there had been no grooming but could you 'prove' there hadn't been.

He knew how resourceful the media could be and to put it mildly did not relish being hauled over the coals like in the aftermath of the disaster.

The prospect didn't engulf him but he thought it wise to take precautions.

For example, he decided to always call her Hope in public places, such as the pub. It might put someone off the trail should they be sniffing around.

There was just one other cloud on the horizon – the six month expiry of her visa.

At the back of her mind was a grotesque scenario whereby she got thrown out of England and sent back to the United States, while the United States turned its face against Kevin joining her there.

The thought of being parted from him, perhaps for an extended period, petrified her.

Like Abby and John, this was the man she wanted to father her children, always assuming, of course, she could have children.

Oh God, why had she been so incredibly stupid to hook up with that bunch of motorbike mobsters.

She didn't want to think about the whole visa situation, but it bothered her.

It bothered them both albeit Kevin thought it unlikely that the worst would come to pass. It would probably take ages for the authorities to pick up the fact that she had overstayed.

And anyway she was still legitimate for two months.

But it could not be ignored for ever.

What to do about it?

Kevin had it all worked out. He was going to marry her.

OK, that would make it more likely that they might get rumbled by the media, but so what.

Critics might say four months was simply not long enough to be sure and smacked of one of those whirlwind romances couples later regret.

But he knew she was the one, she loved him, he couldn't care less any more about the age difference, the two of them were meant for each other.

Anyway, it wasn't four months – it was nearly 20 years.

His mind was made up.

All he had to do now was buy a ring and pop the question.

Tough to find the time during a busy working week – you couldn't just nip out in your 30 minute lunch break. It wasn't as if it was going to buy a sandwich. This was a ring, he would need to take his time, it had to be right.

He told her he was required to work a half day on the Saturday which was a white lie.

But promised her he would take her out to a posh restaurant for lunch which excited her.

All that week he was fidgety. She thought he was acting oddly but couldn't put her finger on it. He denied anything was up.

On the Saturday he made sure he was out of the house promptly and to keep his cover from blowing was wearing his work suit. Then caught a train into Birmingham and onto the city's famous Jewellery Quarter.

The Jewellery Quarter, where he had done a spot of sight-seeing on first arrival in Birmingham, is in easy walking distance of the city centre and renowned as a destination for high quality, bespoke jewellery,

It is claimed to house Europe's largest concentration of businesses involved in the jewellery trade, and produces 40 per cent of all the jewellery made in the UK. It is also home to the world's largest Assay Office, which hallmarks around 12 million items a year.

Safe to say, Kevin knew he would find something fitting there.

He went into several shops searching for inspiration until captivated by a combination of diamonds which, he hoped, would dazzle his prospective bride.

It cost a pretty penny but it was worth it.

He was well satisfied heading back to Tamworth on the train but for some bizarre reason the nerves got going, butterflies in his stomach and all that.

What if she said 'no'? Oh, come on, don't be ridiculous. Of course she's not going to say 'no'. But, hang on, she's only 19 … she might think it is far too soon.

Stop it, Kevin, it'll be fine.

He was so caught up in this bizarre 'will she, won't she' entanglement that he almost missed his stop.

When he got back to the house she was pleased to see him and agitating to know where he was taking her for the promised meal. All for rushing out of the door.

Edgy, he shepherded her into the lounge, saying he had something he wanted to show her.

What was it?

Be patient, he insisted. It was a surprise.

Pretending to go into a huff at his keeping it back from her, she went from grumpy to open-mouthed wonder as he sank down on one knee.

He opened up a small jewellery box. Pointing it towards her, she could see it was a beautiful diamond ring.

"Oh my God," she said, finally realising what was happening.

"Suzanne Duthie, aka Hope Duthie, will you marry me," he said.

She started crying and suddenly he wasn't at all sure of her response.

"Darling, of course I will marry you."

She was standing there, laughing, crying, he slipped the ring on her finger, it was so pretty.

This only happened in fairy tales, didn't it?

They kissed and then they embraced.

But as they held each other she was suddenly constrained – his body was going limp in her arms.

She stepped back slightly, there was this opaque look of shock in his eyes as though he could not believe what was happening, and, as his weight took him, he slipped through her fingers to the floor, the empty jewellery box tumbling from his grasp.

He lay there motionless – he didn't seem to be breathing.

This time her 'Oh my God' was of blind hysteria.

He had collapsed. This couldn't be happening to her. What to do?

A voice was calling to him, pleading with him – it was hers ... "Get up Kevin, you must get up, Kevin, please Kevin, please."

She was on the floor beside him, imploring him. Holding his hand.

There was no response.

She let out the most desperate scream.

She must get help. That was it. She would go round to the neighbours and get help.

More screams as she pressed bells and hammered on doors.

She only knew the neighbours to say hello to and that was it.

A door opened somewhat tentatively.

"Please, please help me – he's on the floor dying. Please, please, we have to save him."

A woman in her fifties stood there. She promised to get her husband and went inside.

Another neighbour, a man in his twenties, heard the racket and came outside to investigate.

He raced round with her to the house.

Kevin was still lying where he had dropped.

Had she phoned the emergency services?

In her flustered state, it hadn't crossed her mind. What was the number? 911? No, that was the United States.

999, he told her.

She found her mobile and discovered it was out of juice.

He rang from his phone.

The operator had a load of questions and he passed the phone to Suzi who was by now in bits and close to falling apart.

What was the address and postcode?

She rattled off the address but couldn't remember the postcode.

"Oh, you are such a dope, what is the wretched postcode?" she demanded, tearing herself to shreds.

Never mind.

What was the phone number she was calling from in case they got cut off – thankfully she could recall the land line digits.

What had happened?

He had collapsed in her arms. He was lying on the floor, not moving. He wasn't breathing.

"Please, please he needs an ambulance urgently."

The operator said she was sorting it out.

The questions kept on coming as Suzi became ever more frantic.

The patient's age, sex and medical history. 41, male, healthy as far as she was aware.

Was the patient conscious, breathing, any bleeding or chest pain. Her rancour boiled over – she had told them all this. No he wasn't breathing and he wasn't conscious.

"What is all this? Just get the bloody ambulance here. Don't you understand – he's dying."

She was now back on her hands and knees imploring Kevin to come round.

The neighbour took over the phone.

He explained who he was.

Was the airway clear? He said it seemed to be.

She took him through the steps for carrying out CPR (Cardiopulmonary Resuscitation).

He said he thought he had the gist of it, told Suzi what he was going to attempt, and handed the phone back to her.

With hands interlocked he began pumping Kevin's chest in regular cycles – one, two, three, four, five, six, seven, eight, nine, ten.

Pause.

One, two, three, four, five, six, seven, eight, nine, ten.

And on and on – it was really quite sapping.

Suzi was just standing there looking horrified, but, hang on, kiss of life, she had seen that take place in a television thriller.

She was down beside the neighbour now and every time he paused she blew air into Kevin's lungs.

From the control room the alert had gone out – cardiac arrest.

Both an ambulance and a rapid response vehicle were on their way, blue lights flashing, sirens blaring.

Suzi heard the whining noise first, immediately jumped up, it had to be them. She raced outside to direct them to the right house.

A small huddle of neighbours were in the street wondering what was going on, whispering amongst themselves, fearing the worst.

The rapid response vehicle hove into view.

They went inside, took over immediately, asked for space while they worked on him.

Medical equipment, stretcher, defibrillation in an attempt to electric shock his heart, but nothing seemed to be working.

Now the ambulance was here.

And at that point Suzi fainted.

She came round as they were getting him into the ambulance, pleading to be allowed to go too.

The rapid responders took pity on her.

She grabbed her bag, the house keys and they were away, blue lights and sirens again warning traffic to get out of the way.

Every minute felt like an hour, then they were there and he was being rushed into A&E where a crash team was waiting.

It was useless. A DOA – dead on arrival.

They took her to a side room – she looked terrible, face streaked by countless tears, hair all over the place, the nice dress she had put on for the lunch ruined.

Seated at a basic table, they took it slowly, gradually weaving the narrative towards the brutal truth.

Cardiac arrests were very serious indeed, first responders and the ambulance crew had done their level best, battling all the way in to bring him back from the brink, but to no avail. He was very sorry to tell her, it was awful news, there was no way of breaking it to her gently, Kevin had passed away.

Clutching at straws, she had been hoping against hope the words would not be delivered.

She rested her head on the table, hands both side of her head, and closed her mind. She didn't cry – there were no tears left – but grieved to herself, just the occasional low moan breaking the silence.

The consultant said he was afraid that there were other matters he must mention.

Almost certainly the coroner would order a post-mortem because of the sudden nature of the death. Secondly, how appropriate might it be to donate his organs – he would ask a member of the organ donation team to speak to her. It would unfortunately require a prompt decision.

He said he would arrange a member of staff to sit with her in her sorrow.

She said she would prefer some privacy while she savoured the memories.

He said that was fine and she should take as long as she needed.

Someone would come to see her in due course and see if she felt ready to discuss matters.

He closed the door.

She was alone; she had never felt so alone ever.

She visualised his features and his mannerisms, his kindness, his playfulness, his devotion to her.

The love of her life was gone – how would she manage, what would she do, it was so unfair.

There could be nobody else after him. She felt bereft.

Time seemed to stand still ... until the knock on the door.

The first hard decision of many which would have to be confronted.

"Come in."

It was the organ team representative. She said her name was Gwen.

She ran through the technicalities about donation – the vital organs quickly become unusable for transplantation but bone, skin, heart valves and corneas can be donated within the first 24 hours of death.

In turn Suzi explained that she was living with Kevin, they had become engaged, but doubted whether she would be classed as next of kin.

His family was in Australia, they almost certainly didn't know she was with him, they definitely would not know he was dead, she hadn't got the Sydney phone number on her.

She had no idea what opinion he might have had on organ donation and she never recalled him raising the subject.

At which point she lost interest in the whole thing.

If they could sort it out they could do what they wanted.

Tiredness all of a sudden overtook her. All she wanted to do was go home and rest.

Gwen said she understood how traumatic it was – Suzi was sure she wasn't even close to understanding. But the woman was trying to be sympathetic.

They would arrange a taxi for her.

While she waited it struck her how hospitals were such a sterile environment in every sense of the word.

She had seen too many hospitals to last a lifetime.

Was there someone who could be with her once she arrived back – a relative, friend or neighbour?

The neighbours had done what they could, she said. But really she would be all right. She would rather be on her own.

The journey was laboured – Suzi was aware the road ahead was going to be so difficult too.

At last it pulled up outside the house. She managed to scramble just enough money together to meet the fare.

Eyes seemed to be on her as she walked to the front door – the neighbours were on watch.

The lady whose bell she had rung first came out – there was no need to ask as to the outcome. She could see from Suzi's tear-stained face and bloodshot eyes.

"I'm so sorry for you, dear," she said, and put a wizened arm around Suzi.

It set the weeping off again as she struggled to retrieve the house keys from her handbag.

"Would you like me to come in and make you a nice cup of tea, love?

Half of her wanted to tell this no doubt well-meaning busybody to go to hell while the other wanted to be hugged and told none of this was happening.

They went in together and the woman headed for the kitchen and put the kettle on.

"Sit down on the sofa – you must be shattered," she told Suzi.

She got the tea brewing and kept her company as they drank it together. It transpired her name was Mrs Wilson.

"I am sure he was a good man," she said. "I feel awful for you. How old was he?"

"41."

"Oh, dear, that's no age at all. How very, very, sad. And the medical people tried so hard."

Suzi had had enough.

"You're being very decent," she told Mrs Wilson. "All the neighbours have been marvellous. But I feel completely exhausted."

Mrs Wilson took the hint.

"No problem, dear," she said. "You get yourself a good night's sleep. Maybe take a paracetamol or two. And remember I'm just next door. If you need anything just knock – doesn't matter what time it is."

She was a good old duck who clearly felt for Suzi in her hour of need.

"Thank you – you've been an enormous comfort," said Suzi as Mrs Wilson shuffled out.

The door closed – it was closing on a chapter of her life.

She sat back down on the sofa in her misery. How could this be happening? She had gone from fiancé to 'widow' in the space of thirty seconds.

It was scarcely credible but it had happened.

She looked at the picture of the two of them together which she had insisted went in pride of place on the bookcase.

They had been so happy – you could see it in the portrait.

The jewellery box was still lying where it had fallen.

She couldn't leave it there. Picked it up. Looked at the engagement ring on her finger.

The ring, the framed picture and her memories – that was all she really had of him. Not much to take away from a relationship of such passion and commitment.

What day was it? Oh yes, Saturday still. The bar would be humming with lively punters and jocular chatter. In contrast, here she was, isolated and broken, in a room which now seemed contaminated by tragedy.

There was no escape from the grim events of the day – she kept on going over and over them in the vain hope that they may have a different ending. But it was the same each time.

She asked herself what more could she have done. There had been no signs that he might be ill. Why had she never taken a first aid course? She must put that right sooner rather than later in case some other poor wretch required help. Could she have done more in those critical minutes after the collapse before brain damage sets in?

Questions which, she was sure would tear her apart in the days, weeks and years to come.

But she must not feel it was somehow her fault – that was the way to madness.

What about Kevin's family – she should be phoning them to pass on the terrible news, but it was late, she hadn't the strength, it would have to wait for the morning.

She thought of phoning Abby – the ever reliable Abby who had done so much for her. Abby would know what to do. Abby would try to console her. Abby was so sensible.

In dismay she toyed with all the formal duties she would have to take on – contact the hospital and the coroner's office, arrange a death certificate if she was allowed one, discuss funeral arrangements. And where would that be – probably not Tamworth as they were in effect just passing through. Probably the body would have to be repatriated to Australia.

And there would be much, much, more on top of that to tackle.

She felt sick to her stomach at the prospect.

How would his parents take it? Would she be able to cooperate with them? Would they marginalise her?

It was all too grizzly to bear.

At some point she must have drifted off into sleep because when she was next aware and looked down at her watch it said 1am.

For her own good she must get herself to bed.

She needed to shut everything out if only for a few hours.

She dragged herself off the sofa, got herself a glass of orange and water, and plodded up the stairs. She would do her teeth – she hated going to bed without doing her teeth.

She put her clothes into the laundry basket and then pulled the sheets over her.

She would pretend he was there, holding her, caressing her, making love to her one final time.

Then, pray God, allow her some sort of sleep.

It took a while but then she was dead to the world. Searching the Valley of the Shadow of Death for him.

Because the next she knew was that she had left the house, undertaken a long walk to reach the main rail line and was tramping across Wigginton Park.

With her nimble frame she was able to scale the protective fence and gain access to the line.

This was it. No more need to grieve, a means of escape from undertakers, forms, family, and the rest, she probably wouldn't feel a thing.

A train was approaching, she stepped onto the line, the briefest of glimpses at the tortured face of the driver, and … obliteration.

She woke up covered in sweat and screaming the rooftops down.

Screaming, screaming, screaming. Until she feared waking the neighbours.

It had been so real she could barely accept that she was still alive and had never left her bedroom.

She thrust her head into her pillow and sobbed, and sobbed, and sobbed.

Shattered, it took her many minutes to pull herself together.

She knew what this was all about. The nightmare had followed the exact same pattern of the suicide attempt Kevin had outlined when they made their confessionals to each other. She had been shocked and appalled at the time – was this some grizzly signage, telling her to get out?

A shiver went down her spine – this was almost paranormal. It scared her.

She sat there rigid.

Until eventually she got it.

She could not remain in this house a moment longer, this house which held the very best and very worst of memories, this house which had now become a ghoul, sucking the life from her.

To hell with funeral, body, possessions et al, she was quitting. His parents would just have to handle it all. A callous way to act perhaps, but she was out of it, it was finished, she had no strength left.

She set about her mission systematically.

Wash, shower, toilet – she wanted to be prepared for what she was about to embark upon. She wasn't sure where she was headed. Probably train to London and flight across the Atlantic. Where else could she go but Normal? It would be a haven for her. Or maybe Toronto. She could stay with Abby. Abby would look after her, tell he she wasn't at fault. She would phone her from London and make arrangements.

Now where had she put the big backpack with which she had arrived?

Think Suzi, think.

It was where she had left it on top of the wardrobe.

She examined it – wiped it with a rag in rudimentary fashion. It was a bit battered and moth-eaten. It really needed a proper clean but it would have to do.

Going into her bedroom she packed as many of her clothes as she possibly could, folding them as neat as possible rather than throwing them in willy-nilly. It meant she could take more.

For protection, she symbolically wrapped the portrait picture of them together in the polka dot undies, then placed it carefully between a sweater and top.

She got her wash things, her make-up bag. She religiously checked off items – shoes, socks, panties, jeans, dresses, tops, shorts ... until she was almost befuddled.

Must not leave anything important behind.

She went into his room. Some of her stuff was lying around and she also wanted to see whether there was any further memento she might salvage to remember him by.

She took a belt from around his trousers – she would wear it with her jeans.

Something to tell her she remained his whatever the future should bring.

She remembered the laundry basket. Items intermingled, she had to separate her clothes from his. It nearly set the tears flowing again. It was like vultures picking the bones of a zebra carcase.

Dragging the backpack down the stairs, she plonked it on the table where they had once indulged so many meals.

Determined to be ultra-efficient, she decided it would not be wise to leave on an empty stomach. She toasted a couple of pieces of bread, put some butter on them, fried an egg, placed it between the slices, cut it in half, and ate carefully, trying to avoid yoke flowing down onto her chin. All washed down with a glass of milk. Even cleaned the frying pan.

Looking out of the kitchen window, she perceived that it was raining ... and raining quite hard.

She found her anorak – it wasn't fully waterproof. She had intended buying something more practical and hard-wearing but had never got round to doing so, too late now.

Never mind, she would have to get on with it.

She was ready though she didn't feel ready.

Something was missing. It was all too sanitised, too regimented, she could not abandon this poky little hovel they had both adored without saying a proper goodbye, acknowledging all that he had contributed.

She did not care much for religion – it was all tosh. But, just as he had said a prayer in the water, putting trust in a higher power, she felt she too must offer up a gesture of sorts, a testament to their union.

Suzi made the sign of the cross, knelt down, put her hands together, and closed her eyes.

She told God to look after Kevin, proffer shelter to a good man, spoke about his devotion and their great love, and asked him to bless her as she headed into the unknown.

She put her coat on, then struggled into the backpack. Goodness, it was heavy.

She opened the front door and was immediately battered by rain and wind, cowered back, forced it shut again and caught her breath.

It was as if nature was reeking its wrath on her for taking flight.

But the house was now dark and brooding in its emptiness. She mustn't change her mind. The place had served its purpose and that purpose was now on a slab in the hospital mortuary. It was time to depart.

She opened the door for a second time and faced down the gale.

Once outside, she tugged hard, got the thing closed, locked it, put the keys back through the letter box and contemplated a long, wet, dreary walk to the rail station.

Not much of a dawn chorus in these conditions – had things been different she would have appreciated some bird song to cheer her path.

She strode out onto the road, walked fifty paces, and looked back.

Tears were pouring down her face, rain was pouring down her face.

She turned and headed away. It was done.

END

About the Author

John Duckers has spent all his career in the media.

Originally from the Wirral, Cheshire, he was educated at Uppingham School in Rutland and Dundee University.

An award winning journalist, he spent 16 years on the news side of The Press and Journal in Aberdeen, a major regional daily across the north of Scotland, and then 18 years as business editor of The Birmingham Post.

Now semi-retired, he still works part-time as a freelance media writer in both PR and journalism.

A widower, with two grown-up children, he lives in Moseley, a suburb of Birmingham.

Lightning Source UK Ltd.
Milton Keynes UK
UKHW041409301118
333186UK00001B/23/P